The Secretkeepers

The Secretkeepers

A Novel

Charles Rammelkamp

Red Hen Press Los Angeles

THE SECRETKEEPERS

Book design by Jacob Williamson
Cover design by Mark E. Cull
Cover art *Monday Afternoon* by David Stowell

ISBN 1-888996-97-8
Library of Congress Catalog Card Number 2004096200

The City of Los Angeles Cultural Affairs Department,
California Arts Council and
the Los Angeles County Arts Commision
partially support Red Hen Press.

First Edition

Red Hen Press
www.redhen.org

For Abby, from whom I keep no secrets—
or only a few

Contents

The Secretkeepers

Vows

Cicadas

The beginning of June 1987. Greenspan was taking over the Fed from Volcker; Webster, the former FBI chief, had taken over the CIA from Casey, who had resigned and then died; in the American League East Toronto had taken over first place from the Yankees, and from the sound of things, the cicadas were taking over Baltimore. Bridgewater lay on the sticky green and white rubber strips of a chaise lounge by the side of the Wyman Park Pool Club pool flipping through *Time Magazine*, glancing at news items with only a fraction of his attention, bored. Restless. Affected, perhaps, by the cicadas' frantic monotony, he felt his angst, too, rising to a pitch.

The high-pitched rattling of the cicadas was like the ceaseless shrilling of maracas, a constant sound that swelled and subsided, coming in waves, a shrill chattering sometimes so intense Bridgewater thought his eardrums would burst; he could feel the pulsing throb as something actual of which the penetrating noise was only a single manifestation: some elemental force of nature threatening to run amok.

Across University Parkway, on the bumpy white stucco walls of a building owned by Johns Hopkins, Bridgewater could see them clustered like dates; they shone brownly with the sheen of dried fruit. Squished bodies like smeared raisins littered the wet cement floors of the cabanas where people changed into their bathing suits.

In the "Milestones" section Bridgewater read that Danny Kaye had died. Although he already knew this, reading the notice in *Time* made him feel gloomier still. Another Jewish humanitarian bites the dust. Frowning, he looked over the edge of the magazine at a cicada on the gray cement wall of the men's shower room. Its transparent wings, textured like a shed snakeskin, shimmered with cellophane wetness. Frangible shafts of light broke and merged kaleidoscopically, reflected from the shiny wings. A real work of nature. A vein of bright orange-red, a sort of racing stripe, laced the upper edges of the clear wings. You saw them on sidewalks everywhere, wrapped in their cellophane cloaks, the bright orange-red ribbon defining the edges like woven trim. High-tech Draculas.

The older cicadas, plump as prunes, resting on curbs or clinging to trees, likewise had a chilling effect: benign as turtles or frogs sunning themselves on rocks, only more intimidating, because less familiar. They had those red bulbous eyes like grains of colored sugar candy that made Bridgewater think of omniscience. Or at least "allseeingness."

An odor of cedar shavings at the pool carried with it an image of a pet store. The sharp, pungent odor teased Bridgewater's nostrils so that he almost wanted to sneeze. The pool, advertised as L-shaped, actually resembled a lopsided J. The odor came from the trees that, beyond a high white fence, buffered the pool from the street. A little oasis in the middle of the city, invaded by cicadas. Mainly conifers—not a cedar in sight, except they were all evergreens, weren't they?—those tall pines were the source of that earsplitting din. The cicadas clustered in the trees, guerrilla warriors waiting for the moment to attack; they swooped around the pool and sometimes landed on the half-clad sunbathers.

The rubber strips of the chaise lounge stuck to Bridgewater's back; his sweat made them slick and stinging. He jounced a little. Like a trampoline, that lack of stability and balance. Or did his impression of a lack of balance come from a different source?

A story in *Time* about Mount St. Helens seven years after the volcano erupted caught Bridgewater's restless eye. Had it really been seven years? Yes, that was the year he and Zippy had bought the Toyota Tercel. The mysterious, almost magical power of nature intrigued Bridgewater. Unfathomable power. You thought that puny man really could subdue it, and then some awesome, uncontrollable thing like an earthquake or a tornado came along to remind you of your essential insignificance. Something like the cicadas served as a more subtle reminder. Craziness at the core of reality. A metaphysical principle.

Bridgewater remembered the little schoolgirls running onto the bus the day before, screaming like characters from *The Birds*. (Bridgewater often found himself thinking of that Alfred Hitchcock movie those early weeks in June.)

"One flew in my face!" shrieked a little brown-haired girl in a pleated plaid skirt with an oversized safety pin. She'd looked like a plastic doll.

"One of them tried to fly up my dress!" another said with horror.

"I had three of them stuck on me this morning when I went into class!"

"Eeeeuuuuwwww!" A little girl with freckles made a face.

Out of the window of the bus, Bridgewater watched an older woman standing on the opposite streetcorner swatting at the air with her purse as she stood waiting for the bus going the other way. Bridgewater knew she was swatting at a cicada, even though he could not see the insect with his own eyes.

"They make that noise by rubbing their legs together. It's the males that do it," an old black lady sitting two rows up said to her seatmate.

"It's in the Bible," her companion replied. "The swarm of locusts. Moses was in Egypt, and he told Fay-row God was gonna send a plague of locusts!"

Moses, Bridgewater thought, as if caught by surprise. The shy, stammering leader of the Hebrews in Egypt, the reluctant representative of the people, a hard-luck case who only got a brief glimpse of the Promised Land in reward for all that work. Husband of Zipporah.

"Seen 'em seventeen year ago back in seventy; seen 'em seventeen year afore that in fifty-three; seen 'em seventeen year afore that in thirty-six. I remember. I seen 'em," an old white man on another seat was saying to the young man in his twenties who sat beside him. He nodded with sage conviction. "Don't remember seein' 'em in nineteen, but I musta been old enough. I was ten in nineteen." He nodded again. "Yep, I seen 'em."

"Notice you don't hear them when it rains?" the younger man said. "Once it starts to get hot, though, those fuckers start to chatter like rattlesnakes!"

"Doug!" a plangent female voice cried, awakening Bridgewater from his reverie. He looked around. A college girl in a bikini was pleading with the lifeguard, her whine in harmony with the cicadas. "What'd you do with the kickboards?"

Bridgewater watched the lifeguard, a tan, broadshouldered college boy, reach behind a counter and bring forth a blue kickboard with the white outline of a dolphin drawn on it. Like a barnyard rooster, Doug strutted about with the kickboard, teasing the girl, refusing to give it to her.

"Dooooo-uuug!" she said in a reproachful singsong. An elaborate mating ritual was going on here, the dominance and submission of animals in nature, the preening of the male and the tail-lifting of the female. The girl stood there helplessly, her arms at her sides. Take me.

Just then a cicada flew into the sensitive flesh under the girl's left breast, and she shrieked, alarmed.

"I hate those damn things!" she cried.

"Hate them?" Doug said, handing her the kickboard. The cicada had spoiled the mood. "Hell, why don't you eat 'em?"

"Did you say *eat* them? Oh! Don't make me sick!"

"Sure," the lifeguard said, smiling boyishly. "Marinate 'em in teriyaki sauce and fry 'em, or put 'em in tacos instead of ground beef. Roast 'em and then crumble them up over ice cream."

"Oh, yuck!"

"They serve 'em over in Mount Washington. At Café des Artistes."

"No thanks!" The girl walked over to the pool, her butt twitching an invitation and a promise, and she dove in. Bridgewater was sure she'd be back. His conviction made him anxious. Could she simply walk away?

Around the pool the sunworshippers lay on chaise lounges with headphones over their ears and shades covering their eyes. For the most part they seemed blithely unaware of the cicadas. The bugs were a nuisance on the street, but they would soon die with nothing left but a memory for the next decade and a half. Their lives were so brief, a frantic mating ritual, somnambulistic; their maturation, after seventeen years of dormancy, was so accelerated you could almost literally see the process happening before your eyes, the metamorphosis from pupa to adult. "*Glut thy sorrow on a morning rose . . .*" An almost frantic impulse to cram all of life's essential processes into the briefest possible duration. You'd scream, too!

The sexual tension in the air, Bridgewater thought, might only be a symptom of his loneliness, an illusion fostered by the jungle-like whir of the cicadas. Or there might be some metaphysical basis to it, some crisis in his own developmental process, paralleling the cicadas'. He was thirty-five, Dante's age at the beginning of *The Divine Comedy*.

When I had journeyed half of our life's way,
I found myself within a shadowed forest,
For I had lost the path that does not stray

Dante's mid-life crisis was more than male menopause; Bridgewater suspected his own was, too. After eight years of marriage, Bridgewater's wife had left him. She'd been gone for more than a month now, and lately Bridgewater had begun to yearn for female companionship. But not only had his wife left him, she had left him for Mick Jagger; that was the crazy thing.

In *Time* Bridgewater read an account of the West German boy who had flown a tiny Cessna into Moscow's Red Square. In the air, the cicadas resembled helicopters or hummingbirds; you could see their wings beating. The clumsy, graceless whirl. Then on the sidewalks, the already spent ones, dying, frantically beating their wings in a futile effort at flight, seemed like airplanes shot out of the sky, sputtering to a stop. Birds with broken wings.

What a crazy thing to do! Fly an airplane to the Kremlin! The kid who did it was sure to go to Siberia or someplace. What a price to pay! The kid claimed he did it in the name of peace! A rational-sounding excuse for what was essentially a fraternity boy prank. Well, what defined craziness, anyway? Who could say?

The doctors Bridgewater had spoken to had told him that his wife, Zippy, "suffered from the delusion that an unattainable man of high social status is passionately in love with her. She desires a sexual relationship with the man." Exactly what *he* had told the doctors! But they went on to give the disorder a name: "de Clerambault Syndrome." They were not sure if the disorder were a clinical entity in its own right or a variant of one of the major psychoses. Under the present diagnostic system, they said, her disorder (they loved to refer to this as a "disorder," like calling shit a bowel movement) was best classified as a manifestation of a more general psychopathological condition, most likely paranoid schizophrenia.

Accusingly, one expert called Zippy's disorder a defense against feelings of depression and loneliness, perhaps a reaction to feelings of rejection. Feeling unloved and unlovable, she tried to overcome this threat to her ego, these narcissistic injuries, by turning them into grandiose fantasies.

But was it Bridgewater's fault they weren't able to have a baby? And why did they think Zippy felt guilty? Was she even "sick," after all?

Another specialist handed him the tired old Freudian line. Zippy sought a safe, eroticized father figure.

Mick Jagger, safe?

"Safe because unattainable," the doctor explained, miffed at Bridgewater's incredulous tone, his lack of respect for scientific hypotheses.

Yet a third explained the problem as a defense against homosexual impulses. Guilt explained everything to these guys. In any case, they had all prescribed mild antipsychotic drugs (drugs that Bridgewater's brother had peddled back in high school). The drugs seemed to help at first—at least Zippy stopped sending Mick Jagger two dozen letters every day and had otherwise functioned normally at her job and in social circumstances—but then just over a month ago she had just taken off. One day at the end of April she just hadn't been home when Bridgewater got there. A few days later he received a postcard from some island in the Caribbean.

Bridgewater sighed, looking at the girl in the pool. Feckless, without real vitality, despite his big shoulders and his tan, the lifeguard, too, followed the girl's movements, a big dumb smile smeared across his face. He had the inside track to the girl's affections. But damned if Bridgewater was going to be jealous. He turned back to his magazine.

"Excuse me, is Saul Bellow's new book reviewed in that issue?"

Bridgewater turned to look into the eyes of the red-haired woman on the chaise lounge next to his. He thought he recognized her from someplace. Those laughing green cat's eyes stared familiarly.

"*More Die of Heartbreak*? I don't know. I think so."

"Can I see it when you're done? I'm doing a paper on Saul Bellow for a summer school class at Hopkins."

"Oh yeah?"

"The theme of plants in his later novels. Plant life, vegetable consciousness. Like deep sleep."

"Sounds interesting." Bridgewater gave her the magazine. *Sounds like a crashing bore!*

"You're sure you're done with it?"

"Sure." Couldn't he say anything but "sure" and "oh yeah?" This was his chance to meet another woman. She had clearly dropped a hankie in asking for the magazine. Bridgewater knew his mating rituals, all right. Talk about tail-lifting. Where had he seen her before?

She gave the impression of being athletic. She probably worked out on metal and naugahyde equipment in a sweat-smelling fitness club somewhere, Bridgewater guessed, played racquetball and squash. Her strong-looking legs were tanned from exposure to the sun (or a tanning booth); flat against her muscular torso, her breasts, the contour visible underneath the peach-colored nylon bathing suit, reminded him of two country-fried eggs. Wholesome. "Good for you." Momentarily, he envisioned oozing yellow yolk on the fabric staining the pinkish orange swimsuit blue-green. Crazy. He blinked his eyes to clear away the hallucination. He eyed the woman critically.

Attractive, yes, but her rich dull red hair would be brassy and toneless in another few years, and with that sort of coloration she would most likely develop moles and warts on her arms and body. But then, he was no great shakes in the looks department himself, would be even less a prize as time went on. Bridgewater was a slender, bony man with knobby knees and fine blond hair sparsely covering his shins and thighs. His hairline was receding; he had a bald spot on his crown. Looking at him, you thought of scaffolding or collapsible aluminum porch furniture, the legs buckled under. Still, he reserved the right to assess women from the perspective of a teenage cocksman. Certainly at this moment in time, she was a delectable piece. No argument there. But where had he seen her before?

"You go to Hopkins?"

"I'm in a graduate program in English. I took a few years off after college," she explained. "I taught English in high school for a while."

Mid to late twenties, Bridgewater calculated, the facts dovetailing with the appearance.

"And you're doing a paper on Bellow?"

"You think it's dumb, don't you?" she accused. "Plant life. Ever read *The Dean's December*, the one he wrote after getting the Nobel Prize? Remember how the dean was a sucker for the cyclamens back in Chicago?" She did not pause for a reply but went on without taking a breath. "Flowers are so complex but so benign. The appearance of design in nature without any apparent intelligence behind it. Of course, the same facts used to be used to prove the existence of God." Her crazy bookish talk both challenged and repelled him.

"Maybe it's innocence he's getting at; the innocence of an absent-minded intellectual in human affairs seen as analogous to the innocent growth of plants. Mystic signs of an unconscious order." She seemed to be talking more to herself than to him, but still she eyed him closely, intently, a cat watching a bird.

"Or like the cicadas," Bridgewater interrupted. "Buried under the ground for seventeen years and then they wake up like Sleeping Beauty to a full-fledged sex life, so natural and unpremeditated it's just like breathing."

"Sure, like the cicadas," the woman said, turning away, and Bridgewater felt from her curt reply, the apparent boredom and distaste, that he had lost points. What had he said wrong? Did he sound too sarcastic, as if he didn't take her seriously? Her aggressive manner put him off balance but attracted him at the same time. He didn't know that much about Bellow. Better leave the topic alone and go on to something else.

"You come here often?" he asked.

"Depends on what you mean by 'often'."

The coy response both pleased and annoyed Bridgewater. He shrugged. "Do you come here after classes or something?"

"I live over there," she said, indicating an adjacent apartment building with a nod of her head. "It's part of the rental agreement. I get to use the pool. How about you?"

"I just joined."

"Did your wife join with you?"

Bridgewater looked down at his left hand with the gold band on it. Then he remembered: he had seen this woman at the store where he bought his monthly bus pass, a dirty, bleak-looking building with MONEY ORDERS FOOD STAMPS CHECKS CASHED painted in loud red letters on the whitewashed brick outside and glowing in eerie blue neon in the window. He and Zippy used to go in together at the end of every month to buy bus passes. They owned a car, but they preferred public transportation.

"No, she left Baltimore about a month ago." He shrugged. What could he say without exposing the great gaping hole in his heart? "She was suffering from de Clerambault's Syndrome."

"Rambo?"

Was she joking? "Maybe I mispronounced it. It's a mental disorder." He shrugged again, hating himself for using that term. Disorder.

"She's in a hospital or something?"

"Or something." After an awkward silence he made a lame clarification "She just . . . went away." He changed the subject. "So you're doing a paper on Saul Bellow." *Wrong move*! He wished he could take it back.

"He has this thing about your elemental self, the way you really are."

"The way you 'really are'?"

Agitated, she gestured with the *Time*, which she had rolled up into a baton, waving it in a semi-circle over her head, and Bridgewater could have sworn her green eyes bulged out past the tip of her nose, big as traffic lights. The cicadas' shrill noise seemed to foster hallucinations. "A basic harmony. An elemental serenity. Mystical and passive, feminine. Like vegetation. Bellow is annoyed by the oscillation of modern consciousness. It's like the restlessness of high-speed computers that constantly poll terminals for input, only it's the senses and memory that are being polled for some new pocket of stimulation, something to fasten the attention on, some nugget of interest. There *are* twenty-four hours to be gotten through every day, after all."

"Too bad we can't live like the cicadas, eh? Just do, don't think." He tried to be agreeable, conciliatory, but apparently he just put his foot in his mouth.

"That's not what I mean." The hollowness of her tone made Bridgewater flinch. "I think there's already too much doing and not enough thinking."

"Just not enough innocence, huh?"

Abruptly, she changed the subject. "Your wife. Where did she go?"

The woman was crazy. Why not try the truth out on her? "Zippy? She went off to marry Mick Jagger."

"Zippy? That's her name? Like the comic strip? Zippy the Pinhead?"

"It's short for Zipporah. A Biblical name. Zipporah was Moses' wife. The name means 'little bird'."

"Moses' wife, eh?"

"She's Jewish. I'm Jewish."

"You? Jewish? Come on! You tell me one lie after another! With that little upturned nose and blond hair?"

"I converted. It's a long story."

"You converted and your wife is marrying Mick Jagger. I hope Jerry Hall has something to say about this."

"All right. I was lying. She's at home. She doesn't like to swim or sunbathe. She didn't want to join." He was sorry now that he'd gotten involved in a conversation with a crazy woman; his loneliness had gotten the better of him.

"I thought so. And you aren't really Jewish, are you?"

"What does 'really Jewish' mean?" he asked, exasperated. His mother-in-law had a hang-up about the same subject. She claimed that the Torah was very explicit on the subject. Who was a Jew, who was a Jew permitted marry, what might happen to a Jew if he or she married a gentile. She said the Torah denounced intermarriage in no uncertain terms. When Bridgewater pointed out that the Torah was full of "mixed marriages," that even Moses had intermarried—Zipporah was the daughter of Jethro the Middianite—Edith Feldman snapped back that Moses married Zipporah *before* the Hebrews had received the Torah on Mount Sinai, and what's more, Moses had not been allowed to enter the promised land.

"Where does your wife work? Zippy?" the woman asked, changing the subject once again. Talk about the oscillation of modern consciousness. But she could probably see that the coy exchange was a cul-de-sac. Ran off to marry Mick Jagger. How absurd!

"Social Security." But why, Bridgewater wondered, was she so concerned about his wife?

"I knew this woman who worked at Social Security," the red-haired woman said. "Hated it. Absolutely *hated* her job. She worked in a building there where everybody complained that their sinuses were being ruined by the office environment, the recycled air. Big clots of gunk and so forth in the nasal passages. Gross."

"Zippy doesn't seem to mind it much." He tried putting on a laconic manner in a feeble attempt to bring the conversation to a close, but face it, he was starving for conversation, even this crazy exchange. How long had it been now? He felt like a Trappist monk.

"My friend at Social Security said her job was very paper-intensive." Which meant, Bridgewater guessed, that she scribbled a lot, made a lot of false starts, wrote a lot of memos. A writer? A computer programmer, like Zippy? A bureaucrat?

"Well, what is your name, anyway?" he asked. A cicada came veering toward his face, and he felt an instant of irrational panic as he slapped at the insect. "God damn bug," he said, embarrassed to have lost his composure. He noticed that the cute girl in the bikini had finished swimming and was lying on a chaise lounge next to the lifeguard.

"Cecilia Nestorick."

The name sounded familiar. Nestorick. Where had he heard it before? You didn't have to give your name to get a bus pass, after all. An anonymous transaction. You told the man behind the glass partition what sort of pass you wanted—the sex of the bus pass owner and the number of zones it covered—and he quoted a price.

"We're distant cousins," Cecilia said, watching him suspiciously.

"Excuse me?" Bridgewater said, puzzled. "Distant cousins?"

"Weren't you going to ask me if I was related to Roger Nestorick? Everybody else does."

Bridgewater's interest revived. So Cecilia had similar problems, he thought, taking heart. Crazy, but on the same wavelength. Roger Nestorick, the infamous sex offender who had molested more than a dozen boys and girls—not to mention terrorizing half the household pets in Waverly, if you could believe the stories—had been convicted on six counts in January after a sensational trial. Zippy may not be an outlaw, she may not even have been crazy, but the doctors had diagnosed both her and Roger as sexual nut cases. Who knows? Maybe Zippy would yet turn out to be the next John Hinckley. He had a quick image of his wife stalking the president with a gun in order to impress Mick Jagger.

"Oh yeah. Now I remember. I followed the case in the papers."

"You and the rest of the city."

"My father knows the prosecutor pretty well," Bridgewater explained.

"Your dad works for the government?"

"City Hall. God, it must have been pretty trying for your family." He tried to sound sympathetic.

"Tell me about it. My mother's on committees down in Annapolis and Washington trying to get research grants and lobbying for money for mental health care."

"Your mother?"

"I said *his* mother."

He wasn't having auditory hallucinations, too, was he? He thought about correcting her but decided not to. Her mother, his mother. What was the difference? Bridgewater shook his head. sympathetically. "So what's become of him, anyway? Was he committed or something? Sent to a hospital?" His curiosity overtook his tact. (Besides, hadn't she asked personal questions?)

But Cecilia took it in stride. "Well, of course he was institutionalized. He'll be in a halfway house soon, though. They've tried a number of treatments on him, from psychodynamic psychotherapies to masturbatory satiation techniques to drug treatment."

"Drug treatment?"

"Antiandrogens. They're supposed to lower the blood level of testosterone."

"Sort of a cold shower in a hypodermic syringe, eh?"

"Testosterone is associated with sexual desire and sexual aggression. The drugs he takes decrease sexual fantasies and the capacity for erection and ejaculation."

"You sound so clinical."

"What do you want? *The National Enquirer*?"

A cicada landed on Bridgewater's bathing suit. He brushed it away.

"Somebody ought to give antiandrogens to these creatures."

"That's nature, not fantasy."

Irritated by Cecilia's didactic tone, Bridgewater finally snapped. "You want natural?" he said. "I'll give you natural."

Cecilia hissed, disgusted. Chastised yet piqued, Bridgewater became insolent. "I bet if you roast them and sprinkle the ashes on a salad it might have an aphrodisiac effect. Like Spanish fly. That wild sexual impulse is clearly genetic, so maybe it would affect humans if we ate them, what do you think?"

"Hah!" Cecilia snorted, sensitive to Bridgewater's aggressive tone. Her green eyes sparkled, vibrant with lunacy. "You know what they make me think of? The dead ones? They make me think of those Halloween candies. The orange and black marshmallow things with the sugar coating."

"They say cicadas taste like shrimp."

She looked dubious. "Probably they taste like whatever you season them with. Garlic or pepper or butter or whatever."

"I bet they get you pretty hot." Bridgewater felt reckless and lewd, carried away by the crazy talk and the cicadas' screeching noise.

"Maybe if you season them with curry powder or coriander."

"Are you feeling hot?" Bridgewater said suggestively. "Would you like to go for a swim?"

"Why don't *you* just cool it?" She regarded him contemptuously.

Excited as a cicada, confused by the fast pace of the repartee, Bridgewater leaned over to Cecilia so that his lips were only inches away from hers. A few others around the pool glanced their way. Doug, the lifeguard, suddenly pointed his nose in the air like a terrier, sensing a hunt. The girl in the bikini's mouth dropped.

"We could go to your apartment over there. We could probably cool down there pretty well."

"I think you've got the wrong station!" Cecilia said toughly. "Why don't you try changing the channel?"

Amazing! Bridgewater had mentally used a similar metaphor to assess his vulnerability to the girl. He thought, he was on the same wavelength, but his carnal desire had jammed the broadcast, and now she was tuning him out.

Bridgewater stood up and walked to the pool. He felt dizzy, vertiginous, reeling like a dying cicada that was spinning to the earth. He dove into the warm, scummy water but with no sensation of relief, shamed by his behavior.

But then he noticed he could no longer hear the ceaseless shriek of the cicadas. He had escaped the noise! Staying under as long as he could, cut off about as completely as if he were in an isolation tank, Bridgewater felt a kind of purgation take place, a cleansing of his emotions. He stayed under until he felt his lungs were about to explode.

A Real Jew

Peter Bridgewater's father, Frank, had an elaborate electric train set. He devoted an entire room of his house to it. There were little towns, train stations, smiling rosy-cheeked white-whiskered plastic stationmasters that actually threw switches and blew whistles, intricate bridges like rollercoasters, tunnels and viaducts, trees, pastures, windmills, cows, a little rippling river with actual water, falls and mill, five trains whose movement around the track was coordinated with split-second accuracy by a timetable Frank had worked out; the trains switched tracks and obeyed traffic signals, sped up and slowed down. Frank Bridgewater wanted to bequeath his train set to a grandson.

Moishe Feldman, Peter Bridgewater's father-in-law, thought Frank Bridgewater was softheaded, a fat, complacent WASP. Frank worked in city government, a bureaucrat high up there in an appointed position; he knew people. A flabby man with high blood pressure, his gnomic, grandfatherly face was red and pale by turns. He pushed papers, and he was an honest government official, but his main interest was his electric train set. It wasn't the privileged WASP aspect that disturbed Moishe when he met Frank so much as the vacancy, the benign expression on his face.

Zippy's father was a short, thin, very tense man. Except for the bald head he could have been cast as Sherlock Holmes. The same hawklike profile. A great noticer. His eyes shifted back and forth as regular as windshield wipers, taking things in. His thick eyebrows had unruly tufts that arched antennae-like with a Mephistophelean flair, like Salvador Dali's mustaches. His small mouth sloped downward in a sensuous look of considered appraisal. He gave an impression of continual evaluation and revision.

The vacancy in Frank Bridgewater's face and the childish obsession with the toy trains disturbed Moishe Feldman for deeper reasons than resentment. Was this a family trait, this childishness? Like father, like son? Moishe's eyes tick-tocked back and forth, observing, weighing, sizing up his new son-in-law, comparing him to his old man.

If Moishe had known about Frank's father, he would have been really disturbed. Peter's grandfather had had Alzheimer's, though he'd died at 80 from an aneurysm. Nobody had a name for his condition, and friends and relatives were shocked by his loss of memory. This couldn't be senility, they reasoned, because the old guy was still very active; it was more akin to something weird and inexplicable, like something from a horror movie. Driving from Philadelphia to Baltimore one afternoon after going to the flower show, Peter Bridgewater had turned to his wife, to whom he had been married fifty-five years, and had said to her quite seriously: "And what did you say your name was?"

Had Moishe known this, he would have felt very uneasy about his daughter Zipporah's marriage. A definite family characteristic, one might infer. You can't argue with genes.

As it was, Moishe already was disturbed, and not surprisingly. Neither he nor his wife Edith had been aware of the Bridgewaters until Zippy had introduced her fiancé to them as a *fait accompli*—a converted Jew.

It was at Zippy Feldman's urging that Bridgewater had decided to convert to Judaism. Not to say he was insincere: Peter had always secretly thought of himself as Jewish, sort of a Morrano, both now and back then. But he did not think of "Jewish" as referring to a religious conviction. Whether he could participate in Jewish liturgical practices seemed vaguely beside the point to him. Yet converting to Judaism meant exactly that, learning the Jewish calendar, the rudiments of kashrut, the Jewish dietary laws, and an acquaintance with Hebrew and with Jewish history. Some of this was already familiar to him and explained why he identified with Jews. Only, he had learned about Jewish history as the "Old" Testament, law and lore that had been superseded by the "New" Testament. Still, he hadn't implicitly accepted the Christian creed; he never *really* believed that God had had a son by a virgin, for example; nor did he actually believe in God or heaven or a soul with an afterlife, though he *had* gone through a phase of believing in ghosts. He had read Hans Holzer and other parapsychologists like a fundamentalist Christian reading the bible, accepting the "proof" of otherworldly phenomena without question. He always pointed out that Holzer's books were classified as "non-fiction" in the public library as evidence of their factuality. The books wouldn't be non-fiction if they weren't true, the teenaged Bridgewater had reasoned.

But essentially Peter did not care about any other world than the one he lived in, and it was in this world that he felt Jewish; it was the this-wordly orientation of Judaism that he identified with, why he "felt Jewish." What did this mean, "feeling Jewish"? It did not mean eating bagels and traditional Jewish food and avoiding pork, shellfish, or milk with meat; it did not mean attending bar mitzvahs and other Jewish social events. It meant being alone, a minority of one, on a sort of personal Diaspora, away from a home where you are not even missed. A sort of Woody Allen character, or a character out of a Philip Roth story who has no blind loyalties, for whom self-consciousness is a curse.

Bridgewater thought it was significant that Kierkegaard had used Abraham as the paradigm of faith. That was what "Jewish" meant to Peter, growing up in Baltimore in the 1960's—strong convictions held in isolation. He would learn many other ideas about what being Jewish meant as he grew older.

Including religious conversion. According to Zippy, if Peter simply converted to Judaism, he would satisfy her parents, who dearly wanted her to marry a Jewish man. At some point in their relationship, when they were both in their mid-twenties and had lived together monogamously for a year and found the life a pleasant one, Peter and Zippy had begun discussing marriage. Of course, it was inevitable that the subject would come up, and indeed, Peter had discussed it with two or three previous girlfriends. (Always, he had approved of the idea, while his partners, perhaps taking the subject more seriously than he as a real proposition rather than a sentimental fantasy, had expressed distaste at the idea, even contempt for his lack of a sense of reality; they were just "friends" those girls had pointed out, even if they had had sex.) But at some point the subject became real and not merely theoretical, and their discussions became more like strategy sessions (us against the world) than abstract, idealized pictures of a life of bliss and equality. The goal was to satisfy everybody's expectations. *Everybody's.*

Peter could not deny that Zippy knew her own parents better than he—after all, he had never met them. Nor could he deny that he wanted peace in the family. Therefore, since she insisted that converting would satisfy her parents' single requirement that the man she married must be Jewish, he saw no reason to refuse to convert to Judaism. He saw no hypocrisy, either: not to say that he wasn't *aware* that his actions proceeded from opportunistic motives, but the gesture was no more hypocritical than any other act meant to promote harmony and peace, like going to school and preening before the teacher or pretending to be fulfilled by your lousy little job, evincing the faith that if you stuck to it long enough, it had to get better (or at least, you'd get used to it) or shamming an interest in the boring affairs of some relative with whom you happened to be trapped for an hour, or even exchanging pleasantries with the grocer while he bags your bread and cheese. You did not have to be a fervent zealot to convert to another religion. Spaniards used to make Christian converts of South American Indians by the tens of thousands, after all.

Of course, religion purports to deal with the ultimate issues—birth, death, morality, eternity, the afterlife—while something like buying a box of breakfast cereal is only a trivial transaction, but you always encounter life on a personal basis, from a private perspective, and while religion might offer some valid interpretations and offer useful suggestions, you can never truthfully buy any one dogma lock, stock and barrel—any more than you can buy cereal without considering that it is made from wheat or has fruit in it or sugar-coating or makes you shit better. You might buy into an idea, but you never truly sell your soul. Like science, religion codifies, and to that degree it loses the personal magic that prompted it in the first place. So Peter consented to convert to Judaism, and he enjoyed the classes and the course of study; he did not feel like a fraud. He felt that he was doing something good.

For twenty-two weeks, Peter was enrolled in a weekly evening class composed of couples who intended to marry, one of whom was Jewish. Half the converts were men and the other half women; there was no sexual bend. Why twenty-two weeks, Peter wondered. Twenty-two letters in the Hebrew alphabet? In cabalistic numerology, the number twenty-two stood for "all things." Whatever the reason, after the twenty-two week course, Peter signed up to go through the conversion ceremony, after which, according to the conservative rabbi who sponsored him, Peter would be Jewish. At that time, Peter would get to pick a Jewish name.

Peter's sponsor, Rabbi Norman Saperstein, a serious young fellow with an enormous social conscience matched only by the gravity of his expression, both of which depressed the hell out of Bridgewater, offered to speak with him whenever he needed guidance, but as passionately as he wanted to *want* to be guided spiritually, Bridgewater could never think of anything to talk to the rabbi about. He called on Saperstein once, made an appointment, and the two sat in Saperstein's gloomy book-crammed study at the shul for half an hour saying practically nothing. Still, the rabbi seemed convinced of Bridgewater's sincerity, and he never questioned his motives.

Finally came the day of the conversion ceremony, the ritual, the vows, the prayers—there was always a ceremony for such events. This one involved immersion in a *mikva*—a ritual purification bath—like a baptism. The *mikva* was in a nondescript gray frame house on Washington Street in Brookline. Peter and Zippy were living in a small apartment in Beacon Hill, in Boston, that winter. They had caught the subway out from Arlington Street, walking through the snow-buried Public Garden to the subway station that cold, bright Sunday morning. Several other people from Bridgewater's class were converting that day, too. They were accompanied by parents and relatives. Bridgewater and Zippy held hands in silence, awaiting his turn, listening to the others talking. They were sitting in a sort of waiting room in the front of the house. An aged Jewish lady had met them at the door and indicated the hangers where they could leave their coats. Then she led them to the small anteroom that was stuffed with ill-matched furniture—straight-backed chairs of all different styles, some wood and some metal, sofas whose upholstery was frayed and splitting, a couple of tatty armchairs.

"I was in the hospital overnight," a shy blond fellow in his middle twenties was saying. Bridgewater knew him; Jeff Elliott was a plump, cheerful man who ran a newspaper stand in Quincy; he was marrying a dark, tiny woman named Susan Nichter. Bridgewater assumed that the bald man with thick, dark-framed glasses was Susan's father.

"It must have hurt," the man said sympathetically.

"Not much," Jeff answered.

Susan looked on dreamily, embarrassed, pretending that she was not listening to her father and her fiancé.

"Well . . . I guess it's necessary," Mr. Nichter said.

"Yeah, it's the—the sign, I guess."

"Although it's not just Jews."

"But for different reasons."

"That's true."

The two men fell silent. Several minutes later Jeff was summoned to the rooms at the back of the house. The older lady came into the room through a squeaky, swinging wooden door and nodded to him, whispering something Bridgewater could not hear. He wondered if she looked ghoulish but could not convince himself she did.

"You're converting too," the man said, part question, part statement. Why else would this other blond fellow be here with a dark Jewish girl?

"Yes." Bridgewater felt some longer explanation was required, but he could not think of anything to say.

"Did you have to go through the same thing as Jeff?"

"No, I already was," Bridgewater said, feeling a little offended that his penis was in the public domain, a subject for all to talk about, even directly to his face. "But there's a ceremony. The covenant of Abraham." He shrugged, feeling his face turn pink with self-consciousness.

Mr. Nichter smiled and nodded his head and looked away. Zippy squeezed his hand and they looked sympathetically into each other's eyes. Zippy had dark, shadowy hair that she cut like a helmet; it hung loose to the shoulders and her bangs came partway down her forehead. In the subdued light of the anteroom she seemed like the subject of a religious painting. A dim light the Dutch painters would have killed for. Bridgewater also thought of Italian Renaissance Madonnas and became excited by the possibilities. It could be solemn or it could be satiric, this Jewish Madonna painting. He gave it a title: *Bris Millah*. A Jewish sister or mother at a male child's circumcision.

With painterly objectivity, Bridgewater took an inventory of Zippy's features: Mediterranean-looking skin, big brown eyes with a subtle Oriental slant, small even teeth, a nose that came straight down from her brows and then hooked (like her father's), hatchet-like, perpendicular to her weak chin that sloped inward toward her neck; the head was propped on a long, elegant neck that sank into a basin formed by big collarbones and small, sloping shoulders. Her dark eyebrows knitted toward each other in a look of affection. Maybe a charcoal sketch, he thought, though a vivid oil painting with the yellow light on her hair, like a halo, would be stunning. But as always, he did not have his tools with him when he needed them, and the inspiration became a monumental burden that finally melted into forgetfulness.

A few minutes later, the old lady came through the swinging doors and looked at Bridgewater. Again she mumbled something he could not understand, but he knew she wanted him to follow her, and he rose from his seat. Zippy squeezed his hand one last time.

Bridgewater was shown into a room where his mentor, Rabbi Saperstein, and two other rabbis awaited him. He shook hands with the rabbis and with the *mohel*, and without further ado was asked to pull down his pants. While the three rabbis mumbled prayers, the *mohel* sprayed a local anesthetic on Bridgewater's cock and then stabbed the hem where the shaft meets the head with a lancet, drawing blood. The other rabbis continued to mumble prayers until the ceremony was over. Then Bridgewater was told he could pull his pants back up.

He was shown into a dressing room by Rabbi Saperstein and told to take off his clothes. When he was completely naked, he took a shower, and then, naked and dripping, he went through a door into the *mikva,* a blue-tiled pool of natural rainwater with steps leading down into the water. The water came up to his chest.

Rabbi Saperstein entered through another door. He asked Bridgewater why he was in the *mikva*, and Bridgewater replied that he was converting to Judaism. This was part of the script, and Bridgewater knew it was coming. In fact, he had rehearsed all his lines many times. Next, the rabbi asked him if he were doing this of his own free will, and he said yes. Then he completely immersed himself, and when he emerged, he put on the black nylon yarmulke the rabbi handed down to him and recited the required prayer in Hebrew and in English: "*Barooch ata adonai, elohaynoo melech ha-olam, asher kid'shanoo b'mitzvotav v'tzee-vanoo al t'vee-lat gayreem*. Blessed art thou, oh Lord our God, Ruler of the Universe, for sanctifying our lives with thy commandments and for instructing us about the immersion of converts."

Immediately afterward came the second prayer. First, Bridgewater dunked twice, then he put the yarmulke back on and said, "*Barooch ata adonai, elohaynoo melech ha-olam, shehecheyanoo, v'keeyemanoo, v'heegeeanoo, la-a'zman, ha-she*. Blessed art thou, oh Lord our God, Ruler of the Universe, for granting us life, sustaining us, and for helping us to reach this day."

And that was it. Already he had chosen his Jewish name, Pinchas. As was the custom, he chose a name that began with the same phonetic character as his Christian name. At the final class meeting the following Tuesday evening, Bridgewater received a certificate of conversion with both his Christian and his Jewish names. Pinchas ben Avraham. Son of Abraham. What had become of Frank?

After the immersion ceremony, Bridgewater got dressed and went out to the waiting room. Peter-Pinchas and Zippy went to a kosher restaurant on Harvard Avenue and had lunch to celebrate the conversion.

That night, back in their Beacon Hill apartment, Bridgewater noticed bloodstains on his underwear when he stripped to go to bed. For several days afterward there was a bruise on his dick where the *mohel* had stabbed him with the lancet. Other than that, nothing felt very different.

Zippy was a secretkeeper. Premonition and secretkeeping usually go hand in hand, and Zippy was to premonition what Houdini was to escape: she was downright mediumistic. Bridgewater was well aware of this propensity of hers to anticipate the future. In fact, her insight and sensitivity had persuaded him that conversion was the most pragmatic strategy for marrying; while they were co-conspirators, Zippy was clearly the "intelligence source." So, lulled by her sanguine outlook, Bridgewater was completely unprepared for his reception into the Feldman family.

But perhaps the whole problem lay with the fact that Zippy *was* a secretkeeper. This was not news to Bridgewater. Early in their relationship, for example, long before she fell for Mick Jagger, Zippy had been gone on a big name sports star whose face smiled at you from billboards and cereal boxes, encouraging you to drink milk. But she wouldn't admit to the crush, as though to say it would be to demean it. Secretkeepers are like that; they know something you don't know, and that's the kick. Much later, after she had gone off to marry Mick Jagger, Bridgewater would remember his introduction to her parents —the revelation to her folks of Zippy's main secret—as the beginning of the end, when he began to lose the specialness for her that had been so central to their relationship.

But at the time he was simply shocked by the confusion into which he had evidently thrown the Feldmans. Maybe he was a Jew, technically, according to somebody's system, but the Feldmans didn't buy it; his parents couldn't be explained away so easily, and after all, the Feldmans met them all at the same time, more or less: introduced to their son-in-law on Monday, they met Peter's father on the following Friday. Moishe's eyes swept with the regularity of a metronome between father and son, sizing them up.

Though the Feldmans had grown up in New York City, Moishe's business had taken him to the middle west after he and Edith were married. Moishe Feldman sold watercraft, used mostly on lakes. The Feldmans were the only Jewish family in Potawatomi Rapids, on Lake Michigan. So among Diaspora Jews, the Feldmans were on a diaspora of their own, exiled from their New York family and connections. Perhaps because she was so isolated, Zippy's mother had striven to act and speak Jewish. "Oy!" Edith loved to say, or "Gevalt!" Saying the Yiddish words made her feel like a "real" Jew from her grandparents' Galician *shtetl*, none of your assimilated American bastardized Jews for her, those Reform Jews just dying to be Protestant. She kept a kosher kitchen as best she could under the circumstances. She was febrile-looking and had a warm smile and quick, judicious eyes, and Bridgewater liked her right away for the character he could see bursting out of her skin, but he was frozen by the coldness she showed him.

But they went through the wedding as planned. Guests were invited from both sides of the family. Bridgewater's uncle, a chemist who lived near Ann Arbor, attended with a lady friend. His father and his brother represented him, too. His brother had come all the way from France. None of Zippy's other relatives came, other than her sister, Rachael. One sent a contribution in Zippy's name to an anti-*shmad* society that opposed intermarriage as an apostasy from Judaism.

They were married beneath a *chupah* by a conservative rabbi from Muskegon, and Bridgewater stamped on the wineglass, shattering it. Putting the ring on Zippy's finger, he recited the prayer: "*Ha-ray aht m'kudeshat lee, b'taba-aht zu, k'dat moshe v'yis-ra-ayl.*" Be thou consecrated unto me by this ring as my wife, according to the law of Moses and Israel. After the wedding, they spent their honeymoon with the Feldmans in Potawatomi Rapids. Frank and Mark went back home to Baltimore, Mark having "completed his business" in France, as he put it, though it wasn't clear to Peter what his "business" was, and Rachael went back to school in Waltham.

Bridgewater's most vivid memory of the honeymoon was going barefoot down the path every morning to the outhouse to do his business, the sound of his feet muffled on the pad of dead brown pine needles that lined the way. Because of the water pressure, the Feldmans' main toilet facilities (they did have flush toilets) were in this building fifty feet down the lakeside from the main house. In the mornings, the narrow path would be crisscrossed with cobwebs spiders had spun between the cedar branches and the juniper bushes overnight, and the filaments clung, net-like, to his face when he walked to the outhouse at dawn.

One morning, when he approached the main house from the outhouse, just as he was about to come into view from around a huge ancient pine tree, its furrowed bark green and mossy, he overheard the Feldmans in urgent discussion with their daughter.

"I just hope he doesn't wind up like his father," Moishe was saying.

"But what's wrong with his father?" Zippy cried, exasperated.

"Oy! What's wrong with his father, she asks!" Edith exclaimed.

"He plays with toys! Did you hear him going on and on about his train set? My God! I thought I was talking to a four-year old boy!"

"He's very important in Baltimore politics."

"What's that prove? We have an actor for president."

"He's not as dumb as you think he is."

"I just hope Gazookis doesn't wind up like him."

"They're very nice people. I stayed at their house when I went down for my interview with the Social Security Administration."

"I'm sure they're fine people," Moishe said, and Bridgewater could feel his inner struggle to make the point he was trying to make. "I don't doubt their generosity. But what's Gazookis going to do when you move down to Baltimore? Sponge off his old man? Play with toys?"

"Freelance graphics."

"But he wants to be a writer."

The heavy irony in her father's voice upset Zippy. "A *painter*!" she exclaimed. "He wants to *paint*!"

"All right, a painter. But how will he make a living?"

"He can get freelance work. Besides, he has a chance to work in the graphics lab at Wyman Park Community College."

"Never heard of it."

"Well, Peter's never heard of Potawatomi Rapids, either."

"You're going to support him on your government paycheck from Social Security?"

"We'll share expenses."

"He'll get his share from his old man. I know the type."

"Gevalt, Zipporah! Intermarriage is Hitler's final victory!" Edith cried then, the though probably triggered by her husband's reference to "types."

"But he's Jewish! He converted!"

"In Israel there are people who would say he's *not* Jewish."

"Israel, hell. The United States. But I was *with* him! He converted! He's sincere about it!"

"But he just doesn't *look* Jewish! He's not from the same gene pool. He's his father's son!"

"What a racist thing to say! *You* sound like Hitler!"

"Gevalt, Zipporah! Such things you should not say!"

"But can't you see I love him? Don't you understand that we love each other? Don't you know what love means?"

"Love!" Moishe scoffed. "Love means whatever you want it to mean. It doesn't have anything to do with this."

"Your concern with the purity of the race?"

"It's not *race*! Unless you want to call it racial memory. It's people! It's tradition!"

"Don't hand me that *Fiddler on the Roof* crap!"

"Oy vey!"

"It's *not* race!" Moishe insisted. "It's—it's—"

"Genes! You keep harping on genes!"

"Genes aren't race, Zippy! Genes are facts! His father plays with electric trains, Zippy! Do you hear what I'm saying? His father plays with toys!"

"At least his uncle seemed intelligent," Edith conceded. "The chemist."

"But his father!"

"His father! Oy vey!"

"Just be nice to him!" Zippy pleaded. "Please just try to be nice to him."

"Nice to him!" Moishe scoffed. "Who's not going to be 'nice' to him? You know, his brother sure looked like a druggie, with that little leather thug hat and the long straggly hair."

"Mark's been in France."

"What was he doing there?"

"I think he had some sort of business."

"What sort of business?":

"I don't know. What if he was just absorbing the culture? Bumming around?"

"Bumming around," Moishe repeated. That said it all.

"Well, look who's talking about brothers," Zippy said. "You certainly have a fine one."

"What? My brother Sid's an elected official of New Jersey, Zippy. Sid's made something out of himself!"

"Uncle Sid's a corrupt bully and you know it. He always has been. He makes Jimmy Hoffa look like a saint."

"Oy vey!"

"You show a little more respect for your elders, Zippy! Besides, we're not talking about Sid. We're talking about Gazookis."

"Well, at least any children you have will be Jewish," Edith said.

"You mean genetically?" Zippy said sarcastically. She knew that a child born of a Jewish woman is by definition Jewish.

"Oy vey! To think this is my daughter! To think a daughter of mine would speak this way to her mother!"

"I'm going to Detweiler's for a newspaper," Moishe said, bringing the discussion to a close. Detweiler's was the general store in Potawatomi Rapids.

Bridgewater leaned against the pine, listening to the door open and then close and then the engine of Moishe's Buick Skylark starting up. What makes a Jew a Jew? Genes? The persecution mentality? Cultural memory? Rituals? Beliefs? Shared values? What makes a Jew a *real* Jew?

Later that day they drove over to Chippewa Landing, near Manton, to canoe on the Manistee. ("Chippewa? The Chippewa were a tribe in North Carolina and Georgia that got resettled on a reservation in Oklahoma," Peter said. "They were never near Michigan!" "That's the Cherokee," Moishe said, correcting him. "The Chippewa, or Ojibwa, were part of the Algonquin tribal system, Canadian Indians." He felt triumphant, demonstrating his superior knowledge, but his doubts about Peter increased; his eyes swept over Bridgewater like searchlights; his frown deepened and his mouth became an "O" of doubt.) When they got out of the car, Peter remembered they'd left the sunscreen and the thermos of iced tea behind.

"There's stuff in the trunk, the trunk, the trunk. There's stuff in the trunk, the trunk, the trunk. Stuff in the trunk! Stuff in the trunk! Stuff in the, stuff in the trunk!" he chanted boyishly.

Zippy laughed, but Moishe looked at him as if he were crazy, his eyes prowling back and forth restlessly, like caged animals. All that afternoon he watched Bridgewater for signs of mental weakness. Peter felt miserable all that day, a bug under a microscope, until he and Zippy boarded an airplane in Grand Rapids to go back to Boston.

A Work of Art

It was a hot summer, heat wave after heat wave rolling in, leaving the city awash in hundred degree temperatures for days on end, saturating every hour of the day with unbearable, damp warmth, flooding every pore with the effluence of frustration, anger, exhaustion. At 6:00 a.m. the temperature would already be 85. Overnight lows never went below 80.

The hot summer had been full of controversy and violence. There were the Iran-Contra hearings down in Washington, Oliver North, Admiral Poindexter, the lawyers and the Senate committee all exchanging heated words and the news media repeating every one of them at least a dozen times. Everywhere you looked, there was something that made people angry, started fights. Pit bulls, the Pope's visit with Kurt Waldheim, the nomination of the new Supreme Court justice. Sikh separatists bombed Hindu buses in the Punjab, and the Persian Gulf boiled over with violence. There was trouble between the Iranians and the French, the Iranians and the Iraqis, the Iranians and the Americans, the Iranians and practically everybody. The Russians continued to duke it out with the mujahedin in Afghanistan. In Los Angeles, people actually shot each other on the freeways.

In Baltimore, the Hadassah convention had just been held and the big name politicians had all courted the Jewish vote—George Bush, Barbara Mikulski, George Schultz, asskissers justifying government policy or promising change. And there was controversy over the governor's plans to build a twin-stadium sports complex in Camden Yards. Controversy over the number of homeruns baseball players were hitting filled the sports pages. Land reform in the Philippines, the prosecution of Nazi war criminals, AIDS, Medicare, Alzheimer's, the court martial of Curtis Lonetree (the marine guard at the American embassy in Moscow), South Korean student riots, the ongoing debate over nuclear power plants, the PTL wars, Jim and Tammi Bakker, medium-range missile curbs, disarmament negotiations. The list was practically endless. Beirut was always a mess, and South Africa was forever the scene of killing and strikes. The airlines were sloppy with near-miss incidents and crashes, and you could always count on a long wait at the airport before your plane took off, seldom on time. Inflation was on the rise again, and gas prices were soaring.

In mid-July, Baltimore sponsored its annual Artscape celebration on Mount Royal Avenue. Originally a festival for the arts, Artscape had rapidly degenerated into a beer brawl with high-priced, big-name bands playing outdoors on the Decker Stage. Practically every restaurant in town had a booth and sold everything from sandwiches and pizza slices to tandoori chicken and ice cream sundaes. To be fair, there were juried art exhibitions, crafts booths and a writers' tent, but the main thrust of the activity was in performance, entertainment. In addition to the singers and musicians, there were poetry readings and plays, and the streets were rife with musicians, jugglers and acrobats, all vying for attention, most with little boxes or hats for donations. The lemonade stands and the beer trucks did a brisk business. The carnival atmosphere even extended to people dressed up in strange costumes and dancing in the streets. The poor man's Mardi Gras.

Bridgewater lived in the adjacent Bolton Hill neighborhood, and he strolled over in search of some distraction from the heat Friday after work. He looked at the paintings in one of the art college's buildings and felt depressed because he had nothing to display himself, not that there was anything being shown that he really admired. But before he was overcome by frustration, he left the air-conditioning and wandered, brooding, among the jugglers and the clowns and the hurdy-gurdy men. He recognized a storyteller from Boston, Brother Blue, a black man dressed entirely in blue from beret down to running shoes. Years before he used to see Brother Blue telling stories in Harvard Square.

Walking among the booths like a traveler in a foreign land, an American tourist at the casbah in Tangiers, say, gawking at hashish sellers, Bridgewater did not at first recognize Cecilia Nestorick when she walked up to him and enthusiastically (it seemed) said hi. Like old friends long separated. Dimly troubled by memory, he tried to recall where he had met this person before. Then he knew: The crazy woman!

"Oh, hi. How are you?" Like individual characters parading onto a stage, his emotions followed one after the other: uneasiness at his impression of her craziness, excitement at the memory of his attraction to her at the pool a month before, guilt or apprehension at the vague recollection of an unpleasant parting, gratitude at her apparent forgiveness (how *un*forgiving women can be, after all!), pleasure at a diversion from the heat: above all this, pleasure, the essential reaction within his consciousness, in his cells, like something ultimately electrical and having only to do with impersonal molecules become suddenly sentient. Nothing judgmental, just motiveless awareness. I think, therefore I am.

"You've got that 'nobody's home' look," Cecilia said.

"Nobody's home?"

"Vague. The lights are on but nobody's home."

Bridgewater smiled. "It must have to do with the heat." He was still basking in the thrill of the encounter, the sense of wonder it provoked in him. A man dressed in a bear costume walked by. *He must be suffocating*, Bridgewater thought.

"It's interesting how extremes of temperature reduce you to your animal elements, isn't it? Your basic self. Don't you feel like all you're doing is surviving? Enduring?"

"You can say that again." Gradually, Bridgewater recalled in a new wave of thought how wordy and pretentious and confused he'd found this woman to be the first time he'd met her. How crazy. His uneasiness grew.

"Bellow cites several accounts of arctic explorers in his fiction and their observations of the effect cold has on human behavior, how it reduces you to your ultimate selfish impulses. Even fantasies respond to the cold. Some of the wish-fulfillment myths of arctic tribes reflect that."

"How's your paper on Bellow coming?" Already, part of Bridgewater's mind was looking for an escape. *Well, nice meeting you again. Have a good time at Artscape. Hope the heatwave breaks. Bye! Nice seeing you again!* "You're doing it on plant life in his later novels? The consciousness of rutabagas or something?"

"I decided to write instead about the arctic images and the presence of winter in his fiction. The Amundsen expedition in *Humboldt's Gift* that Humboldt and Charlie Citrine write their script about, the significance of arctic lichens to the botanist in *More Die of Heartbreak*, the importance of the Jesup Expedition to the arctic in the short story, "Cousins," the austere mystical presence of winter in *The Dean's December*. Even in *Henderson the Rain King*, which takes place in Africa, Henderson at one point says that if he didn't go to Africa he'd have gone to the arctic. He was fascinated by the Eskimos and Wilfred Grenfell. In fact, the novel *ends* in Newfoundland on a triumphant note."

"What's the point?" Bridgewater interrupted. He wondered if he should refer her to the good intentions department. He remembered so well the shifting chaotic search for a thesis, a point-of-view, when he was writing term papers in college, the need to make a point, to say something significant. But this Saul Bellow stuff sounded like an obsession. The woman might be dangerous. But how? Just because she prattled on about a novelist? Still, it indicated a character trait. The fanatic. Or did it?

"It's the redemptive quality of suffering, I think, and the need to stay in touch with your elemental self. Take Henderson. He's a great sufferer. He says, truth comes through blows, makes a point of it. Eye-eee, truth comes through suffering."

"Huh, that's interesting," Bridgewater said. His mind darted from excuse to excuse in search of a graceful way to leave her. He was going to see the "Thunder Thighs Revue" at the Fox building, he could say, or "Lambs Eat Ivy" at the University of Baltimore. Or he was going to a movie. *Roxanne* and *Revenge of the Nerds II* were showing at the Rotunda; some Woody Allen films were playing at the Charles.

"But you're not that interested, I can tell," she said, reading his mind.

"No, that's not true," Bridgewater protested lamely. He softened toward her. Perhaps she just didn't have good conversational skills. "I was just wondering what it all means to you."

"Do you want to sit down?" she asked, gesturing toward an empty bench in the park across from the Lyric. They had been walking slowly in that direction. The sun was already behind the downtown buildings. Evening had begun to fall, even though the heat remained.

Bridgewater hesitated but then followed her to the bench. She was wearing white shorts that came halfway up her thighs and a faded blue Wyman Park Pool Club tee-shirt. Her arms and legs were deeply tanned. Bridgewater guessed she spent a lot of time sunbathing beside the pool, reading Saul Bellow novels. Bridgewater himself had never returned, ashamed by his behavior.

Cecilia was attractive, he could not deny it. He told himself she was probably not crazy, but he didn't feel convinced. Oh, how he would love to run his hands along those smooth tan legs!

They walked past the writers' tent, where a skinny man with acne scars called out to the casual passersby and book browsers.

"If it's poetry you're looking for you've come to the right place," he drawled in the soft-pedaling voice of the easygoing carny. "Surrealism, eroticism, poets in exile from repressive governments—Chili, Iran, the Soviet Union—we've got 'em all! And then there's my own book of love poems. I'd be glad to sign it for you if you want a copy. It's about a real love affair, too, not just some made-up story. It lasted about a year and a half. The earlier poems are the happy ones. The ones at the end are sad." He laughed self-effacingly, having bared his soul to total strangers just to sell a book.

"There's even a couple that rhyme," he chuckled. His manner was implicitly boastful. The romantic gypsy poet. But to Bridgewater he just came off as a *schlemiel*, telling this sort of stuff to the luscious young girl in cut-offs and a tube top who had stopped by to look.

"In both the short story 'Cousins' and *More Die of Heartbreak* Bellow has a character say the phrase, 'You are as you see,' or 'As a man sees, so he is.' The emphasis is on sight, almost like the Italian Neoplatonists , love entering through the eyes and all that, only, Bellow goes beyond all that. Truth is a personal experience. He emphasizes the subjectivity of it. I mean, how you take it all in determines your behavior. You see what I'm saying?"

"Does anybody have a corner on truth or awareness? Or is everything relative and solipsistic?" Bridgewater did not really care, but he wanted to sound intelligent. He noticed how many of the trees had clumps of dead leaves, hanging from the branches like ornaments, where the cicadas had been earlier in the summer. Clusters about the size and shape of cheerleaders' pompoms. From a distance and in the diminishing light, they looked like bunches of grapes, and Bridgewater had a sudden idea for a painting called *The Garden of Eden*. But like most of his ideas, it slipped away forever like a breeze through the trees.

"Certain characters, the autobiographical ones who are really stand-ins for Bellow himself, seem to be clued into the way reality really works, the deeper mysteries of existence; they grasp the big picture. In fact, Alfred Kazin reviewed Bellow's new novel in *The New York Review of Books*, and that was one of his complaints: the super-intelligent protagonist. The review is called 'Trachtenberg the Brain King,' which is kind of interesting since both Eugene Henderson and Kenneth Trachtenberg, the narrator of *More Die of Heartbreak*, have impaired hearing in one ear."

"What's interesting about that?"

"Oh, nothing." Cecilia's manner was abrupt. She was suddenly sick of dealing with Bridgewater's skepticism and boredom. She looked around, as if for escape, and in that gesture Bridgewater felt his own panic index rise. He was about to lose her. He was about to be alone again.

He'd been feeling particularly wretched about his wife, Zippy, since the evening before, after he'd received calls from his father and from Zippy's sister Rachael, one right after the other, a one-two punch.

His father set him up to feel helpless and ineffectual by talking as if nothing had happened, a blustery, cheery monologue about Uncle Ben, who had just left Ann Arbor for a two-month trip to the Soviet Union, and comparing himself and his brother Ben to Peter and Peter's brother Mark. On the one hand, Bridgewater appreciated his father's tact in leaving the subject of his son's estranged wife up to the son to bring up, if he chose, but on the other he hated all this substitute talk about his prepubescent relationship with his brother, how it seemed to repeat the pattern established a generation before. Then Rachael called so soon after Peter's father that Bridgewater thought it was the old guy calling back with some new revelation about his childhood.

But it was Rachael, calling from Kalamazoo, to tell him that Zippy was in Barbados with a friend. Her parents had just got a card from her. She was full of sympathy, and, seeing himself through her eyes—big-titted, motherly Rachael—Bridgewater saw what a pathetic creature he must seem to others. Normally striving for a certain stoicism and convincing himself that he had achieved it, listening to Rachael's reassurances made Bridgewater see himself a basket case, quivering on the brink of hysteria, in danger of throwing himself in front of an oncoming subway train. Goodbye, cruel world. Curiously, her soothing attempts to restore his confidence only made him feel his loneliness more. She said she knew exactly how he felt, her voice oozing condolence. She compared his unhappiness to hers. Rachael was in love with a man her parents would never approve of, if they'd ever known about him. Secretkeeping was a family trait.

When Bridgewater got off the line, he almost *did* feel suicidal, certainly not reassured. It was partly to evade any other possible phone calls that Bridgewater had decided to go to Artscape. Now he confronted his loneliness in yet another form, its urgency indistinguishable from the other bouts of panic. He spoke quickly, almost ingratiating himself to Cecilia.

"From what I've read about him, lots of characters have wide gaps between their teeth, just like Bellow. You think maybe he has a bad ear, too? Henderson and Trachtenberg share that with him? It's really Bellow's bad ear?"

"Maybe."

The gypsy poet's voice drifted over. He was talking to two young women. "It's about a real love affair, too, not just something made up."

"Listen," Bridgewater said, unable to disguise his urgent sense of a crisis coming to a head. "Are you doing anything? I think *Round*

Midnight's playing at the Langsdale Auditorium, if you're interested. It's supposed to be pretty good."

"It is. I saw it at the Charles last week. Actually, I was on my way to the poetry readings at the Law Center."

"Poetry." The disappointment in Bridgewater's voice was almost palpable.

"You don't like poetry?"

"I was an English major, but somehow it never excited me. I think I could never get the names of the carriages straight in nineteenth century novels. I could never form a picture in my mind. The hansoms, the victorias, the broughams, the barouches and the landaus—God, I don't even know if I pronounced them right. I mean, a Chevy, a Toyota, a Cadillac—I could see something like that. Maybe it's a failure of imagination."

"You mean you get lost in the language? Well, I'd like to see Leon Redbone, but he's not playing until tomorrow."

Did she want to make a date for tomorrow? Was she giving him a gentle brush-off? "*Snow White* starts today. We could go to a movie."

"Where's it showing?"

"I don't know. Golden Ring and Perring Plaza. Glen Burnie. No place nearby." He thought. "Kubrick's new film's at the Senator, the art deco theater on York Road they just declared an historic site."

"Another Vietnam movie? No thanks."

Bridgewater and Cecilia sat on the bench, not sure what to do next. Bridgewater continued to debate with himself about Cecilia's sanity, but he no longer saw her as crazy; he just wondered if she was worth the effort, if he really cared to know her after all. Just then a tall man with a dark wig and pancake makeup on his face, obviously dressed up in a sort of costume, approached them from the lemonade stand on Dolphin Street. He was accompanied by a vampish-looking female, heavily made up and scantily dressed. The two were meant to represent some celebrities, but Bridgewater could not guess who. Jim and Tammy Faye?

"Gary, honey, do y'all know these folks? I hope they aren't reporters!"

Ignoring the woman, the man spoke to Bridgewater and Cecilia. "My big mistake was that I didn't get Teddy Kennedy to drive her home."

"Hush your mouth, Gary! Where's the beef?"

Bridgewater wondered whether Donna Rice really spoke in a Southern belle accent. He realized he had never heard her on television, though she had been on several late-night talkshows to tell her story.

He and Cecilia smiled at the clowns, who lingered by them after delivering their lines. Did they expect a handful of change or something?

"I don't want to run for president anyway. I think I'm better qualified to run the PTL."

Bridgewater and Cecilia both began to feel oppressed and instinctively drew closer together on the bench. He put his hand on her shoulder.

"They didn't believe me when I said I had some new ideas!"

"Pretty old ideas, if you ask me, Gary, honey. They been around a l-o-o-o-n-g time!" They both laughed at their wit, and then they moved on. Bridgewater removed his hand from Cecilia's shoulder, and she moved away from him, though not as far as she'd been.

"That was kind of amusing for about ten seconds," Cecilia said.

"I know what you mean. They must have gone to a lot of trouble over it, it looks like."

"I guess Artscape only comes once a year," Cecilia conceded. Bridgewater liked her wit. Crazy? He'd have to be crazy to think she was crazy.

"I'll sign a copy for you if you want to buy it," they heard the gypsy poet declare. "It's about a real love affair I had a few years ago. It's not just a made-up story."

By now the light had practically faded, and although Artscape was well lit, the bench on which they were sitting was beneath a tree, and each appeared shadowy to the other. Moreover, the abundant sounds of music and people talking contributed to the feeling of intimacy, and for the next few minutes they sat quietly on the bench without talking. Something like contentment almost settled in. Then Cecilia said:

"You know, I don't even know your name."

"You don't?" Bridgewater was surprised, and he told her his name.

"That's nice. Like a bridge over troubled waters." After a moment she said, "Have you listened to Paul Simon's new album?"

"*Graceland*? I've just heard a few songs on the radio. It's pretty good."

"I have it at home. Would you like to come over to my apartment and listen to it?"

Wondering at the coincidence of the associations of words that led up to the invitation, Bridgewater looked closely at Cecilia to see what she really meant by it. But she remained a mystery; he could not tell. At the same time they rose from the bench together.

"If you want me to," he said. "Yes."

Really Jewish

When Peter and Zippy Bridgewater moved to Baltimore, they considered moving to Pikesville or to one of the northwest suburbs where the Jewish community was centered, but they decided instead to find a place downtown. They wanted to replicate the urban environment they had found so attractive in Boston, and besides, they felt that living downtown would give Peter more options in finding freelance work. They moved to an apartment in Bolton Hill, partly attracted by the name, so similar to Beacon Hill that they took it as an omen, and Peter had always been charmed by the wide streets and the nineteenth century architecture, when he was growing up. Also, the 28 bus came right through Bolton Hill and went out to Social Security, where Zippy worked. (They preferred public transportation to driving.) They vaguely decided to wait until they had children before moving out to the Jewish suburbs. Since there were no synagogues nearby, the old temple on Eutaw Place having been sold to the Masons, they did not attend *shabbos* services regularly. During the High Holy Days they went to Rosh Hashanah and Yom Kippur services at Johns Hopkins.

Two years after they had been living in Baltimore, Peter and Zippy decided to have a child. Zippy stopped using her diaphragm, and the tube of contraceptive jelly remained in the headboard drawer over the bed. When two months passed and she had not missed her period, Zippy consulted a friend who worked in a biology lab at the University of Maryland breeding rats. Melanie mapped out a program whereby Peter and Zippy would have sex every twelve hours during the critical period of Zippy's fertility, between the tenth and seventeenth day of Zippy's menstrual cycle. Peter would not take any hot baths or sit in the sauna or perform any strenuous activity, to ensure healthy sperm.

They did not completely obey the instructions—sometimes they were just too tired—but sure enough, two weeks later Zippy had not started to menstruate. They waited another week before buying a "QTest" kit at the Rite-Aid, but the next morning, Zippy collected a small vial of urine and inserted the strip into the urine. Like alchemists, Peter and Zippy watched for a change in composition; like primitives, they gulped in awe when the strip turned blue: she was pregnant! A gynecologist confirmed this a few weeks later.

Peter and Zippy told their parents. True, Zippy had her qualms about revealing the secret, as if she might be relinquishing some essence of her soul, but how could she keep quiet about it? Frank Bridgewater was elated. Now he would have a grandchild to pass his electric train set on to. The Feldmans exulted in their good fortune at having a Jewish grandchild to look forward to. For once, everybody was pleased. Peter assured the Feldmans that the child would receive a Jewish education, at least until he or she was old enough to have the choice to accept or reject religion, after becoming a bar or a bat mitzvah.

After the second appointment with her doctor, Zippy informed Bridgewater that he would have to have a blood test for the Tay-Sachs gene. Doctor's orders. Though mildly annoyed, Bridgewater consented. At eighty-seven dollars for a blood test that was going to be negative it wasn't that easy to justify; always pinching pennies, the thought of his cheapness made Bridgewater feel guilty. Better be safe than sorry. But how was he going to have the gene? Absurd! The gene only affected Ashkenazi Jews. Sure, he'd converted, but this was a genetic consideration and had nothing to do with religious convictions or allegiances. How oppressive doctors can be with their orders!

Bridgewater was not allowed to eat anything the night before the test, not even a cup of coffee in the morning. He had to be at the Wyman Park Community College graphics lab at eight to meet somebody who was going to repair the typesetter, which was on the blink. He was tongue-tied and incoherent without the cup of coffee, but what could he do? He felt inarticulate and stupid and he cursed the blood test and the doctor who ordered it. Rain was falling in a steady mumble from an endlessly gray sky when he caught the bus over to the clinic on 33rd Street. It had been falling all night, and the leaves were plastered into sewers and against curbs like machine-gunned corpses; it added to his sense of desolation. He arrived at the clinic at quarter to seven. Two women showed up shortly after he got there to stand in the rain with him, waiting for the nurse to arrive. Bridgewater felt grumpy and impatient but tried to conceal it from the others. At last the nurse showed up at ten after seven, late for work. But her cheeriness disarmed Bridgewater, and he did not dump on her. One of the other patients was chattering away to him about how she and her husband were determined to have a baby. Apparently she was coming to the blood clinic because she was in the process of an in-vitro birth.

"My boss is going to kill me. I take so much time off work to come down here!" she giggled, and Bridgewater suddenly repented his shitty thoughts. He was the lucky one, after all. Maybe he didn't need to have the test, but shouldn't he be thankful for that?

Technically, Bridgewater had arrived before either of the other two patients, and he took advantage of their deference to have his blood tested first. The nurse asked him to fill out a card about his ancestry. He checked the box marked "Protestant" for religion at birth. Then the nurse mopped his arm with a cotton swab saturated with disinfectant, injected the hypodermic needle, sucked up a red tube as if by magic, sealed the tube and wished him a good day. Bridgewater in turn handed the nurse his insurance form (he was still working on the deductible, though, so it didn't do him a lot of good, he'd already noted with some irritation), and he wished her the same. Passing through the waiting room on his way out he smiled at the chatty woman.

"Good luck!" she chirped. "I hope you and your wife have a wonderful baby!"

"You too!" he replied, sounding as cheery as he could.

"Have a good day!" she called as he stepped out into the rain, and for a moment Bridgewater felt blessed. Apart from needing a cup of coffee, he was done with the test and would probably get to work on time after all. But outside his umbrella would not open, and he got soaked waiting for the bus to take him to school.

A week later, when Bridgewater came home from an appointment with a client for some freelance work designing a brochure for an environmental public policy campaign to save a neighborhood park from being sacrificed to a housing development, Zippy told him, almost proudly, "You've got it! You're a carrier!"

"Got what?" Then he remembered. She had just been to the gynecologist. The results of his blood test were in.

"There must be a Jew in your past after all, Peter!" Her brown eyes twinkled a secret knowledge to him, their private language, shared meanings.

On his mother's side, his ancestry was Dutch-German. Peter wondered if one of those Lutherans had married a Jew sometime in the past. The Jew in the woodpile. Or really, were genes ever really the exclusive property of any one ethnic group? It sounded like the nineteenth century theories of racial distinctions, only with twentieth century scientific language. Sure, by definition, only black people have the genes for dark pigmentation, say, but a genetic disease was different, wasn't it? Sickle cell anemia also predominantly affects blacks, but the genetic predisposition is not essential to their racial makeup or exclusive to their race. Tay-Sachs a Jewish gene? Did it mark you as a Jew to have it?

"Shouldn't we be worried?"

"Well, there's not much chance I have it," Zippy said. She did not seem worried. "I mean, sure, it mainly affects Ashkenazi Jews, but they do survive. They aren't being wiped out. Jews have been around a long time."

"But the very fact that you *are* Jewish makes it more likely you've got it, increases the likelihood of the baby having it."

"I think it's 400 out of every million Jewish babies that die from it. Those are the statistics. Pretty good odds if you ask me."

"Yeah, but what if you *do* have the gene?"

"It's a recessive gene, which means the odds are still only one in four that the baby will have it. Don't worry! We'll deal with it when we have to. There's nothing we can do about it now. I'm having a blood test next week."

Zippy's fatalism was persuasive, and Bridgewater relaxed. What *could* he do about it? Still, he felt a confusion of emotions—vindication, guilt, injustice; he remembered the overheard conversation among the Feldmans at Potawatomi Rapids. Genes! What would Moishe Feldman say now if he learned that Bridgewater carried a "Jewish gene"? *Well, Moses and Edith, the good news is that I'm Jewish. The bad news is that your grandchild has an incurable disease that's one hundred percent fatal by the age of four. Mazel tov!*

"Tell me," he said to Zippy, "who put the 'nazi' in "Ashkenazi'?"

What Moishe had to say, when he learned that Zippy's tests had also been positive, that an amniocentesis had shown the child had the disease and that Zippy was going to have a second trimester abortion, was: "What do you mean Gazookis has Tay-Sachs? He's not even Jewish."

Of course, Moishe and Edith were just as devastated by the news as everybody else and they were supportive and sympathetic, but Bridgewater felt bitter when he heard this. All the trouble he had gone to converting, and for what? Harmony in the family? Some harmony! Bridgewater wasn't trying to be Jewish; he wasn't seeking admission into some sort of club; he had no particular yen to wear a skullcap or a prayer shawl, and although he fasted on Yom Kippur and abstained from leavened bread during Passover, he did not advertise it or wear it like a badge.

The reason he had converted was to please Zippy and her damn family. Yet they eyed him suspiciously, as if he were a spy in the house of David, a thief in the temple, the secret anti-Semitic goy come to corrupt them from within. Fine, if they didn't think he was Jewish despite the circus act of his conversion, that was their business; he didn't care. What did it matter that they had immolated his flesh? Jabbed at his prick with a sharp object and had him submerge himself in water? Anybody can do that. Take away the symbolism and the events mean nothing. He just wished they'd lay off with the hostility and derision. The suspicion. Being Jewish was not the sacred distinction in his eyes it apparently was in theirs. The label meant nothing. Jewish. What did it really mean?

In his conversion course, one of the assigned texts had been called *A History of the Jewish Experience*. Looking through it after hearing Moishe, Bridgewater wondered *whose* Jewish experience? What defined the experience? Suffering? Nobody had a corner on that or on persecution either.

The Jewish experience, according to the author, was a living dialogue between God and His people. God acted in history through His people. What shit! Ask for a straight answer and they give you mysticism instead! Jargon and sophistry. Bridgewater didn't ask for empirical proofs of God's existence, he just wanted something more characteristic of experience. Maybe all you really needed to do to be a Jew was to call yourself a Jew, live like a Jew, associate with Jews. It was just a word, after all. Jew.

> I am a Jew. Hath not a Jew eyes? Hath not a Jew hands, organs, dimensions, senses, affections, passions? Fed with the same food, hurt with the same weapons, subject to the same diseases, healed by the same means, warmed and cooled by the same winter and summer as a Christian is? If you prick us, do we not bleed? If you tickle us, do we not laugh?

Shylock meant to show the Jewish experience as part of the universal human experience. Bridgewater's question was just the opposite. What distinguishes what is purely *Jewish*? Apart from the ritual and prayer, apart from simply hanging around with "real" Jews, what made a real Jew "real"? Genes? Couldn't be something as ephemeral as a "lifestyle," could it?

Comparing Jews to Christians wasn't a valid way of approaching the matter, rather beside the point. Yes, they were different systems of belief and worship, but that had nothing to do with *people*. Comparing Jews to Christians was like comparing the Orioles to the Yankees or the Bears to the Giants: team psychology. After all, you could be traded from the Blue Jays to the Cardinals, analogous to conversion, and you would *be* a Cardinal. But despite joining the team, Bridgewater was not a Jew—not a "real" Jew, anyway. A convert, a born-again—like a member of the team with an asterisk by his name on the roster.

To the extent he separated her loss from his, Bridgewater felt genuinely sorry for Zippy, who was fatalistic and unemotional throughout the ordeal of the blood tests and the abortion. He felt more than pity—he felt guilt; he felt responsible. So did she. They tried a second time, but again the amniocentesis revealed that the child was fatally stricken, and Zippy had another abortion. After that, they decided not to try again; the risk was too great, the disappointment too devastating.

For a time they felt closer to each other than they ever had before, a little cell of life in Bolton Hill, and each was extra-attentive to the other's needs. They began to attend synagogue services with a Conservative congregation on Park Heights Avenue, but the consolations of religion were inadequate to their emotional needs. It was like taking a bath in sorrow, a poor substitute; the solemnity of the services exacerbated their loss; the sympathy was cloying. Then, when they stopped going to synagogue, they started to drift apart. Each tried to become absorbed in his or her own work. Bridgewater took up painting again. But he found himself drawn to images of pregnant women and nursing mothers and headed into abstract doodling that failed to capture his imagination. From memory, he tried drawing a picture of the woman at the blood clinic, the one so hopeful about an in-vitro pregnancy, but it made him feel bitter and cursed to be married to Zippy. Each saw in the other the source of sorrow, the unwitting cause of personal pain.

Their sexual relations dwindled and disappeared. There was so much sorrow and pain associated with the act, so much danger and risk, that neither responded to the prospect in the usual way. When they tried to have sex, the overemphasis on birth control was so unromantic, methodical, ultimately anti-aphrodisiac, that often they did not finish what they'd started. Finally, Bridgewater could no longer achieve an erection and he and Zippy stopped trying, though they continued to sleep together in the same bed. It began with the old joke about having a headache, but more often than not, it was Bridgewater suffering from the migraine, and Zippy who felt rejected, unworthy.

Zippy took Bridgewater's failure to get a hardon as a sign of her own inadequacy as a lover. Introverted Zippy, the secretkeeper, receded further into herself. The faraway loneliness in her big brown eyes made Bridgewater think of the pictures of missing children on milk cartons and on the signs plastered up in grocery stores like wanted posters. Images he might have painted; dark eyes like a vortex sucking him into their bottomless pain.

One evening she came naked into the living room, where Bridgewater was drawing a picture of a woman pushing a baby carriage over a cliff. She pressed her pubic bush against his right arm, with which he was steadying the drawing pad. (Bridgewater was left-handed; she had come from the bedroom to his right side.)

"Oh, hi," he said, looking up at her and hastily covering the image with his left arm. He refused to acknowledge the implicit offer, and Zippy saw the image he was drawing, and now she knew with a certainty she could not deflect that it was all over between them. She started to cry, and Bridgewater jumped up hastily and drew her toward him.

"I'm sorry, Zippy, I really am," he said, but he did not know what he was apologizing for.

Zippy began writing letters to Mick Jagger. At first, Bridgewater thought it was a joke, the impulse of a bored woman, and even when he asked her about it and she replied that she couldn't get no satisfaction, he merely took it as an idle expression of her frustration, weird, sure, but nothing psychotic. He was frustrated, too, wasn't he? But before long, Bridgewater began finding dozens of them in the mail in the evenings, stamped RETURN TO SENDER, ADDRESS UNKNOWN. He never opened them, but once or twice he had seen a letter in the typewriter and had read the lurid sexual fantasies they contained. How could he not see these aimed at him? Maybe she left them around so he could read them, so he would know without a doubt that he was the author of her misery.

They began to see a marriage counselor, a woman named Mary Higgins, but she very quickly homed in on Zippy's depression, and they consulted other doctors for psychiatric counseling. That was when they hit on the de Clerambault Syndrome, the re-formation in different words of the very thing about which he'd told them. Medication was prescribed, mild anti-psychotic drugs and anti-depressants. Zippy objected to the drugs. She didn't like the way they made her feel, and the side effects were intolerable—constipation and fatigue, or diarrhea and vomiting. She did not believe she was sick. Finally, if anything, the drugs made her more remote, more difficult to talk to; she even became hostile at times. Zippy regarded Peter suspiciously, as if he were a jailer. The secretkeeper in her came out in spades. He couldn't ask her anything without immediately being asked why he wanted to know, and then her response was always vague, evasive.

Then one day Bridgewater came home from work and she just wasn't there. The postcard came a few days later, after he had made calls to her parents in Potawatomi Rapids, to her friends at Social Security, and to her doctors. He did not consult the police. She was not crazy or criminal. Maybe, in fact, getting away from him would do her some good, he reasoned. He admitted guiltily to himself that he felt some relief. A sneaky sense of survival or escape. No doubt about it.

As for Zippy's parents, Bridgewater seemed to sense a secret feeling of vindication. On the occasion of the second abortion, Edith had even wondered aloud if God weren't punishing their daughter for marrying a gentile. Or did Bridgewater imagine this feeling of triumph? Feeling contradictory emotions himself, did he attribute the same ambivalence to others? He had never really forgiven them for the overheard conversation during their honeymoon. Yes, it was funny how guilt operated. Never in a pure form but always cut or chased by relief and then reacting to the self-interested responses even more cruelly, but sometimes, too, being defeated or overwhelmed by the exultation inherent in the selfishness. A powerful emotion, guilt. It made you see yourself and the world differently, but ultimately it changed *nothing*. Too much emphasis was placed on guilt, just as too much emphasis was placed on love.

In his train room in Baltimore, Frank Bridgewater grieved privately. He would never have a grandchild to whom he could bequeath his elaborate railroad, no young mind whose fascination with the motion of the toys would revive and justify his own.

Charles Rammelkamp

Toot! Toot! The electric trains swarmed around the tracks like moiling mindless vipers coiled and writhing in a snake's den. There no longer seemed any purpose to the coordination of their movement.

Death

Bridgewater rode the elevator up to Cecilia Nestorick's sixth-floor apartment overlooking the Wyman Park Pool Club on University Avenue. During the past month they had seen a lot of each other. They met at the pool, had dinner and slept together regularly, and lately, Bridgewater had been using Cecilia as a model for a painting, making sketches of her in her living room, reclining on a couch or sitting at a table.

The arrangement was very convenient for them both. A summer romance. Or was it? Though not as secretive as Zippy, Cecilia nevertheless had a private life that she did not always like to discuss. She did not like to talk about her family, for instance. Who could blame her, given the embarrassing publicity? But what did it mean, that she drew the line there? Would she blow him off in the fall? For now, though, the undefined terms of their relationship seemed to satisfy both of their needs and desires. No commitments. No strings attached. She knew about Zippy, and he was still married to her, after all. Bridgewater wondered what sort of future Cecilia thought they had together. Did she even *want* a future with him? He was afraid to ask. She kept part of herself off limits, gathered it within herself, but she clung to him in bed like a little child.

Originally drawn to Cecilia by his loneliness and her good looks, Bridgewater, though still ambivalent, found her fascinating in an almost morbid way. There was that cousin of hers, for one thing; Roger was definitely off-limits; you could not talk to Cecilia about Roger. She changed the subject whenever Bridgewater brought him up, and she lost her temper if he pursued the subject. While not the same person, they still came from the same stock, the same gene pool. Was Roger's problem genetic? Was he somehow predisposed to that sort of behavior? Just add water and watch it grow. If so, the same affliction might be latent in Roger's cousin—though from all appearances, her sexual proclivities seemed orthodox enough to Bridgewater. Still, there *was* the cousin, and though Bridgewater found his "case" fascinating, he did not want to get too chummy with the other Nestoricks—not that Cecilia had invited him to a family get-together or anything.

In this sense her secretiveness protected him. And while she was definitely *not* her cousin, her relationship to him gave her an air of danger with echoes of Zippy's "case" implicit in this perception. Hey, babe, take a walk on the wild side.

And what *did* she see in him? The convenience? The no strings? Convenient their arrangement certainly was. No denying that. She had classes nearby at the Homewood campus, and his walk from work at the WPCC graphics lab took less than five minutes. A lot closer than Bolton Hill. Her sixth-floor perch was like a secret little nest to which they both flew for stimulation. Maybe she just regarded him as a pal, no special claims. In the latter part of the 20th century, sex has ceased to be a claim; just another activity for which you need a partner, like racquetball or tennis.

Bridgewater had just been speaking with a client about designing a brochure for a safe-sex ad campaign, depicting various sorts of condoms and explaining their use. Good old rubbers, Bridgewater mused in the elevator. They're not just for birth control any more.

When he knocked on her door (the formality implied distance), Cecilia called out over the whir of a blow-dryer to come in. Even over the noise she recognized Bridgewater's familiar tap on the door—the implied intimacy. He tried the knob, discovering the door was unlocked. The sound of the blow-dryer grew louder as he entered the apartment. Cecilia stuck her head around the corner of the bedroom door, the Vidal Sassoon 1500 aimed at her head, the trigger depressed. The electric cord was looped around her neck like some sort of noose.

"Sounds worse than the cicadas," Bridgewater said, raising his voice above the noise. He walked into her apartment, a spacious one-bedroom affair with high ceilings and off-white walls, an institutional color described as "eggshell" in the advertisements. The walls were thin, and the apartment gave the impression of a flimsiness in construction, as if you could stick your hand through the plaster, but for all that there was an atmosphere of delicacy and even, oddly, of elegance to it.

The living room was sparsely furnished. A television was balanced atop a bookcase at one end of the sofa. Books were piled on the floor beside the card table on which a blank computer monitor perched like some blind Cyclops on the CPU box, which was crammed tightly next to a printer loaded with a continuous roll of paper that likewise struck Bridgewater as something out of Greek mythology. Sisyphus? Several directors chairs flanked a teak coffee table by the picture window. Under the table were boxes and boxes of games—card games, dominos, games involving marbles and pick-up sticks, "Trivial Pursuit," "Backgammon," "Monopoly," "Parcheesi," "Clue," a Civil War strategy game called "The Blue and the Gray," etc. Occasionally, Cecilia tried to get Bridgewater to play with her, but board games did not interest him. "Chairman of the Bored" she called him, and "Chairman of the Board" he called her during their bedroom games and pillow talk. It was usually after sex that she wanted to play games. Like a post-coital cigarette.

"You're lucky you found me." Cecilia said in a voice loud enough to be heard over the blow-dryer, which she was rooting around her scalp now, up under the lush red hair. "I've been working out at the gym."

She pressed a button and the blow-dryer stopped whirring, but only to be replaced by the buzz and rumble of other machines. Outside, a delivery truck at the Wyman Park Deli cleared its throat, while inside, the refrigerator and the air conditioner murmured together in a conspiratorial undertone. Lawn mowers growled angrily in the distance, and in the rush-hour traffic on University Parkway the car horns threatened and complained. A siren screamed by, warning the others off. Cecilia emerged from the bedroom. She was wearing only a loose cotton T-shirt and panties, and Bridgewater suppressed a desire to take her into his arms. *How easy it would be. Why didn't he just do it? What was the harm?*

"God, it's hot out," he commented.

"Not as bad as yesterday. Yesterday it got up to ninety-six. It's only about ninety today."

"Only." Bridgewater looked out the window at the L-shaped pool at the club. From this perspective it looked like a wavering comma.

"Iced tea?" Cecilia brought a couple of glasses of tea over from the kitchenette and they sat in the directors chairs.

"Where were you twenty-five years ago yesterday?" Bridgewater asked, smiling at some memory. Already the arrangement felt domestic and, to that extent, claustrophobic. Claustrophobia led to restlessness, and restlessness made him irritable. There was some kind of trap here, if only he could identify it. Cecilia's near-nakedness made him wary. He tried to keep a conversational perspective on things.

"Twenty-five years ago? What is this? Some kind of trivia quiz? I thought you didn't like games. Let's see. Twenty-five years ago I was two years old. Why? Where were you?"

"Funny you should ask. Twenty-five years ago yesterday I was visiting my uncle in Michigan. I was ten years old. It was a Sunday, and some guy he knew in Ann Arbor called and invited us to go to a doubleheader at Tiger Stadium, Detroit versus Cleveland. Detroit was like thirty or forty or fifty miles down the road, and we went in this guy's beat-up Chevy convertible. He was one of those perpetually youthful student hangers-on you find in university towns; my uncle knew him in graduate school. He drove over from Ann Arbor and picked us all up.

"We had seats along first base in the second deck. The Indians won the first game and the Tigers won the second. After the game, this guy took us to the locker room—he knew some of the Detroit players——and I got some autographs. I got Don Mosse's autograph and some others, but none of the ones I really wanted, like Al Kaline or Stormin' Norman Cash or Rocky Colavito or Frank Lary, 'the Yankee Killer.' I think I lost them all even before we got back to the car. When we were driving back home that evening we stopped at a filling station on I-94 and heard the news over the radio. Marilyn Monroe had just died."

"Death!" Cecilia rolled her eyes and shuddered. "God, it's always death that gets remembered. In another week we'll be inundated with details of Elvis Presley's life. It'll be the tenth anniversary of Elvis' death on the sixteenth. Today, you know, is the forty-second anniversary of Hiroshima."

"That's right. I'd forgotten." Let down because she was not impressed by his memory, Bridgewater felt a little peeved. His father-in-law, Moishe Feldman, a big Tigers fan, had been enthralled when he'd heard the story years ago. He even brought it up when he and Edith called Bridgewater a couple weeks earlier with the latest status report on Zippy, from whom they'd received a postcard postmarked Barbados.

Bridgewater watched Cecilia idly brushing her red hair and asked, with the barest trace of sarcasm, "Does Saul Bellow have anything to say about death?" Having quit her teaching job, Cecilia had devoted her entire energy to Saul Bellow. Bridgewater could not decide if this was pathetic or admirable. He saw his role in her life as that of midwife, drawing out the insights into the writer's life and work. But he felt more like a martyr—or a victim. The subject bored him to tears, though lately he had tried reading a few of Bellow's novels and had found them vivid and comical.

"Plenty. Take Henderson. Henderson describes himself as 'kissing cousins' with death. And in his latest, Bellow writes about the macabre obsession with death that's so pervasive in our culture. Here," she said, reaching for the gray-jacketed novel and turning the pages:

> Death also, while you enjoy a viewer's immunity from it, is entertaining, as it was in Imperial Rome, or in 1793. As today, Sadat is murdered, Indira Gandhi is assassinated, the Pope himself is gunned down in St. Peter's Square, while personally unharmed, *you* live to see more and more and more, until after many deferrals death gets personal even with you. The jumpmaster says, "You bail out next."

Cecilia closed *More Die of Heartbreak* and smiled at Bridgewater. "Then there's *Mister Sammler's Planet*. Artur Sammler, a survivor of a Nazi death camp, reflects that nobody makes sober, decent terms with death. It's always a surprise and an intrusion."

"Don't tell me. You've changed your topic again! Death according to Saul Bellow."

Cecilia laughed but did not answer him directly. "I'm almost done. The paper's due next week."

"At the age of ten I didn't have any special feelings for Marilyn Monroe," Bridgewater said after a moment. "I just remember the day, how it was marked by death. It was the only time I ever went to Tiger Stadium, though, so maybe that's why I remember it so vividly. I don't know what I was doing when Elvis died, except that I was living in Boston and taking courses at Emerson College, and down by the Charles River, on a cement wall, somebody spraypainted:

ELVIS IS DEAD. LONG LIVE THE KING.

"*Some Like It Hot* was on TV last night."

"Wasn't Marilyn great in that? You watch it?"

"I liked George Raft better. But I'd already seen it a couple of times. Besides, I was working on my paper."

"Death," Bridgewater said. "God. You read about all those Iranian pilgrims that got killed at Mecca last week? Four hundred of them. Trampled to death or machine-gunned or something. During the *haj*. That's like shooting the Pope in St. Peter's Square."

"What do you think when you pass a graveyard on a highway?" Cecilia seemed to be baiting him. Like a game. Trick question. He grew wary.

"What do I think? What do you mean, what do I think?"

"What crosses your mind?"

"Just that. Crosses," Bridgewater responded quickly, but he knew that wasn't true, and he said, "No, I think of fingernails. The tombstones all in a row make me think of giant fingernails, like somebody's trying to claw his way out. They say the fingernails and hair continue to grow after death."

"Do you really believe that? When I pass a graveyard I think of a chessboard. I guess I have a different image of tombstones. They seem like ornate carved chess pieces to me, and the fenced-in cemetery is like a game board."

"Does Bellow have any images?" It was like poking at a rotten tooth to feel the pain again, but he asked anyway. It might provide the clue to whatever game she was playing.

"In *Henderson the Rain King* Henderson says he thinks of graves as envelopes, and the tombstones are like postage stamps licked by death." So that was it! She'd been leading up to another Bellow-ism!

"Let's stop talking about this. It's getting to be depressing."

"Death and everything?"

Saul Bellow and everything, Bridgewater thought grimly. He changed the subject.

"I was just talking with a client before I came here about doing a brochure to promote the use of condoms."

"Who wants a brochure on condoms? Planned Parenthood?"

"The Coalition for Alternative Lifestyles."

"Coalition. Sounds like a grassroots political movement. Who are they?"

Bridgewater shrugged. "I answered an ad in the paper. It pays all right. The guy I talked to was named Troy MacArthur. I'm pretty sure he's gay. He had on this cloying aftershave. Smelled like a girl at the senior prom." Lest he be suspected of low-consciousness attitudes, Bridgewater added, "He's a nice guy. I think I'll like working with him."

"They're worried about AIDS? What a creepy disease! It's like death on the installment plan."

"We can't get away from the subject of death, can we?"

"I guess it happens to us all, sooner or later."

"We try to put it off as long as we can."

"Why do you think I work out all the time? I want to stay fit, healthy."

"You look good," Bridgewater said, and saying so quickened his desire. Cecilia saw this and smiled to herself.

"God," she said. "It feels so good to take a sauna." The suppleness of her limbs made Bridgewater melancholy with desire.

"I sit in the one at WPCC sometimes." Bridgewater's face twisted into a glum smile; he had just been ambushed by memory once again. "When Zippy and I were trying to have a baby I didn't sit in the sauna during our week of procreative sex because the heat can kill the sperm in the testicles, and I was trying to improve my odds, like memorizing cards in a game of blackjack." He had already told Cecilia pretty much all there was to know about his relationship with his wife. Sitting side by side together in the chaise lounges at the pool, as if he were lying on a psychiatric couch, he had told her all the intimate details of his life with Zippy. Cecilia occasionally talked about her cousin Roger, the convicted sex offender, but she was vague when he probed her for details, and he tactfully shut up, ashamed at his own rabid curiosity about the case.

"You didn't want to keep one? I mean, it must have been hard to make the decision. To get an abortion."

"Would you have any qualms about an abortion?" Bridgewater's radar had gone up, and only after he'd blurted the question did he realize how tactless he sounded.

Cecilia made a wry face. "Don't worry. I don't want to have your baby."

"No, it's not that, it's just—" He returned abruptly to their previous conversation, seeing he was in a cul de sac.

"No, it wasn't easy, but we didn't have a choice, really. Tay-Sachs is always fatal. Victims usually die between the ages of two and four. They're perfectly normal for the first six months, and then the progressive physical and mental retardation sets in. Kids who have it lose the capacity to learn anything new, and what they do know they start to lose. They just fall apart. Spasticity, dementia, paralysis, blindness. The works. The whole nervous system breaks down. Death must come as a reward or a release."

"God, that's even scarier than AIDS."

"It's caused by a lack of an enzyme called hexosaminidase A," Bridgewater said. He still remembered all the details. "The lack of that enzyme results in the pooling of sphingolipids in the brain."

"That's so sad." She really seemed to mean it. Oddly, this made Bridgewater even more restless. A cloying sympathy. He was reminded of his sister-in-law's sympathy. Rachael called every week or two to "cheer him up" about Zippy and to convey whatever news she had, which always sounded the same. Still in Barbados. Then she'd start talking about her own complicated love life, how she wished she could tell her parents about her boyfriend, Docina Brown. (She called him "Dody." Bridgewater wondered if she had made it up herself or if he was know generally by that nickname.) Somehow the self-pity got mixed up with the sympathy, and Rachael would end up in tears. Then Bridgewater wound up reassuring *her*. Strangely, although he could not quite put his finger on it, there seemed to be a similar vein of melancholy running through Cecilia that evoked a similar response. Had she been involved in a long heartbreaking affair that had left her scarred? But this was another aspect of her private life that she chose not to discuss. Sometimes it really did seem like he was on the psychiatric couch talking about his life; there was no mutual confession.

"I wish we could change the subject, but we keep coming back to death."

"Even when we talk about birth."

Death served a purpose of illumination, Bridgewater thought, clarifying things. An illumination like that of art or insanity. The event drew attention to itself and shed light on its surroundings. Zippy's actions, for instance, had drawn so much scrutiny, like a magnet attracting iron filings. Was Zippy "insane," though, just because her behavior was, well, unconventional? Could you call it pathological, her behavior? Was "unorthodox" too tame, an understatement? But she wasn't the first woman to dump her husband, he reflected. Happens all the time.

By contrast, take a commonplace confused intellectual sort like Cecilia. Once he had gotten to know her she was all-right, though at first his impulse had been to run away. She had seemed loony when he first met her, and he still had his doubts from time to time, but essentially she had normal ambitions and desires. You could call Cecilia subtle or you could call her boring, but the effect was the same—she did not stun you by her abnormal behavior or appearance. Still, he didn't see or know everything about her, Bridgewater reminded himself. He wondered if death would reveal more. Would it shed a light?

But the point was that though he had come to like her, Bridgewater had difficulty recalling her face. (He looked at his sketches at home to refresh his memory, though they, too, like his memory, were distortions.) One Friday evening in the Giant he had become aware that he had passed her going down the cereal aisle without acknowledging her presence, and his conscience had troubled him that entire evening.

He had even called to implicitly apologize, but she had not answered her phone. Had she noticed him, he wondered, or had the woman just been some redhead look-alike? She'd been with a man, he recalled, but when Bridgewater tried to picture the man's face, all he saw were Cecilia's red hair and green eyes. If she had died that evening, how would the incident in the grocery store have played itself out in his memory?

Her name was already associated with illuminating tragedy, death. St. Cecilia, patron saint of the blind. Her saint's day came on November 22, a day forever etched in American memory, at least for some generations, as the day Kennedy was assassinated in Dallas. Where were you that day? In a sixth-grade classroom, aware from the serious expression on the face of the fifth-grade teacher, Mrs. Thompson, who came in to borrow the television set, that something was terribly wrong. (There were only three television sets in Craycombe Elementary, used on a rotating basis by the different classes.) A few minutes later, the principal announced over the public address system that the president had been shot. So in the midst of tragedy, Mrs. Thompson duplicitously, selfishly took the television set so that her class could watch the news bulletins instead of Mrs. Boucher's. Death and tragedy vivify the minute details. Would Bridgewater otherwise ever have noticed, recalled Mrs. Thompson's behavior, except in the light of the assassination? Would he, despite his lack of interest in Marilyn Monroe, ever have remembered the baseball game in Detroit, the autograph from a journeyman pitcher on a mediocre team? And what role do love and guilt play in this, those two great motivators?

Meanings are revealed in their multifaceted ambiguity; illumination, more a function of showing than of telling, provides the key to the riddle of each moment, the secret workings of the here and now. Inadequate to tell things you didn't even realize you knew, language fails to communicate these essences; everybody knows this; hence, speaking in tongues, nonsensical gibberish to all who hear, is said to be divinely inspired speech. God talking. Beyond the capacity of human understanding. A whack on the skull, like death surprising you. Bridgewater chalked this up to fundamentalist wish-fulfillment, the urge to have access to ultimate mysteries. Hence the secret desire to believe the crap the grocery store tabloids print. *If only it were so! If only it were so!* Woman walks away from graveyard after she is pronounced dead. "I just woke up!" *If only it were so! If only it were so!* Government satellites photograph Heaven, confirm its existence. *If only it were so! If only it were so!* Man recalls past lives. *If only it were so! If only it were so!*

But take the lessons of the Zen Buddhist monks instead—enlightenment comes through non-verbal experience. (*Or yes, okay, take Saul Bellow's Henderson—truth comes through blows.)*

"I knew this guy in high school who was really into hard rock. It was all he seemed to live for. Pot and rock concerts. Posters of rock stars and T-shirts. His name was Jim Rector. He worked as a salesman in a Radio Shack because he loved stereo systems. He could talk rings around you with that tech talk jive about woofers and tweeters. He went to Central America for a vacation—this was during the seventies some time—and he was in an earthquake in Guatemala. It really shook him up, if you'll excuse the pun. All that death. Bodies and rubble everywhere. He helped in the clean-up, uncovering dead bodies, burying the dead, consoling the grieving, breaking the news. He came back when it was all over and resumed working at Radio Shack, but then the next thing I knew he'd gone off to India to follow some guru. This was ten, twelve years ago. I think he lives in a hut by the Ganges these days."

"And your wife ran off to marry Mick Jagger. God, if I didn't know better, I'd say you were the biggest liar since Munchausen."

"And you're the biggest bore since Saul Bellow!" At once he knew he'd said the wrong thing, calling her a bore. An almost unforgivable insult. But it was out of his mouth and he couldn't take it back. Apologizing would only make it worse.

Cecilia's expression was angry and hurt; her green eyes glistened like marbles with the tears.

"You're always ragging me about my paper on Saul Bellow, like I'm some indecisive twit. I don't kid you about your drawing and painting, do I?" Incipient hatred smoldered in her green eyes like something poisonous, a glimpse of her voracious id. Bridgewater saw his sarcasm really had been a little too pointed. He softened toward Cecilia, realizing he must annoy her at times, too. People get on each other's nerves. It's the nature of relationships.

"Sorry. It's just that I was making a point about death, being a witness to death, and its impact, and you just trivialized me. Called me a liar."

"I was just marveling at your story." She sounded like a petulant child, and it annoyed him.

"At least I tell you about things. You act as though your private life is off-limits, a subject we can't talk about."

"Like what?"

"Well, there's your cousin, Roger, for instance."

"Okay, Peter. You want to know something? Roger's not my cousin. He's my brother."

"Your brother?"

"That's right, I'm Roger Nestorick's sister. Feel better now that you know?"

Bridgewater was stunned, and for a moment he couldn't speak. He looked out at the shimmering blue pool at the club, and then he recovered his composure.

"See? You're the one who tells lies, not me," he said, and he reached for her, but she pulled away. "A distant cousin, you said."

She still refused to meet his eyes. "Do you blame me?"

"A lie is a lie. That's all I'm saying. We all lie. Sometimes, you know, I find myself lying to people when it doesn't really matter. Like, 'Where have you been?' and I'll say, 'Oh, no place,' evasive, even though where I've been isn't of any importance. You know what I'm saying?"

Cecilia shrugged and looked away.

"So what about Roger, anyway?" Bridgewater said after an awkward silence.

"What do you mean, what about Roger?" She looked cagey all at once, her green eyes alert as a cat's watching a mouse.

Bridgewater shrugged again. "How did he get the way he is?"

"How did Zippy get the way *she* is? How did any of us get to be the way we are?"

"I mean, was he abused as a child or something?"

"Look, let's not talk about *this*, either. Even death is a more pleasant topic that this."

"Sorry." Bridgewater wanted to reach for her again. The little dispute had aroused him, but he did not want to be rejected again. He fidgeted. "Must be genes," he said.

After another moment, Cecilia said, "So, do you want to make love?" She knew he was worked up.

"Do you?" Bridgewater's hand went reflexively to his belt buckle. He moved it away and scratched his leg, hoping she hadn't noticed his eagerness, but she smiled knowingly at him, the look at once of a martyr and prison guard. In control. Pussy power.

"Want to draw some afterwards? I like to pose best after we've fucked. It's restful." She really enjoyed teasing him. Another of Cecilia's games, he thought.

"Want to go to a movie later on?" he asked, struggling to get back some of the power. The psychological edge of decision-making. Calling the shots.

"What's showing?"

" '*Swimming to Cambodia*' is at the Charles. '*Who's That Girl?*' starts tomorrow."

"Madonna, huh? Marilyn Monroe manqué, speaking of dead people."

"You don't like Madonna? I think she's sexy."

"See what I mean? Where's it showing, anyway?"

"Harbor Park, Jumpers, Greenspring, Columbia – places like that. Three-cinema complexes, typically in shopping malls, the ones that serve up three of Hollywood's latest junk movies and two-dollar boxes of Milk Duds and Good'n'Plenties."

"Want to see '*Swimming to Cambodia*' tomorrow night?"

"Okay. And just hang around tonight?" She was calling the shots, after all.

As if to prove her control of the situation, Cecilia stood up and started to undress. "Maybe we can play a game of Scrabble later on."

"Sure," Bridgewater said, standing to unbuckle his trousers. He'd agree to anything about now. Cecilia had his number. Checkmate. His pants fell to the floor, bunching up beneath his kneecaps and making it awkward to follow Cecilia's naked swaying buttocks into the bedroom.

Fathers and Sons

The anemic early-September sky and the air, heavy with misty drizzle, rinsed the city in a pale wet light. Driving out past Loyola College to his father's house, Bridgewater felt like an underexposed negative, smudgy and indistinct. Like the weather outside. Morbidly self-conscious, his hands sweating as they gripped the steering wheel, he saw himself as one of the characters in an old *Twilight Zone* episode, about to enter a world over which he had no control, a world in which he returned to the peculiar powerlessness of childhood. Spiritually disenfranchised. His lanky frame folded over S-like into the tiny Toyota Tercel, packed in tight as a portion of intestine; his arms draped over the steering wheel like a truck driver's in his rig. Little Zippy's idea, the Tercel. It made sense economically, gas mileage and all that, not to mention the unobtrusive, almost apologetically unadorned appearance that would discourage vandals from breaking into it (as it was, he and Zippy woke up one Halloween morning to discover that all the cars parked on Bolton Street for two blocks on either side had had the windshield wiper on the driver's side torn off and carelessly discarded like an insect's broken antennae), nor to mention the fact that Zippy made all the car payments. Still, had he known his wife would be leaving him in a few years, he would have insisted on something more roomy, like a tank.

Every child must experience that feeling of a loss of autonomy, spiritual integrity, no matter how old, when he or she enters the parental home. Having read Hemingway in college, Bridgewater had decided long ago he was a "separate peace" type. (One soul, one vote!) He always had this strong reaction when he went home, as though the sanctity of his equilibrium were being violated, his interior gyroscope upset. Why had he let Zippy persuade him to return to Baltimore? He was sure he'd lost a great deal of respect in her eyes when she saw him with his parents, solving the riddle of his personality, seeing him as the overgrown child he was. No wonder she kept secrets! Not that he'd particularly viewed her any differently once he'd met Moishe and Edith. Still, there was no denying the *Twilight Zone* sensations of a loss of control, of being a stranger in an all-too-familiar setting.

For one thing, he could still recall with a keen intensity the claustrophobia of growing up. His relationship with his younger brother Mark. Very archetypal, like Jacob and Esau. (In fact, all those handy, clichéd ideas of family relationships occurred to him, the ones with classic, dramatic precedents and labels, convenient grooves into which his mind settled. The curse of being educated! You no longer saw things for what they were but as examples of some transcendent law! Bridgewater recognized, or tried to recognize, that these models only obscured reality, but they influenced his thinking nevertheless and triggered unwanted visceral responses. A crybaby's sense of injustice. Understanding this, he was yet helpless to stop it.)

Or did the Jacob and Esau story of unequal love and stolen birthrights clarify rather than blur the experience? That could always be the case, after all. Favored by their mother, Mark had sought their father's blessing just to please her, while privately expressing contempt for the old guy in the Oedipal manner. Mark had succeeded, too; he had stolen his brother's birthright of affection, hogged all the parental attention for himself. Bridgewater hesitated to call Mark's tactics underhanded, but while secretly ridiculing their father, Mark had always shown such deference that you'd have almost called him Chinese. Hypocritical, but no more so than anybody else, he had to admit. One of the sublimations of civilization, if you wanted to get Freudian about it.

Bridgewater recognized that his resentment was simply going over old ground, and he even occasionally wondered if he hadn't made the whole thing up, the preferential treatment bit. ("You like Mark better than you like me!" The old Smothers Brothers routine, standard sibling rivalry.) But he could not stop the resentment from welling up, blurring his vision. Mark of all people!

The apple of the old man's eye, Mark had had a checkered history. Dropping out of college, he had gone overseas to bum around, and in Paris he had gotten involved with a couple of guys from Australia whose racket was to befriend tourists and then slip them a mickey—knockout drops in fruit juice. They'd rob them blind once the tourists had passed out; they'd take everything—cash, cards, passports, jewelry, items of clothing. When he got back to the States, he rode out the waterbed boom in the bedroom communities in the Beltway, combining a water-furniture store with a head shop, until selling drug paraphernalia became illegal. Then he briefly managed a Burger King in Newark, Delaware, until a rash of mysterious robberies caused him to lose his job. Now, at the age of 32, he sold real estate, and he was making a killing. He had the gift of gab; he could bullshit his way through a sale, and ever since interest rates had gone down, he had been hauling money in hand over fist. He had invested money in a hotel in Miami thought to be run by the Mafia—at least, that's what his brother suspected. In a word, Mark was pretty successful these days, and that exacerbated Bridgewater's sense of injustice. His little brother!

But by the time he pulled into his father's driveway, Bridgewater's bitterness had spent itself, and now sentiment had taken its place. So much for *The Twilight Zone*. Time to indulge in a little *Lassie*. The usual reaction, inevitable as the swing of a pendulum. The tree in the yard greeted him silently as an old friend. *Welcome home, Pete! Good to see you, fella!* Good old vegetation. The tales that old maple tree could tell. The time Mark had pushed him out of the lower branches and broken his wrist. An accident. He hadn't meant to. The nights during high school when Mark had sneaked out of the second floor window and gone down the tree to go on a futile search for pussy. What had he been thinking? The police had always brought him home. Of course, they knew who Mark's father was, and they never pressed charges.

Bridgewater remembered the pets they'd had as children. The dogs, the cats, the hamsters. All named and anthropomorphized. The poignance of their deaths. Run over by cars. Distemper. Cancer. Old age. Fluffy, the old cat down whose throat Mark had once forced a tab of LSD. The way its head had bobbed about like a puppet's, the glassy green marble eyes dizzy with cosmic consciousness.

Stepping out of the car onto the gravel driveway and unfolding himself like a new vacuum cleaner sack, his eyes as misty as the day outside, Bridgewater walked up the front walk where decades ago their tricycles and wagons and scooters had stood. Oh, what schmaltz! Get a hold of yourself, man!

As always, he hesitated at the front door, feeling he should knock, to establish a little barrier to separate his personality from the all-consuming entity of "family." But he knew his father would insist that he simply enter—it was still his house; he was always welcome—and finally he pushed the front door open and strode in. The maple newel on the banister at the foot of the stairs going up to the second floor, a wooden globe, like a crystal ball brought a vision of another world, his childhood. Growing up. The bird's eye at the top of the newel was as familiar to him as the scar over his left knee where his flesh had been gouged in a bicycle accident during his adolescence (Mark, an impish kid even back then, had stuck a broom handle in the spokes of the bike's wheel as Peter rode past, ruining the wheel and injuring Peter.) A sacred object when he had believed in ghosts; he had touched the bird's eye on the maple newel post reverentially, superstitiously, before going to bed at night to ward off evil spirits. The accordion-like radiators their father had ritualistically bled every fall with the key that was kept all year long in a tool drawer in the basement. Those knocking metal relics from another age, an obsolete technology. Frank refused to have central air-conditioning installed, though he had finally consented to buy a couple of window units.

Finally, stepping inside and pulling the door closed behind him, Bridgewater remembered his mother's death. The memory always came back to him on overcast days like this when the gloom of the living room had the sepulchral, dust-suspended, musty air of a funeral parlor. She had died from a massive heart attack after going swimming at the athletic club. Standing naked on the scales to weigh herself, she had simply keeled over. Wham. Dead. Thirteen years ago this November. Peter had just turned 23.

Why was he being so melancholy? So shaky emotionally? His own rotten love life, sure. But he refused to admit it. Who doesn't have affairs? Who doesn't break up with a partner? A part of life. He tried to put it out of his mind. He and Cecilia hadn't even officially *been* a couple, he thought, grabbing at some kind of consolation.

Frank was in the sunken den at the rear of the house, a room you descended into like a wading pool. He was parked in front of the television set watching the local news. A couch potato. To his credit, Frank did make an effort to work out at the athletic club where his wife had died over a decade before, riding the exercise bicycles while reading the newspaper, but the tendency of his molecules was to rest. The cells inside his body wanted to go on strike. A phlegmatic guy. A human paperweight.

Frank watched the news and read newspapers on the homeopathic principle. Administering minute quantities of remedies that in massive doses will kill you, cause the very disease you're trying to fight. A vaccination of the consciousness. A booster of information before getting to the crossword puzzle or to the canned-laughter sitcom. Only his elaborate electric train set could get him out of his chair.

"Pete! Have a seat! Something to drink? Help yourself." Frank did not take his eyes from the television set, and Bridgewater felt his own drawn to the screen. A story about the Pope's imminent visit to the United States. All across the nation, Jews, gays, nuns and priests geared up to register protest, bombard the pontiff with complaints. "The Pope just doesn't know what it is to be a Catholic," one young woman told a reporter. She was the live-in lover of a priest out in Calvert County someplace. The modern age. The shrinking capacity for abstinence, the increasing reluctance to endure restraint for its own sake. Discipline? Who the hell needs it? What's it good for?

"You want anything?" Bridgewater asked, headed for the kitchen to retrieve a beer from the refrigerator. His father had still not looked at him.

"Help yourself!" Frank said, still watching the screen.

When he came back from the kitchen with a National Premium, Bridgewater asked his father how he was doing. A perfunctory question, but now Frank did not even reply; more important than the Pope's visit, evidently, the National Football League was threatening to go on strike; Frank's attention was absorbed in the story. The couch and chairs in the sunken den surrounded the television set like supplicants at an altar, and Bridgewater took a chair against one wall so that he had a full view of Frank's profile. *Old Man in a Chair*. A seventeenth century German shopkeeper dozing in front of the fire after a day's work. Subdued light. A dog at his feet, likewise snoozing in the warmth of the fire. Oil on canvas, thick as tree bark.

Frank knew the names of all the young girls who came to the athletic club for aerobics classes. He greeted them enthusiastically from his perch on the exercise bicycle. "Hi, Maureen!" "How's it going, Janet?" "How you doing, Pam?" "Hi there, Gail!" A fond foolish old man, his son's affectionate assessment. When they asked him in turn how he was doing, Frank always replied in a cheerful voice, "Terrible! Couldn't be worse!" Then he'd call them by little nicknames, like "Mo" and "Jan-honey," "Pammy" and "Gail-babe." ("Your father slobbers," Bridgewater could still recall his mother saying, chiding Frank for his sentimentality.)

Frank had back trouble, and occasionally he wore an elastic orthopedic corset around his middle, like an elderly lady wearing a girdle. In profile he looked rather well, though the flesh on his arms was starting to come away from the bones and hang loose, wagging like a beagle's jowls.

They sat this way without speaking—without *needing* to speak—for another ten minutes while they listened to the stories about the West German Siamese twins that were being separated at Johns Hopkins Hospital that weekend, forest fires out west, and the pennant races in major league baseball. Then, a story about Pat Robertson's presidential campaign finally provoked a reaction. Apparently, Robertson's campaign was doing well in Iowa.

"Pat Robertson! Jesus!" Frank said. "I thought the PTL scandal last spring would have undermined his candidacy."

"Wasn't his father a senator? From Virginia? Robertson's?"

"I'd have thought the secular humanists would have lumped them all together and ridiculed them off the face of the map," Frank said, not hearing his son. Never admitting to religious or political preferences—probably not even having any—Frank showed what a political person he really was, after all his years in city government. For this reason, Frank's exclamations always interested Bridgewater, but when he asked Frank his views pointblank, he always had a way of deflecting the questions. Typically, he'd say, "Well, what do *you* think?" But didn't this reference to secular humanists (a fundamentalist Christian's way of calling you a son of a bitch, even more lowdown than "liberal") reveal something? But in the next breath Frank said, "That guy Oral Roberts was something, though, wasn't he? Making God out to be some kind of Iranian terrorist holding him hostage for a ransom of ten million dollars!" He chuckled and reached down beside his chair. His hand came up with a National Premium of his own, and Frank's Adam's apple bobbed up and down as he sucked at the bottle.

Bridgewater recalled Moishe Feldman's rantings about Pat Robertson during a visit he and Zippy had made to Potawatomi Rapids the year before. "Elect him and he'll wipe out the Jews, you watch," Moishe warned. He had just received a plea from the American Jewish Congress for contributions. The letter warned about the Christian right and Pat Robertson in particular. "He's even said that the moment you turn the Constitution over to non-Christians it destroys the foundations of society. What an anti-Semite! What a son of a bitch! Elect that bastard and we'll be having pogroms right here in America!"

"Oy vey!" Edith chimed in.

Frank switched off the television and turned his attention to his son just as a pretty woman reporter with a sincere expression on her face told the camera that sex offender Roger Nestorick's appeal of his conviction on several counts of child molestation would soon be heard in court. "Paroled in a half-way house in Jessup, Nestorick has been performing community serv—" *Click.*

In his father's gaze, Bridgewater could feel himself—his personality, his individuality—shrinking to invisibility. Frank did not see *him*; he saw a child. Bridgewater tried to make his voice sound husky, as if to inflate his diminishing sense of self, blow himself back up to human proportions. He was afraid, speaking, that his voice might come out as a child's falsetto.

"My father-in-law is a little apprehensive about Pat Robertson becoming president."

"Is he? I imagine he is. What's the Jewish holiday that's coming up in a few weeks? Passover?"

"Rosh Hashanah, then Yom Kippur."

"That's right. New Year, isn't it?"

"Rosh Hashanah, yeah, that's the New Year. It's 5748 this time, I think."

"Is that right?" Frank had already lost interest. But the subject had raised his curiosity about his daughter-in-law. Diplomatically, he asked, "Have you spoken with them lately? Any news? About Zip?" *Zip*! His father's annoying nicknaming habit took Bridgewater by surprise again, but he tried to ignore it.

"Not since the end of July. The national governors' conference was going on in Traverse City when I called. Moishe was doing a booming business down in Potawatomi Rapids, selling and renting boats."

"Did they have any news?"

"They got a card from her around Independence Day."

"Where from?"

"Barbados? I think they said Barbados. Mick Jagger's been doing some recording down there. He's coming out with a new solo album called *Primitive Cool*."

Tacitly admitting that their daughter had "done him wrong," the Feldmans were more inclined to be sympathetic toward Bridgewater since Zippy's departure. Still, Moishe reserved a judgmental edge in his tone when he inquired about Bridgewater's efforts at making a living.

"Got any prospects?" he asked, and Bridgewater could almost see his father-in-law's eyes flickering back and forth.

"A few."

Rachael even said her parents were inclined to take his side the last time she called. She told Bridgewater that her parents were proud of the courage and the patience and the devotion he displayed. They did not know about Cecilia Nestorick, of course, nor did Rachael. Rachael said it made her feel more hopeful about telling Moishe and Edith about Dody Brown one day. "One day soon."

Frank did not know about Zippy's obsession with Mick Jagger and did not respond to Peter's comment. He regarded his son for a moment before speaking. Then, probing, he remarked affably that Bridgewater seemed to be taking it all rather well. Thirteen years as a widower had given Frank a kind of insight into the ways of coping with loneliness, and by his cagey comment, Bridgewater guessed that his father wondered if there were another woman, that he was fishing around for clues.

"I've been keeping busy," Bridgewater replied, thinking of Cecilia and feeling depressed.

"Painting?"

"Working."

Bridgewater recalled his last meeting with Cecilia earlier in the week. It came flooding over him in vivid detail. Lying naked on her couch in her apartment while Bridgewater drew, she had told him, almost proudly, that she had not handed in her paper on Saul Bellow. The professor had given her an incomplete; she had the next semester to complete and hand it in—though it could be extended indefinitely, at the professor's discretion, she surmised. Her manner as she told him all this made Bridgewater remember Zippy telling him he carried the Tay-Sachs gene.

"Why not? Why didn't you hand it in? You've been working on it all summer."

"I just realized that what I was writing about arctic images wasn't what I really wanted to *say*."

"And what did you really want to say?" He had been wishing he had an orange crayon to color in the pubic triangle, several shades darker than the hair on her head. Inspired, or enchanted, by the prospect of painting a nude, Bridgewater's mind dwelt on the possibilities. What should his approach be? Like Botticelli's *Birth of Venus*, the figure undulant but idealized, decorous and chaste while being voluptuous and sensual at the same time? Or a luscious female body, an adoring portrait like Renoir's *baigneuses*, earthy and sensuous? Or again, there was Matisse's *Blue Nude*, more abstract, less concerned with ideal form and proportion but no less erotic in the posture, the prominence of the thighs. Which line should he take? He could do all three! And more! Yet he knew he would probably never get around to any actual painting. "Art" interested him more, finally, than painting; painting was so messy. All those fumes and chemicals. The turpentine. Besides, a work of art is always more perfect in conception than in execution. If only he had an oeuvre attributed to him already, a controversial inventory of paintings that had all the critics arguing, all the galleries drooling, all the patrons fawning!

But this news of Cecilia's strangely upset him.

"I want to talk about Bellow as a *thinker*," she said. "What he has to say about humanity, about life, about death. The whole thing. I don't want to just write something clever or something precious or insightful. I want to say what really *matters*."

Bridgewater had always found this kind of talk exasperating. But now he had an urge to spank her. He put aside his sketchpad and asked her what that was. What really "mattered," as she put it. He could not conceal his impatience; he sounded contemptuous.

Cecilia gestured with her arms, as if to embrace the universe. The white of her breasts, surrounded by the tan flesh, cooked from a summer of sun beside the pool, glowed luminescent in the shadowy late afternoon light like neon blobs. "Just everything," she said. "Like the way Herzog writes to dead people or the way Sammler keeps recalling Nazi death camps, crawling out of a mass grave where his wife is, through layers of dead bodies. The way that novel ends with Sammler talking to God about the knowledge of moral responsibility embedded in human consciousness, while he stares at his nephew's corpse."

"Death? You mean you really are going to write about Bellow's views of death?" Bridgewater recalled the conversation they had had a month before.

Cecilia laughed, shaking her head.

"You know, Bellow's Jewish—" Bridgewater began, not really sure what he intended to say next—perhaps something about the absence of a conception of the afterlife in Jewish thought—but she cut him off anyway.

"Oh, that's nothing! He's way beyond all that. Take Augie March. He starts his story saying, 'I am an American, Chicago-born.' An American! Not a Jew! You're trailing the wrong scent if you try to tackle Bellow as a Jew."

"You ever read an essay by Philip Roth called 'Imagining Jews'?"

"Yes, and I think it's rather narrow. Roth tries to fit Bellow into his own little theory about the moral Jewish protagonist. Bellow's fiction is full of Jewish hedonists as well as the ultra-moral types. Just like the rest of humanity. Take Artur Sammler's nephew and niece, for instance."

"So you don't think Jews have a unique experience?"

"Historically, maybe, but not existentially. Judaism isn't that much different from any other western religion. You just think it is because you converted. But it's all pretty familiar, isn't it? God and redemption and all that. Converting to Judaism must be like emigrating to Canada."

Going to Canada! How he yearned to slap the smug little know-it-all bitch! Sure, it wasn't like joining a Zen monastery in Tokyo or signing up with the Dalai Lama in Tibet or something, but it *was* different nonetheless! Bridgewater changed the subject back to Cecilia. Put the spotlight on her. "So what *are* you writing about, now? What is it that 'matters'?"

"Well, I guess I'm back to plants, really. Right where I started. Should have trusted my instincts. Mysticism, really. I think that's the way to get at him. Higher states of consciousness. The *structure* of consciousness, really. Like a floorplan, a blueprint. All the emphasis in his later novels on William Blake and Swedenborg. Mister Sammler devotes himself to 13th century religious thinkers, like Meister Eckhart, for instance, and Charlie Citrine, the narrator of *Humboldt's Gift*, studies Rudolf Steiner's mystical philosophy. And Benn Crader, in his latest, is into William Blake—"

Bridgewater interrupted the recitation of the catalogue. "Does Artur Sammler love plants, too?" He was unable to keep the sarcasm and the disappointment out of his voice.

Cecilia lowered her eyes; Bridgewater's scorn vexed her. "No, but Doctor Govinda Lal speculates that the kind of vegetation that could thrive on the moon is a hybrid of lichens and cacti, and Sammler's niece, Margotte, has odd plants growing in her parlor. Potato vines, rubber plants, avocados."

"Potato vines." Bridgewater could not control the ironic tone; his voice quivered with scorn.

"Herzog speaks disdainfully of 'potato love'," she added. "The insincere kind. Low consciousness."

Had this observation about "potato love" been aimed at him? He wondered this now in Frank's sunken den. It had not occurred to him at the time. Yet he had realized that his behavior was priggish, like an offended schoolteacher, and he had tried to relax a bit. He smiled, but his lips had an unconvincing warped look, the line of the smile crooked and wavering. Unaccountably distressed by Cecilia's failure—he had had such faith in her as a scholar, he almost felt betrayed—Bridgewater asked her if she didn't have the will to complete her paper. It sounded foolish. Will. Centuries back they talked about Will as some metaphysical force. Plato and Aristotle, Schopenhauer and Nietzsche. Medieval philosophers like Augustine wrote endlessly about man's free will and God's omniscience, free will and predestination. Now, if you ever heard the will spoken of at all it referred to things like quitting cigarettes and sticking to diets.

His reference to will had evidently seemed smug to Cecilia, too—as if he had finally taken the step overboard into an ocean of conceit. Sitting upright, she looked at him crossly and said, "Well, what's it to you whether I hand my paper in on time? You're not my father. Don't give me that 'will' bullshit! I don't criticize you because you haven't started painting yet, have I?" She started to get dressed.

"I'm still making sketches. I'm still drawing."

"Bullshit. I bet you just want to look at me naked. You'd rather look than fuck me."

"You want me to fuck you?"

"Oh no you don't. You're not going to get me to beg for it so you can square it with your conscience."

"Square what with my conscience?"

"Your infidelity to your wife. You've been mooning about her all summer."

"I have not been 'mooning' this summer."

Already in her underpants and shorts, Cecilia reached for her bra but then flung it aside and pulled on one of those Hard Rock Café T-shirts, this one with Istanbul written underneath the orange circle. Was there really a Hard Rock Café in Turkey?

"You did it just now with your talk about this Jewish bullshit, and then there's all this shit about Mick Jagger. I'd say *you* are the Hinckley type around here, not your wife. You just couldn't take the fact that she dumped you for some regular guy. Or for nobody at all."

"Look, I'm sorry I criticized you about your holy brilliant paper. I'm sure you'll get a Pulitzer Prize for it when you write it."

"Ha ha ha."

"*If* you write it."

"Why don't you sketch it for me? Then you can paint a masterpiece."

"Maybe Saul Bellow will fuck you if it's good enough."

"Who I fuck is none of your business."

"You fucking somebody besides me?"

"Wouldn't you like to know."

"Now that you bring it up, yeah. *Are* you fucking somebody else?"

"What if I *am* fucking Saul Bellow?"

"Right, and I'm fucking Elizabeth Taylor."

"Wouldn't you like to know," she said. "Wouldn't you like to know."

"You're probably fucking your brother."

She lunged out to slap his face, but he dodged her. "You slime!"

"Does Roger put it up your ass when he's not molesting ten-year-olds?"

"You bastard!"

Cecilia finally ordered him out.

"Why don't you just go now, Peter? I'd better work on my paper." Now her sarcasm made him smile; it was all so ludicrous! But, his vanity wounded by her remarks about Zippy and his painting, he got up to leave. Underneath it all, moreover, he felt emasculated by her insinuation that his tastes were voyeuristic. Hadn't she enjoyed the sex? Hadn't she come, too? She *had* begged for it.

"I'll sell you one of my paintings when I'm done with it," he said at the door. "Your big beautiful red-haired pussy, oil on canvas!"

"Well I hope you remember what it looks like, because you won't be seeing it again!"

That's when the finality of it hit him. What had he done?

"Working? Doing anything besides your job with those other kids at WPCC?" A mild, benevolent man, Frank Bridgewater could still get in an editorial dig at his son. Equating him with college kids. His job, anyway. Young and dumb and full of come. Bridgewater thought of the two work-study students who helped him in the graphics lab, a Chinese boy named Wing Lee and a Jewish girl named Lee Wing, both of them nineteen. Lee called him "Mr. Bridgewater," even though he told her to call him Peter.

"Well, I designed a safe-sex brochure for one client last month, and earlier in the summer there was a design project for some people in Ocean City, a resort client, and I did some photography work for a weekly tabloid a couple weekends when I was there. I also wrote a little feature article," he added, remembering the little sidebar he had written about some "colorful character," a hustler on the boardwalk, that was part of a larger article about resort society.

"Freelance?"

"Of course."

"Would you like to move there? Ocean City? Maybe settle in for a while, get a job with an ad agency?" Frank always came up with these suggestions when his son visited him, always trying to "cure" him of some existential illness from which he saw Peter suffering. He had Bridgewater pegged as a guy who was still becoming, still on his way to adulthood, not yet grown up. Bridgewater, on the contrary, felt himself decaying. Falling apart.

"No." No need to elaborate. Simple question, simple answer. The urge to clarify, to explain, to establish a space for himself in the world, foamed behind his lips, but he kept his mouth shut. Still, he could not prevent the involuntary shudder at the prospect of living in Ocean City. Depending on the tides and the prevailing winds, you could almost always count on those near-invisible insects, the kind that float past your eyes like hallucinations and then wind up in your ears and mouth. The vacuous self-satisfaction of resorters and the chaotic depression of youth culture.

"Anything else?"

"That's kept me pretty busy. But I did do some layout and copyfitting work for an art museum."

"BMA?"

"A place called the Maryland Council for Avant Garde Expression. They have a little gallery downtown. Privately owned."

"Never heard of them."

"No? They've been around. MC-AGE? Ever heard that title?" Bridgewater knew what his father was up to by this line of questioning. Part of the cure. The city sponsored the BMA. Frank, in city government, could put a little work his son's way if he'd let him.

"Doesn't sound familiar. Now, the BMA –"

"So what do you hear from Mark?" Bridgewater asked to divert his father's attention. Frank's face relaxed into an expression of fondness.

"Knockin' 'em dead in Miami Beach."

"He's down there for his hotel business?"

"Now *there's* a successful guy."

"From Burger King to the Gold Coast, eh?"

"Do you still hold a grudge against Mark for being the prodigal son?"

"He's not the prodigal son. He's Mark." Bridgewater resisted his father's tendency to blur his brother's identity in these mythic categories. "He's a criminal."

"He deals with some rough customers, I'll grant that." Frank was not aware of Mark's Jean Genet activities in Paris, and he attributed the Burger King fiasco to bum luck, sheer coincidence. The head shop was just smart business. Mark had seen an opportunity and seized it. He'd understood there was a market and he exploited it. Simple as that.

"Well, I'm glad he's doing all right," Bridgewater said, the grudge still in his voice.

"I just wish he'd settle down and get married. I might never have a grandchild!"

"He's got a girlfriend?" Bridgewater wondered if Frank's comment were aimed at him. A rebuke. There was still that electric train set to be bequeathed, after all.

"He's always got girlfriends. That's his trouble. It's too easy for him. He's such a charming guy."

"A real Casanova."

"But he's been seeing a lot of a gal called Bambi Warner lately. A real knockout."

"I'm sure she is."

"Say, I just got a real neat replica of a B&O locomotive," Frank said. "Want to see it? Mark really loved it when he stopped over before going to Florida."

Before he could answer, the telephone rang. Saved by the bell! Frank reached over and picked up the receiver. It was for Bridgewater. It was Zippy. She was back in Baltimore.

Repentance

Bridgewater stood at the bus stop on Howard Street waiting for the bus out to Social Security. He had taken the day off work and arranged to meet Zippy for lunch. The MTA had changed the route of the 28 bus so often because of construction on Howard Street that Bridgewater no longer knew where to catch it. Not on Park Avenue where he and Zippy lived, that's for sure. How convenient it used to be to step outside the door and practically be at the bus stop. Yet another reason to regret. So he had gone down past Maryland General Hospital, beyond Antique Row to a bus stop near the Little X porn theater (lurid posters advertised movies called *Playgirls* and *Neon Nights*) and the discount electronics stores that proclaimed STEREOS-TVS-VCRS, where he found a group of people waiting for a bus. Here he stopped and, assuming a posture of waiting—weight thrown onto one hip, knees locked and shins concave—he examined the manuscript he held, *The Collected Poems of Franklin Wood*. Music from ghetto blasters swelled and then subsided as first one and then another pedestrian passed by lugging one of the valise-like gadgets. The sky crowded low into the street, and even though Bridgewater's watch said half past eleven, the streetlights glowed overhead with the jaundiced yellow-fever light; they were the high tech kind that came on if the ambient light were insufficient. They snored with the monotony of alarm clocks. In the space where the bus stopped a shiny red sportscar was illegally parked. Two bumper stickers on the rear said I ♥ JESUS, red letters on a white background, and B104 MEANS MUSIC with a Coca-Cola logo on one end, white letters on a red background. Bumper stickers chosen as decoration.

Bridgewater turned the pages of the book to a poem that began:

> I live in the land
> Where bumper stickers
> Have replaced ideas.
> Instead of hearts
> We have tee-shirts
> To show our devotion . . .

This small man, Wood, with a flowing pompadour had come into the WPCC graphics lab one day looking for somebody to design the dust jacket of his book. He was publishing it himself. Vanity press. Evidently he had inherited a pile of dough from his family and did not have to work. Bridgewater had taken the design job himself, attracted to Wood for reasons he could not explain; Wood seemed like another outsider. Bridgewater envisioned a rustic scene for the cover. Wood's poems had that romantic reactionary tone, going back to a time before computers, when-life-was-simple-and-the-rivers-weren't-polluted sort of thing.

Bridgewater put aside the book and delved into his thoughts instead, hypnotized by the buzzing streetlights. Zippy had been back more than a month, but he continued to marvel at how rich his life seemed to have become now. Never a dull empty moment. No more desert-like loneliness, wondering what to do next. How had his father stood it all these years? But as always, Bridgewater tried to sort out his real feelings from the ones he thought he ought to have and the ones that simply seemed efficacious to him, the ones that helped him avoid pain. Shouldn't he, after all, feel betrayed? Indignant? Hurt?

The thought of betrayal brought other thoughts. Zippy had been in Barbados all summer. Not only did she come back with a tan, but she came back pregnant to boot. The baby was due in December, which meant she had been knocked up in March, and as far as Bridgewater knew, she had not been unfaithful to him while she'd been in Baltimore. So he was the father, right? But hadn't they scrupulously used birth control on those rare occasions that winter when they *had* been able to overcome their fears and sadness? Zippy had had an IUD inserted; another Tay-Sachs abortion would have devastated them both.

Zippy said the reason she left was that she realized she was pregnant and she kind of flipped out precisely because of the possibility of another Tay-Sachs fetus and another abortion. Not even IUDs are foolproof. She had stayed with a woman she had known in college who lived in Barbados, Liz McEver. Zippy had kept in touch with Liz over the years, and she had sought refuge with her to "get her head together." It wasn't a phrase she usually used, which made Bridgewater suspicious, but he let it slide. What else was she supposed to say? She did not mention Mick Jagger, and Bridgewater did not ask. She seemed somewhat contrite, or repentant, or regretful, but she did not grovel or apologize too excessively. Fine. He did not require it.

Zippy had found the nude sketches of Cecilia in his dresser drawer when she went looking for blank checks. She remarked that the model looked familiar. Bridgewater told her she had probably seen the woman when they had gone to buy bus passes. Zippy said she must be a warm, generous person. Bridgewater wondered what had led her to draw that conclusion, but he said nothing about their relationship. He grudgingly admired the way Zippy had turned the tables on him on the fidelity question. Not that there were any overt accusations or any arguments. (Actually, Bridgewater was secretly thrilled to have her back, felt some of the old, original love that he'd thought was gone forever; he reviled in his sappy sentimentality, which had become his reference point for "normal"—an attitude he'd inherited from his father, he thought with a kind of alarm, but then reflected that it probably had more to do with "the human condition" than any specific genetic or environmental influence. Zippy seemed happy to be back, too.) But the climate of guilt being what it is, the onus of hanky-panky was more on Bridgewater than on Zippy. Yet *she* had left *him*, right? So didn't that mitigate his transgressions? And why had she left him, anyway? Was there some more elemental reason than "getting her head together"?

Bridgewater recalled a conversation he'd had with Rachael in May or June, soon after Zippy's departure. In attempting to explain her sister's behavior, Rachael told him about the time when, as a twelve-year old child, Zippy had found a stray dog near her parents' home in Potawatomi Rapids and brought it home with her. A mongrel with brown and white fur and floppy ears that she named Ernie, after the butcher at Detweiler's, the general store, Rachael said. But Zippy overheard her parents talking about Ernie the next day; they'd made arrangements to give the dog to a farmer up the road. So Zippy took the dog and "ran away" with him. She hid out on the beach with her dog and a small bag of Lender's bagels she'd taken for nourishment. Though amused by the note their child had left, the Feldmans became worried when it started to get dark and Zippy could not be found. They mobilized their neighbors to search for the little girl. Eventually, Sue Truckenmiller, a teenage clerk at Detweiler's, discovered Zippy by the lighthouse on Potawatomi Point. The Feldmans were overwhelmed with relief when they had their daughter back, but she did not get to keep Ernie. The dog was still given to the farmer.

"Do you think she ran off with a loveable little mutt?"

"No, that's not what I meant at all, and you know it! It's just that in our family we sort of go off by ourselves to work things out." Bridgewater had wondered aloud why his wife had not consulted him if anything was disturbing her. That had prompted Rachael's reminiscence about Ernie. "That's why I haven't mentioned Dody to Mom and Dad yet. And you know Zippy didn't tell them about you until after you'd converted."

"Do you think she's hiding out in Barbados with another man, then, instead of a dog?" *Mick Jagger*?

Again, Bridgewater's sarcasm annoyed Zippy's sister. "I mean, we don't *know* what the matter is, Peter! Whatever it is, she probably has a very good reason, and we just have to reserve judgement until we find out."

Well, pregnancy hadn't been what he'd expected at all, that's for sure. Whether Zippy had "betrayed" him or not, she was carrying his child. And hell, why not just admit it, he was glad to have her back. Was there some sort of principle involved that he wasn't aware of? Some cinematic reaction he was obligated to portray, perform? If so, he hadn't read the script. Or maybe his role really *was* the blind cuckold? The possibilities crowded his brain.

Zippy's parents had come to visit them during the High Holy Days. Just before they arrived, Zippy had brought home a black cat with white feet, the kind you would probably name "Boots" because of the coloring. Only, Zippy had another idea.

"Let's call him Azazel," she said, and her brown eyes sparkled with mischief. Azazel, the scapegoat mentioned in the Torah, upon which the Hebrews had piled their sins before banishing it into the wilderness with its unenviable cargo. Part of the Yom Kippur symbolism.

"Are we going to keep him?"

"Can we? Of course, you'll have to clean his litterbox since I'm pregnant." Remembering Rachael's story about Ernie, Bridgewater consented.

So they kept the cat, Azazel. What sort of symbolism did that suggest? That they kept their sins about them like dirty secrets that won't go away? Standing at the bus stop, he flipped through Franklin Wood's manuscript.

> I carry my sins
> Like a bag of seeds,
> Scattering them where I walk.
> I refuse to be ashamed
> Or to apologize for nature . . .

Bridgewater closed the book and tried to picture Franklin. He was a shy little man with a faintly southern accent, a Kentuckian transplanted in the north—if you considered Baltimore north. His clothing was baggy; shirts billowed out around his waist. They were the clothes of a person who had recently lost a good deal of weight. He looked up at you through the upper edge of his black frame glasses, from just under the opaque rim, like a little boy peeking around a corner. A guy who looked at the world from the outside. He seemed to fancy himself a 20th century Walt Whitman but without the sexuality. A fairly substantial omission, come to think of it.

When Moishe and Edith had come to Baltimore they immediately expressed their horror at the cat and told Zippy and Bridgewater that they would have to get rid of it. Edith said it would smother the baby. But by this time Bridgewater was rather attached to the animal, whom he called Ozzie.

"In *A Moveable Feast* Hemingway says that only stupid people believe those superstitions about cats. He says they're very good with children."

"Hemingway! Oy vey!"

"Well, I'm the one who's cleaning out the litter pan, anyway."

"What else are you doing besides cleaning out litter pans?" Moishe asked. His eyes went back and forth like go-go dancers in suspended cages. But at some point in his relationship with Moishe, Bridgewater realized, looking at his father-in-law, the non-stop shifting of his eyes had ceased to be "like" this or that and just simply *was*, the way heartbeat or breathing simply *are*—the way the cicadas had simply *been* that summer; his eyes were distracting, perhaps, calling attention to themselves, but they were just *there* in their essential beingness without reference to other, more familiar things. They had become familiar themselves, everyday, like old friends he recognized and no longer feared.

"Well, I'm the one who feeds him most of the time, too," he answered, being obtuse. "He likes Nine Lives' Choice Cuts 'n' Cheese and Fisherman's Stew, mostly, and this low-ash dry food we buy at Gil Miller's Pampered Pet store on Falls Road—"

"I mean, what do you do besides care for the cat?" He looked at Zippy. "Does Gazookis do anything besides care for the cat?"

"Oh, right." Bridgewater blushed. Got one in the oven, so you'd better be responsible, his father-in-law was saying. Bridgewater told Moishe about Franklin Wood.

"A book of poems?"

"Sure, why not?"

"It's deadend. You'll get your name around as somebody who works with subversives and nuts, if you get your name around at all. Who *cares* about poets, for Chrissakes? This isn't Renaissance Italy or Elizabethan England! This is 20th century America!"

Bridgewater could not believe what he was hearing. Totally unanticipated. Why argue? But he said: "Milton Glazer designed the jacket of Philip Roth's latest novel."

"Philip Roth! Gevalt!" Edith exclaimed. "That assimilationist Jew!"

"I just mean, it's a legitimate business and potentially very lucrative." Bridgewater tried to appeal to the pragmatic Moishe, but he could not help thinking he was pandering to the stereotype of the money-grubbing Jew. Shylock. Phrases from childhood buzzed in his memory: "Did you Jew him down?" "Did he Jew you out of your money?"

"Peter also has his job at Wyman Park," Zippy said.

"The community college, right." Moishe sounded disdainful. You'd have thought he had graduated from Harvard from his tone, though he'd only completed high school. Still, why begrudge the man his standards? Besides, Moishe had never regarded Bridgewater's graphics-lab work as "real" employment.

"I've had some pretty good freelance jobs lately. My brother just got into the hotel business in Miami and he might put some advertising business my way."

"He's in real estate now, your brother? The hobo at your wedding?"

"Well, we all have marginal relatives, I guess," Bridgewater said mildly. Moishe looked away. His brother Sid was a corrupt politician and now a fugitive from the law as well. "Look at Nixon, Reagan, Carter. They all have screwball brothers, too."

Mark had come back from his trip to Florida wearing an expensive silk suit and talking like a big-time criminal. To Bridgewater he seemed more like a play actor auditioning for a role in "*Some Like It Hot.*" Toothpick Charlie, maybe, the guy who rats on Spats Columbo to the cops and then gets riddled full of holes by the mob.

"We had to pay off some city officials to change the zoning restrictions," he said grandly, basking in the glamour of his big-shot hoodlum connections. "Five grand here, five grand there. But we got beachfront property, and we ought to make a bundle, especially since we own the construction contracts."

For years Mark had seemingly been unconcerned about clothing and appearances; for more than a decade he had worn torn dirty jeans and a greasy leather bop cap, the kind with the brim so narrow you had to look twice to be sure there was one. It was like his trademark, that bop cap, pulled down jauntily at an angle over his brow, reminiscent of the early Marlon Brando. To go along with the bop cap, a frayed gray cotton vest, the kind gamblers wear, only shabby. Back then, Mark had cultivated the image of a minor thug in a grade B movie. Thin gold wirerim glasses, the kind worn by rock star intellectual poseurs, a square chin, receding hairline, deep horizontal furrows in his forehead—not really worry-lines but the lines of concentration of somebody who lives by his wits. A character. His scrawny neck, the Adam's apple working overtime like a hydraulic pump, brought to Bridgewater's mind the image of a noose. His hunched shoulders, sloping back down his spine, like a hunkered frog set to spring, also aroused thoughts of torture and punishment. Poor posture. A hunchback in the making, Notre Dame. The Bastille. French Revolution. The guillotine.

Now in his tight cream-colored silk suit, a carnation in the lapel, and gleaming patent leather loafers, he looked like a white guy doing a Motown imitation, perhaps revealing a secret ambition to whirl onstage in choreographed movements, lip-synching a song.

For years the bop cap had covered his thinning hair, a concession to vanity, but now Bridgewater expected his brother to have hair transplants and cosmetic surgery to narrow his chin—a la Michael Jackson. If there were a way, no doubt he'd get rid of the green and gold speckles that shot through his blue irises. Maybe he could buy tinted contact lenses.

"Construction's where's the money's at," Mark had said. "Building. The real estate business taught me that much. Contracting and subcontracting. After the hotel we've got our sights set on a shopping mall. Talk about big bucks. That's why we had to get the zoning right."

"We?"

"Me and my partners, Tony Bommarito and Nick Asaro." His eyes twinkled devilishly, the green and gold spots flattening out to green and gold bands, and he barked a short laugh. "Listen, Pete, I know what you're thinking, but they are *not*, I repeat *not* Mafia. I guaranfuckin-*tee* you they are not Mafia." The bad-boy look in his eyes made Bridgewater remember the prank he had pulled at a college dance fifteen years before when, as a high school student, he had come to visit Bridgewater in Boston. Somehow Mark had rigged up a microphone in the girl's restroom, and the boys were able to overhear their private conversations. "There must be fifty yards of cock out there," one girl had exclaimed to her friends, "and all I want is six inches!"

"Having a baby's an expensive proposition," Moishe was saying, "and you'll need some extra money with that." Zippy's father always slightly skewed the prepositions; Bridgewater sensed something wrong but could not put his finger on it. "Of" and "from" and "as" and "while" and "with" all got mixed up somehow; it was as if he'd put a coin in a gumball machine and took whatever flavor popped out, approval on, comments to, where it's at.

They'd all gone to Yom Kippur services at Hopkins, in the glass pavilion of Levering Hall. Bridgewater and Zippy had gone there to the Rosh Hashanah services the week before. Like many nonobservant Jews, Zippy and Bridgewater only attended synagogue services during the High Holy Days. (All this would certainly change when their child began to walk, Bridgewater reflected grimly.). Even this minimal observance felt like an unnecessary burden to Bridgewater, who had never attended church services during his life as a Christian; he shrank from group activities with a kind of horror, feeling his freedom compromised by the behavioral demands, the custom and conformity. His lonely feelings of being an outsider were exacerbated in group situations. Odd, his original feelings of Jewish identification stemmed precisely from this self-consciousness of being an outsider, a pariah, on a personal diaspora from a mythical homeland.

But while Bridgewater usually met the service as something to endure, he found aspects of it interesting nevertheless. The stories, for instance. The Torah portion on the first day of Rosh Hashanah deals with Sarah having a child in her old age. Birth and perpetuation, a theme of the New Year. Sarah having a child at such an advanced age was nothing if not miraculous; similarly, Bridgewater thought, Zippy's pregnancy was miraculous, after two abortions, two fetuses with Tay-Sachs. The conservative rabbi, a woman visiting from New York, spoke of Sarah's embarrassment at finding herself pregnant, and Bridgewater thought of the way that perfect strangers will often stop pregnant women on the street and talk about their condition. Everybody's business. The rabbi fleshed out Sarah's embarrassment at finding herself pregnant in those terms. What would people say? She could almost hear them whispering and snickering. Hey, Grandma! Was it something you ate? The *National Enquirer* headlines:

> WOMAN GIVES BIRTH TO BOY AT AGE 100!
> Miracle Baby Named Isaac by Parents

What Bridgewater found irritating about it all was the slavish way in which God was given all the credit. The human dimensions were so much more touching, so much more compelling than the divine.

They had arrived at the service during the pre-Torah reading prayers, before the scrolls had been removed from the ark. The congregation was singing, "Avee-noo Mal-chenoo . . ." Our father, our king. The blind hero-worshipping depressed him. He felt trapped, even victimized.

The hyperbolic qualities they attributed to Him! All-merciful, wise, forgiving, etc. Even if you bought the superstition about a "supreme being," you couldn't say that stuff with a straight face. Look how fucked up the world was! Not that Bridgewater was fingering God or society or any political or economic system for the mess. Everybody was a victim. He just felt an aesthetic revulsion for the idolatry and the phony humility. Who was this Adonai but a jealous, demanding martinet who required sacrifices in return for vague promises? It made him think of the Third World dictators who demanded complete obedience, had their faces put on currency and posters in the city squares.

Outside, as they approached the makeshift synagogue, Zippy and Bridgewater had encountered a group of boys, Hopkins students, wearing yarmulkes. They, too, were on their way to services. As the boys walked, they improvised lyrics to a 50s rock and roll song:

> Let's go to the shul!
> Let's go to the shul!
> Let's go to the shul! (Oh, baby!)
> Let's go to the shul!
> You can listen to the chazan,
> You can see the rabbi davan
> At the shul!

Bridgewater smiled—no overdone solemnity here, he was glad to see—but Zippy looked at them contemptuously. It was not that she felt they were sacrilegious, Bridgewater thought, but she did not like young Jewish males. She had no brothers and only one sister, still unmarried. Resisting the gravitational pull of her religion, Zippy had sought alliances with non-Jewish men after two unhappy relationships with Jewish boys early in her college career. Zippy found Jewish men too domineering, demanding, whiny and censorious, at least the ones she'd known. JAPs. Moishe and Edith had raised their daughters to be independent and certainly not subservient to their male counterparts. In contrast to Zippy, Bridgewater had always been drawn to Jewish men. They were usually intelligent and witty, decent people, and often very companionable.

The Torah reading on the second day of Rosh Hashanah, the akedah, is the story of Abraham's sacrifice of Isaac.

> MAN CLAIMS GOD ORDERS HIM TO KILL SON!
> Miracle Baby Spared at Last Moment
> Angel Appears with Lamb

The rabbi spoke about the old Kierkegaardian interpretation of the story—expressed long before Kierkegaard in talmudic literature—that God was testing Abraham to see how obedient and faithful he really was. She also mentioned Elie Wiesel's reading that had it the other way around: it was Abraham who was testing God to see how "just" He really was. Put up or shut up. God blinked. Looking at it from the other side gave Bridgewater a feeling of insight. The nugget of wisdom mined from the vein of tedious ritual. But of course, after the thoughtful consideration the mindless liturgical worship came as inevitably as night follows day.

Each day at the conclusion of the Torah service, the rabbi paraded down the aisle carrying the Torah scrolls in her arms, like a baby, accompanied by the cantor. People crowded up to the edge of the aisles when they passed, to touch the tassels of their *tallit*, their prayer shawls, or the corner of their *mahzor*, their prayer book, against the scrolls and then to their lips. Watching them push and strain to touch the Torah caused a visceral reaction in Bridgewater, as it always did, a shuddering repugnance. His intestines contracted, and his skin constricted into goose flesh. Was it the idolatry or the hypocrisy, the sheeplike gesture, that repelled him? Religion always forced this false humility down your throat, no matter what religion. Catholicism thrived on it. Repent!

Each day they had left after the shofar service, when the ram's horn is blown to arrest the congregation's attention. A grating, goose-pimpling sound. Hear, O Israel, indeed.

You hear about the gay rabbi who drove past in his limo? He was blowing his shofar. Chauffeur. Bridgewater toyed with the joke, while the rabbi chanted the prayer and the cantor blew the shofar.

When Zippy and Bridgewater went to the solemn Yom Kippur service with Moishe and Edith the following week, Bridgewater watched his parents-in-law thump their chests during the recitation of sins. A restrained tapping at the heart, a toned down version of the operatic Old World beating of the breast. Again the observer, the outsider, he watched the gyrations of the davaning Jews, like the bearded fellows at the Wailing Wall but not as fervent, bending and swaying to right and left. Who was to say which was authentic? Those guys in Jerusalem or the college kids in high-topped sneakers, observing the proscription against wearing leather on Yom Kippur, clothing made from slaughtered animals? What fervor these budding young Chassids displayed! In a confused rush of longing, Bridgewater felt envy tugging at him at the same time that he found their devotion ludicrous.

Then, during kaddish, the mourners' prayer, Bridgewater's mind wandered irreverently again.

"*Yit-gadal, v'yit-kadash, shmay rabo b'al ma-dee . . .*" the congregation mumbled. Yit-gadosh, b'gosh, Bridgewater thought. Jewish jeans. Jewish genes. He looked around. Yes, there was a discernable type. Your basic yid—potato nose, dark, kinky hair, beady dark eyes. The cute Jewish girls for whom Bridgewater had always been a sucker. Their tawny skin, red or dusky hair, an occasional blond, thick-featured faces and mysterious charm.

After the service, they went back to the Bolton Hill apartment, and Moishe turned on the television to watch his beloved Detroit Tigers duke it out with the Toronto Blue Jays for the American League East division title. Moishe was an avid Tigers fan. He and Edith drove across the state from Potawatomi Rapids at least twice a season to catch a game at Tiger Stadium.

"Come on, Gibson!" Moishe urged. "Hit one outa there like you did last weekend in Toronto!" Moishe privately confided to Bridgewater that synagogue services gave him a headache, and though Yom Kippur was the holiest day in the Jewish calendar, he could not pass up the crucial ballgame. But this sort of everyday hypocrisy did not bother Bridgewater. Parched from the fast, he licked his dry lips, feeling the strips of dry skin curl upward like flaking paint, and he wished he had a chapstick.

"Here come the bus," an elderly black lady said wearily. She wore a heavy coat; gloves covered her hands and disappeared up the coatsleeves. She wore a hat pulled down over her ears, as though dressed for a blizzard.

"I swear to God," another lady who was waiting for the bus said. "We pay more and more and it still don't come on time." The bus riders' complaint. A litany as ritualistic as the Kaddish prayer.

The owner of the illegally parked sportscar rushed out of a pharmacy and dived into the car. A Desi Arnaz-looking guy with cold Cuban eyes and a dark pompadour. A variety of gold and silver chains hung around his neck. He revved the motor a few times and took off with a squeal of tires. A real shitkicker. Bridgewater glanced down at the manuscript as if to make sure he still had it, and then he got into line to get onto the bus, pulling his pass out of his pocket to flash at the driver. A member of the club.

The bus was about half full. Bridgewater took a window seat near the front. Setting the manuscript down on his lap, he reached for a discarded copy of the *Baltimore Sun*. Jerry Falwell had resigned from the PTL board, he read. The front page was full of news about the Bork nomination to the Supreme Court. Bork. Bork. Bork. It sounded like a dripping faucet, unsound plumbing. Downtown near the courthouse on Calvert Street the other day Bridgewater had heard lawyers saying the name in passing conversations on the street. A ubiquitous syllable. After a while the word began to sound like a mating call or some secret code, a communication from which he felt excluded. Bork . . . Bork . . . Bork.

An item on the op-ed page caught Bridgewater's eye. The headline said that today was the twentieth anniversary of Che Guevara's death. Bridgewater remembered the posters. You saw them in head shops and on dorm room walls. Revolutionary chic. A cat-whiskered dude in a beret with a submachine gun. Mark had had one in his room at home, along with a poster of Patty "Tania" Hearst in front of the SLA emblem, the seven-headed hydra.

Bridgewater remembered his friends in college talking about "Che" and "Fidel" as if they were old friends, drinking buddies. He had tried to speak familiarly of them himself once or twice, but ultimately he felt too self-conscious. Power to the people. Peace. Love. Woodstock. Revolution. The code words always stuck in his throat. He was never able to convincingly refer to policemen as "pigs." They did not make him feel angry, those big beefy fellows with the guns and clubs; they only bored him. "Stormtroopers" and "Gestapo" exaggerated the case, even glamorized it.

Bridgewater became aware that somebody in the seat across the aisle was staring at him fiercely. Instinctively, he knew the glance was hostile. He looked around casually. Cecilia Nestorick was giving him a you-son-of-a-bitch glare.

"Cecilia, how are you doing? You know today's the twentieth anniversary of Che Guevara's death?" he said lamely, hoping she would get his allusion to their death conversations the summer before, but she just continued to contemplate him as if he were a maggot and then turned her head away, too disgusted for words.

"My wife's back in Baltimore. She's pregnant." Though Cecilia did not turn, Bridgewater could see his words had an impact, as if he had smacked her in the back of the head with a snowball. Her neck cringed slightly, and the red hair at the back bunched against her collar, and then her hand went back to smooth it out. When she continued to play the aloof bit, ignoring him, Bridgewater turned back to his newspaper. "U.S. Helicopters Sink Three Iranian Boats in the Persian Gulf." Talk about hostility.

Riding the bus out, Woodlawn Ave. to Social Security, Bridgewater almost forgot Cecilia as an individual; she became abstracted as a "problem," one of a nexus of headaches, and looking out the window at the vines that braided the ironwork of a fence, he felt his own life tangled and strangled by sinuous tentacles reaching out to wrap around him. Squeeze the life out of him. Oh, the complications! His impulse was to shift the blame; if only Zippy hadn't run out on him, if only this, if only that. How he yearned for a simpler life. But was there such a thing? Or was it just a romantic fancy? He flipped through the manuscript until he came to the poem he was looking for:

During youthful summers my pleasure
Was to strip naked as a savage and run
Free through orchards and fields.
The sun warmed my body. I sweated
Like a beast, and all under my skin
I felt the electric sensations
Of a wild man. Beneath my feet
My sole shaped the cool dirt,

Smooth and round as marble carving.
I ate fruit from the trees,
Little knowing the cherry I crushed
Against my lips, filmy with
The dry dust of pesticides, engendered
The runaway growth of cancer cells.

A hand on his arm startled him, and he almost dropped the manuscript. He looked up into Cecilia's hard green eyes. He'd just been imagining a cover for Wood's book of a vineyard with densely twisting vines. Now the noose had tightened.

"I'd like to talk to you," Cecilia said. Her tone was neutral, or, more accurately, dead. "You're going to Social Security to see Zippy, aren't you." A statement of fact; she did not pause for a reply. "I'm going to a movie at the mall. Can we get off and walk a little way together?"

"Sure!" Bridgewater said eagerly. He wanted to show her he could be accommodating. He did not like antagonism. Guilt drove him to it, too.

They got out of the bus at the corner of Richardson Road and walked slowly toward Security Boulevard. Cecilia jumped in right away.

"So you were just using me until your wife got back, is that it? I was just your little slut. Just a piece of ass. Something for you to stick your dick into until your wife got back. If you knew I was temporary all along why'd you have to do this to me? Why'd you put me through this? God. It feels like I've been raped."

Her accusations made him catch his breath. The woman was crazy! She really was. "In the first place, Cecilia, I thought our break-up was mutual, and in the second place it happened before Zippy even came back. I never thought of you as temporary, but then I never thought of our—our relationship—" The word sounded hokey to him, and he refined his meaning: "our 'arrangement'—I never thought it was permanent, either. It was just a fling. You knew that. Don't act like you didn't. It was summer. You were writing that endless piece of shit about Saul Bellow."

"And you?"

"I was just doing time."

"Thanks a lot."

"Oh, fuck you, Cecilia! I'm not going to play the ogre to your victim. Fuck that. We're both adults and we knew what it was all about.

Don't come on like some fucking high school ingenue, the innocent girl next door."

"I'm not the churl next door, either!"

"I never said you were."

"Well God damn it! How do you think I feel?"

"About what?" When she turned away, he grabbed her arm and made her look at him. "About what, Cecilia?"

"God damn you, Peter! Just God damn your ass!"

"Look, I'm sorry that you're upset, but it's not my fault, and you know it! We broke up after a summer romance. I know that sounds like a pop song, but it's true, and you know it's true. I even remember the last words you said to me just before you slammed the door in my face. You said I'd never get to look at your pussy again!"

"You're really an asshole, you know it, Peter? A big flaming asshole."

"Look, what do you want me to do, marry you?"

"Peter, I'm pregnant."

Bridgewater waited for her to tell him she was just kidding, but when she said nothing, he asked the inevitable: "Are you sure?"

"My period is three weeks late."

The little bitch! What was she trying to do? Wreck his life? What if he just bashed her head in with a big rock and left her body by the side of the beltway? A random traffic accident. Nobody would ever know the difference. He felt like some desperate loser in a murder mystery, thinking it through like that. But oh, if ever there *was* a moment to go homicidal! Hadn't she used birth control? Hadn't the dumb cunt used birth control? He couldn't believe it.

"I'll pay for half the abortion," he blurted.

"How generous of you."

Her sarcasm stung him. He felt foolish and guilty. "Okay, I'll pay for the whole thing."

"Won't you need money for your baby?"

"I've just gotten a job designing the dust jacket for somebody's book of poems. A little windfall."

"What if I want to keep *my* baby?"

Bridgewater's impulse was to break down and whine. ("*Oh, why are you doing this to me, Cecilia? Why? You know you can't keep that baby!*") But instead he lost his patience, almost became angry. "If you want to keep it, you're on your own!" He felt trapped, cornered, like a dog, and he barked at her viciously, "With your genetic background you ought to think twice about having a baby, unless you want to produce another pervert like your brother!" His cruelty appalled him, and he fought off an impulse to apologize. When he started to stammer, Cecilia cut him off.

"I couldn't keep it, anyway. I just resented your assuming I would . . . never mind."

They walked silently together for a few moments. In another fifty yards they'd be parting ways. Bridgewater did some rapid calculations. If her period was three weeks overdue, that would mean it should have come around the 17th of September. The last time they had fucked was around the third or fourth of September, just after a swim at the club. The club! Closed now until next spring. The pool empty, drained as his dreams. She must have been ovulating then. Given a twenty-eight day cycle, more or less, that would put the day they fucked right in the middle, around the fourteenth day. Without even thinking about it, he had slipped into his old habit of pinpointing fertility periods. Oh, why hadn't the fucking cunt used birth control? The bitch!

Finally, he broke the silence, asking lamely, "So what movie are you going to see?"

Cecilia looked at him with that supreme impatience meant to shrink him out of existence. "*Fatal Attraction*," she said.

Bridgewater couldn't help but laugh at the irony, and then Cecilia did, too. It wasn't clear to Bridgewater who felt more embarrassed for laughing under the circumstances, but Cecilia's neck reddened, and quickly she'd regained her composure; the bitter expression returned to her face, dilating the nostrils with fine indignation and pulling the corners of her dry mouth down. Bridgewater could see what she'd look like in thirty years, and he turned away from the vision.

"Are you working?" he asked. "You said last summer you might be substitute-teaching this fall."

"I sub sometimes, but I'm looking for a full-time job. I had an interview for a P.R. job, but I don't think I'll get it."

They reached Security Boulevard and stopped by the side of the road.

"I'll be in touch with you about the abortion," Bridgewater said. "Give me a call, okay?"

Cecilia nodded curtly but said nothing. She turned and walked away from him.

"I hope you enjoy the movie!" He was aiming for a light, cordial, civilized tone, but he came off sounding flippant, and it only enraged her.

"Fuck you!" she thundered, her eyes savage with hatred, and she turned away abruptly, walking rapidly, agitated. Bridgewater stifled an impulse to run after her and smooth things out.

An abortion! Christ! He thought he was through with abortions! Bridgewater walked glumly through the maze of computer programmers' cubicles to Zippy's. Glancing into some of them he noticed the usual array of framed family photographs arranged across desk tops with the same sort of implicit narrative of cave drawings: the wedding photograph, the baby pictures, the son's graduation, the family vacation. Some cubicles had little plaques on the walls with witty quotes: "Cubicle, Sweet Cubicle" or "Genius Has Its Limits, Stupidity Does Not." A "Miami Vice" calendar hung on the wall of another, Don Johnson's boyish stubbled face smiling beneath the word, OCTOBER.The chance that Cecilia was just trying to scare him still seemed plausible to Bridgewater. She'd get a kick out of making him squirm with the little trick, like out-foxing him in one of her board games. She was a malicious little bitch; she'd put his balls in a vice if she could. How she'd loved to make him squirm at Checkers or Monopoly! Could she be lying, to make him squirm all the more, or to get some money from him? How would he ever know? He seesawed back and forth between suspicion and guilt. But no, deep down he knew it was probably true and he was only wishing it weren't so, that he'd wake up from the bad dream.

The way he'd learned about Zippy's pregnancy was just by looking at her when he drove home from his father's place on Labor Day. She hadn't mentioned it over the phone, but when he saw her there hadn't been any doubt. She looked like a sumo wrestler.

At first Zippy had been shy with him, but then she gave him her version of the events that had led up to her departure, when they were lying together in bed. They had sex, but it wasn't much good for either of them. More like a ritual of some sort. A goodwill gesture. It hurt Zippy, who lay on her back like a beached dolphin, and Bridgewater made quick work of it, hastily getting his squirt and tingle and then rolling over to his side of the bed, away from the wet spot. It wasn't the best, but it was good enough to make him feel cozy and talkative. If he had been a spy, he'd be putty in the hands of a female enemy agent if she used sex to get secrets from him. He'd spill his guts in a second!

When he reached Zippy's cube, he saw her sitting thigh-to-thigh with a sandy-haired man in a three-piece beige pinstriped suit, going over a computer printout. Briefly he tried on the thought of somebody like this man as the father of Zippy's child, an adulterous affair of which Bridgewater had been totally ignorant. But he couldn't convince himself. A guy who dealt with the pathology of microcomputers? Symptoms and causes, development, consequences and cures of computer failure, hardware-and software-related. (What had the sign said in the cubicle a hundred feet back? Something about how computer programmers "do it." Lawyers do it in briefs, teachers do it with class, etc. How did computer programmers "do it"? If he remembered, he'd check on his way back out.)

"Hi, Zippy," he said, knocking on the thin gray metal strip in her entryway. A plaque outside the cubicle said: Zipporah Bridgewater.

"Peter! Hi! I'll just be a minute. Peter, this is Ted. Ted, this is my husband."

"You new here?"

"Just started in June during Zippy's leave of absence."

"I didn't think I'd seen you before, not that I get over here that often." Yes, before her seemingly abrupt departure, Zippy had arranged with her managers to be away for an extended period of time. Unspecified medical complications. Not the behavior of a crazy woman at all. Too prudent, too methodical.

"So you're going to be a papa!" Ted said. He had sincere blue eyes, wet and faintly bloodshot. A sandy-colored mustache came down over his upper lip, the mustache of an adolescent who longs for facial hair. A crust of acne gave texture to the skin on his chin. Rough terrain. "Picked out any names yet?"

Names! There had been a minor battle over who got to name the baby. Bridgewater proposed that he name it if they had a daughter and Zippy name it if they had a son. Zippy said no, she was taking the first name no matter what. After all, he already got the last name. She'd let him choose the middle name. He said, what if he changed his last name to Bridgewaterowitz, but she did not think it was very funny.

Moishe and Edith had lectured Bridgewater on naming the baby, too. "In our religion—well, I guess it's your religion, too—the custom is to not name a child after anybody living, and preferably after a recently deceased relative."

"Gevalt!" Edith exclaimed. "I won't have my grandson named for your cousin Howie! Howie was such a swine, Moishe, such a big nothing! I'd die before I saddled a baby with such a name!"

"There's your mother's brother, Shlomo," Moishe pointed out.

"I won't name a child 'Shlomo,' and that's that!" Zippy said. "I'd rather drown him first!"

"What's wrong with Shlomo? Shlomo's a fine name."

"Mom, it is not! Everybody I've ever known named Shlomo has been a real drag. I will not curse a child with that name!"

"You're anti-Semitic is what you are, Zipporah! A self-hating Jew!"

"How else would she have come to marry Gazookis?"

"Dad!"

"I was just kidding!"

"Well it wasn't funny!" Zippy turned to her mother. "Because I don't like the name Shlomo I'm a self-hating Jew? Come on! Don't be ridiculous! Besides, I might have a daughter, remember."

Bridgewater thought of Hollywood first-name-last-names. Brooke and Morgan and Whitney. He thought of the outrageous names people in the 1960s named their children, defying middleclass conventionality. Grace Slick named her child god with a small G. Frank Zappa named his daughter Moon Unit. David Bowie called his son Zowie. Children had been named Shit and Piss and Fuck and Cunt back then. But later on they got respectable middle-class monikers anyway, as their parents realized what they'd done to their kids, set them up for ridicule. Zowie became Joey; god became Susan or something like that; Shit became Sheila and Fuck became Fred.

"Nothing definite," Bridgewater answered Ted.

"Honey, we'll just be a minute," Zippy said. "We're trying to locate a bug in this program. Your brother called here for you. Mark. Why don't you call him back? I'll be ready when you're done."

"You can use my phone," Ted said. "Mine's the next cube over."

Bridgewater smiled and nodded in thanks and stepped into the adjacent cubicle. A sign on the wall said: "TO ERR IS HUMAN . . . IT TAKES A COMPUTER TO REALLY LOUSE THINGS UP." The plaque outside gave the full name of the occupant: Theodore J. Harmon. Bridgewater sat down in the swivel chair and picked up the phone. He shouted over the partition, "Do I dial nine first to get an outside line?"

"Yeah!" six voices from surrounding cubicles cried in unison.

Mark picked up the receiver in the middle of the first ring. His office was in his house. He had bought this house in Lutherville, just north of Towson. He was on the phone constantly, making promises, making deals. He could have been the politician their father Frank never was.

"Pete, the reason I called you at Zippy's is I've got a hot proposition, and it can't wait."

"Hot proposition?"

"Stock market investments. A computer firm out in Silicon Valley that's about to go public. We can get it now and just count our money later."

"Where'd you learn about this? From Big Tuna or Scarface or one of your other colleagues?"

"I wouldn't have called you if this weren't strictly legitimate, Peter. I know what a pussy you are about these things. I'm trying to do you a favor, man. You've got a family on the way. You're gonna need the bread."

"The stock market's been going down since August, hasn't it?"

"But look how it's been going the last five years! The last six weeks is only a blip on the screen! Besides, the lower prices mean bargains, you know that."

"I don't know. You look at the huge federal deficit and the trade imbalance."

"Pete, basically everybody *wants* the market to succeed. That's what counts. That's why it keeps going up, and that's why it's going to continue to go up. People *want* to make money!"

"Can you give me a few days to think it over?"

"A few days to think it over! Man! You sound just like our father! If that old fool could tell his ass from a hole in the ground he would have invested years ago and got some for us, too. Especially in the foreign markets and money accounts. Instead of diddling himself with those God damn electric trains."

"He does all right financially. He's comfortable. He can retire."

"You know there are forty billionaires in America today? That's twice as many as there were last year! They *all* invest; that's the only way to make it. Sam Walton, John Kluge, Henry Perot, David Packard, Samuel Newhouse—" Mark rattled off the names of America's wealthiest men like a kid spouting statistics off the backs of baseball cards.

"Just let me think about it, won't you?"

"You've got to seize the day, Peter."

Seize the day! Cecilia had spent one afternoon in bed after sex telling him about a Saul Bellow novel by that title, about a guy who gambles on the stock market and loses his shirt! It seemed like an omen, and Bridgewater demurred again, until his brother began to lose patience.

"Are Mushy and Edith still with you? He might like to go in on it if you won't." Mark spoke with the same fervor, the same urgency, that Bridgewater recognized from years back when he would put together a sort of buying consortium for a kilo of marijuana, the same sort of yammering speed freak urgency to his tone. He could almost see the white froth collecting at the corners of Mark's mouth, as when, spittle spraying, lips dry, he'd cut his friends in on so many one-ounce bags of dope, persuading them that if they just sold a few lids they'd get their smoke for free, wheeling and dealing in this penny ante way until he had a few free ounces of pot of his own and some walking around money in his pockets to boot.

"No, they left for Michigan on Tuesday. Moishe had tickets to see a playoff game against the Twins at Tiger Stadium."

"Okay, I'll give you until Monday to decide, and that's it," Mark said. "Think it over. I've got to go now. Bye." He hung up his phone.

Bridgewater put the receiver back into its cradle. He bet that if he dialed Mark's number now he'd get a busy signal; Mark was probably trying to deal a few more people into his stock scheme. He went back to Zippy's cubicle. She and Ted were standing by the entrance, waiting for him.

"I'll submit the job after lunch and see if it will run with these fixes," Ted said. "In a test mode, of course."

"You'll have to modify the disposition parameters on the DD statement of the JCL," Zippy reminded him.

Ted nodded. A secret message seemed to pass between them. Again, Bridgewater tried on the idea of an illicit liaison. Zippy thrived on secrets, after all. Again he drew a blank; only, that very fact disturbed him. Not that he expected Ted to be parking in his garage, but the way things were going, something *had* to be wrong; innocence went against the rule. A worm in every apple.

"Nice to meet you," Ted said, offering his hand. "Have a good lunch!" He seemed to really hope that they had a good meal. The hopeful attitude of a doctor talking to a terminally ill patient. He smiled at Zippy and went to his cubicle.

"You look worried," Zippy remarked as they headed down the aisle. "What did Mark have to say?"

"It was one of his get-rich-quick schemes. He wants me to go in with him on some stocks. A firm in Silicon Valley's about to go public and he can get a deal."

"You aren't going to, are you?"

"I said I'd think about it."

"Along with all the other things you have to think about."

He looked at her sharply. What did she know? But she only laughed and hefted up her swollen belly like a sack of flour. He tried to smile. Oh, yeah. The baby.

"My father said that now's not a good time to buy in the stock market."

"Really? When did he say that?"

"When they were here. He said he thought the market was too volatile."

"Huh," Bridgewater grunted. But where was he going to get enough money otherwise? He had to pay for both a baby and an abortion at the same time! Not even Franklin Wood's pockets were going to be deep enough for that.

"You look troubled," Zippy said, inviting him to confide. "Is anything wrong?"

They passed the last cubicle in the aisle and Bridgewater peered in. The sign said:

COMPUTER PROGRAMMERS DO IT IN CODE

"I feel like the furry little guy in one of those *New Yorker* or *Mad Magazine* cartoons picketing Wall Street with a sign that says, 'The End of the World Is Coming! Repent!'"

Zippy laughed and squeezed his clammy hand. "You exaggerate your problems, Peter! Just say 'no' to Mark. It's too risky."

"Sure," Bridgewater said. They walked past the security check, and with an awful jolt of panic Bridgewater remembered where Cecilia was going when he left her. "Hey, Zippy, let's go someplace else besides the mall for lunch today, okay?"

Thanksgiving

Thanksgiving Day blossomed as bright and promising as an autumn flower, a golden chrysanthemum, say, or an aster, its pink and white flowers shooting triumphantly outward. Despite the dire predictions for rain and snow, the day had bloomed to perfection. Over at the playground on Mosher Street, Bridgewater could see shirt-sleeved teenagers playing a game of football, and on the asphalt basketball court, another group of lightly clad kids tossed a ball through the bent netless hoop. The trees were gaunt, bare, austere; dead leaves choked the gutters. But the day radiated a friendly warmth from which all foreboding was absent. Bridgewater needed a day like that. Red graffiti, on the wall of the elementary school, proclaimed:

> Jermaine + Tyrice
> 2-Gether
> 4-Ever

Bridgewater had noticed the bold message for weeks, but this morning, instead of being a trite, hackneyed act of teenage vandalism, it contained a vague, wonderful promise. Things were going to get better.

Fog had shrouded the streets of Bolton Hill the night before when Bridgewater went out to get a bottle of red wine at the corner grocery. The dank evening air, particularly heavy for the end of November, felt like a damp glove against his face. The sliver of moon had risen. Waxing toward its first quarter, it shone in the clear sky overhead. But crossing the park to get to the store, Bridgewater passed through thick, smoky fog. A mist covered the grass, rising to a level of about eight feet. The tree trunks rose out of the fog like prehistoric animals, a scene from the dawn of history. Bridgewater had not been surprised to see Cecilia Nestorick emerge from the mist, swaddled in a cape like a Hollywood vampire. It was as if he were haunted by her and had expected her to appear all along, as in a dream or a trance of the undead. He called her name, but just as suddenly she disappeared, and Bridgewater, disoriented by the thick, smoky fog, continued to the store. He bought a bottle of merlot, lingered over the first morning edition of the newspaper, full of the news of Chicago mayor Harold Washington's sudden death, and then he returned home, half expecting bats to come swooping down out of the sky. Returning back through the park, he lingered by the fountain, dry now for the winter, the waterworks having been shut down; he hoped Cecilia would reappear. He sat on a bench for ten minutes before going back to Zippy. Maybe it had been a dream, after all, or an hallucination.

In the last seven weeks, Bridgewater had made at least half a dozen attempts to get in touch with Cecilia. But she hung up the phone whenever he called and refused to speak to him when he sought her out. Once he went over to her apartment and she slammed the door in his face. The next time he went, he was informed that Cecilia had moved and left no forwarding address. Her new telephone number was unlisted. Several weeks earlier he had seen her standing beneath the MONEY ORDERS FOOD STAMPS CHECKS CASHED sign at the money exchange where he and Zippy got their bus passes. He and Zippy were holding hands as they approached the store, and Cecilia, seeing them, fled. He did not dare to chase her, and he worried that Zippy had noticed, too, but apparently she had not. Bridgewater concluded from Cecilia's evasiveness that she had been lying about the pregnancy, but he wished he could be sure. Or perhaps she'd had the abortion after all. He wished he knew. All that night, after he got home and went to bed, he was tormented by dreams, his brain wreathed with images of Cecilia: Cecilia posing naked on her couch, holding a baby to her breast, Cecilia reading aloud from a paperback copy of Bellow's *To Jerusalem and Back*, a baby suckling at her nipple.

But today, Thanksgiving, was so bright and benign, he could imagine nothing sinister lying in store for him. Moishe and Edith had come to Baltimore to spend the Thanksgiving holiday with them. They had arrived Tuesday evening; they were staying at the Comfort Inn on Franklin Street. They were all going over to Bridgewater's father's house at noon. Mark would be there, with a guest, and so would Bridgewater's Uncle Ben, the chemist from Ann Arbor.

Beachball round in the belly, wearing a brightly colored smock, Zippy came over to Bridgewater at the window and put her arm around him. He hugged her back. In three weeks she would have the baby.

"It's such a lovely day," she murmured. "Isn't it?"

"Isn't it?" Bridgewater echoed. "How do you feel?"

"Fine. I never really had morning sickness. Just a little nausea the first few weeks."

"When you were still in Baltimore?"

She hugged tightly for a moment, the pressure signifying that she understood the undercurrent of reproach. "How are you?"

"Hopeful."

Zippy and Peter walked into Frank's house without knocking, went past the bird's eye maple newel post and through the dust-suspended living room to the sunken den, where they found Moishe and Frank watching television. The Thanksgiving football game in Detroit. Zippy went into the kitchen, and Bridgewater stepped into the wading pool.

"Who's ahead?"

"Kansas City," his father replied without looking up.

"The Lions!" Moishe said, shaking his head in disgust. "I thought they'd be able to beat the Chiefs, at least!"

The game looked boring, and Bridgewater followed Zippy into the kitchen. Pushing through the swinging saloon doors, Bridgewater saw his Uncle Ben bent over the stove, staring intently into a pot that he was stirring with a spoon. Zippy stood behind him against the counter, and at the walnut kitchen table sat Edith, Mark, and a heavily made up blond woman wearing a shimmery silver low-cut dress that displayed miles of cleavage. The three seated guests were looking away from Zippy and Peter. Though nobody was actually talking—one of those lulls in a conversation—they obviously formed two separate groups. Bridgewater walked over and placed his bottle of wine on the table.

"Happy Thanksgiving," he said.

"Peter! How's it going?" Mark said, looking up. "Let me introduce you to my friend Bambi. Bambi, this is my brother, Peter. Peter, this is Bambi Warner."

"Hi, hair you?" she said, and by the curious dipthonging accent, he knew her to be pure Baltimore. Hampden or Remington, possibly Dundalk. "Mark's tole me so mucha bouchew!" Bambi bubbled, pulling him toward her when he extended his hand. Bridgewater stumbled and, to regain his balance, wrenched his hand away from hers and grabbed the back of Mark's chair. A fortuitous stumble, as he avoided the awkwardness of a kiss.

"What's he said?"

"Oh, I own no. Boucher cats. When you's grown up and everthin'."

"My cats?"

"When we had Fluffy and Jeff, you remember," Mark said. "She just means she feels like she knows you. Give it a break, Pete. Don't always be so suspicious. Christ! My brother can turn 'good morning' into a death threat."

"Peter! How are you!" Uncle Ben said, coming over from the stove. His attention had been absorbed by the pot, and he had not noticed his nephew's entrance. He stretched his arms out and hugged Bridgewater.

"Uncle Ben, how are you?"

Ben Bridgewater was five years younger than his brother Frank, but he looked, if not older, at least more time-worn; a frizzy, unkempt mane of shaggy, uncombed gray covered his head, and his eyes were sunken into his face, the sign of a scholar who has spent his life in study. His character, too, seemed more seasoned; he bore himself with a certain unselfconscious sangfroid that nevertheless seemed acquired, if not exactly cultivated.

Now pushing sixty-five and thinking about retirement, Frank had probably found the strength to endure his widowerhood from his brother's example. Ben had never married. Now a putative celibate, he had once been engaged to a woman, but the details of the affair were foggy, shrouded in mystery. The story involved a flashy rival, an unfaithful woman and a broken heart, back in postwar Ann Arbor. Ben had never completely recovered from the heartbreak and his shattered faith, beyond a timid (timid or courtly?) worship of the female form. The chemist was an avid photographer who occasionally exhibited his work in college galleries throughout southern Michigan—silver-print photography, mainly nudes. He engaged youthful college girls from the university to pose for him. In his obsession for nudes, Bridgewater felt a professional kinship with his uncle, and now, hugging him, inhaling the stale smell of terminal bachelorhood, he thought of the sketches of Cecilia tucked away in a desk drawer at home.

His uncle seemed to have survived the broken heart rather well. At least, he had no financial burdens or family responsibilities to tie him down; he had been able to travel extensively—Europe, China, Japan, Africa, Latin America, the Middle East. He always had a fund of stories to draw upon when conversation wore thin. And who knows? He probably got as much sex as he needed from the models who posed for him. He probably didn't think about it that much any more, anyway.

Once Uncle Ben had been a contestant on "Jeopardy!" He played four nights running during a trip to California. For three straight nights he had won the trivia quiz, accumulating over forty thousand dollars. The first night he had bet his entire eleven thousand-dollar total on the Final Jeopardy question in the category of "The Fifty States." Who could possibly have known as much as he did about the fifty states to ask a question too obscure? Having traveled throughout the country and read extensively, his confidence was high. Besides, he trailed the returning champ, a schoolteacher from Dubuque, Iowa, by a couple thousand. The clue read, "The two states that border on each other named 'Red' in Spanish and 'Red People' in Choctaw." Ben was the only person to respond correctly. "What are Colorado and Oklahoma?"

Though he led most of the fourth night, he finally lost to an accountant from Schenectady, N.Y. (a woman with whom he had subsequently carried on a prolific correspondence). In Double Jeopardy he had bet everything on an audio Daily Double in the category, "Facts and Figures," and then he was unable to identify the Miracles' second number one hit. While he recognized the melody of "I'll Second That Emotion," and, living in the Detroit area, only a deaf person would not have heard the Motown tune at least a thousand times, he was not able to identify the song by name, and he randomly guessed, "If You Feel Like Givin' Me." Even as Alec Trebec was shaking his head, he futilely corrected himself, "I Second the Emotion," but he was too late, and though he was able to gain back another couple of thousand dollars, he just did not have the points to top the accountant in Final Jeopardy. (The category was "Cheeses," and both answered the clue correctly. "What is bleu cheese?")

Watching his uncle on television, Bridgewater had been most astounded during the second game when he rattled off a number of answers in the "Bowling" category. How had Uncle Ben come into possession of those arcane facts? What kind of wood the pins are made of, the number of consecutive strikes you need to get a perfect score of 300, the date the nation's first bowl-a-drome was built.

When Bridgewater told Cecilia Nestorick about Uncle Ben, she was sure he was lying. With her reverence for games she simply could not believe he had an uncle who had actually been on "Jeopardy!" Not to mention one who had come within one victory of automatically qualifying for the tournament of champions. A wife who chased after Mick Jagger, maybe, but an uncle who was a television game-show winner, no.

"You're looking fine, Peter! What's it been? Six, seven years?"

"Did we see you after we got married?" He turned to Zippy. "Zippy, when was the last time we saw Uncle Ben?"

"At our wedding."

"When did you get married? How long's it been?"

"Eight years. Nine years in April."

"I came back from France for the wedding," Mark told Bambi. "I was having a great time over there."

"I'ze gonna say!" Bambi said, looking at Mark with worshipful eyes. Noticing this, Bridgewater reflected that he would feel uncomfortable with a woman that regarded him that way.

Edith muttered something that Bridgewater could not make out where he stood, but his brother's reply explained it.

"I do dress much better now."

"Nine years!" Uncle Ben exclaimed, shaking his head fondly. In that instant he looked just like his brother Frank, but the vision passed so quickly his nephew doubted he'd actually seen the resemblance. The genetic giveaway. "How time flies. Carter was still president. That's right, I remember now."

"You've been abroad a lot since then."

"A few places. Mainly Iraq. I did some consulting work for an oil firm. And Russia, the Soviet Union. But mainly I've been home, in Michigan. Working on my photography. As much as I can."

"I saw you on television, of course."

"Oh, yes," Uncle Ben blushed modestly, and he reached up and brushed the tangled gray furball that was his hair. But if he felt self-conscious, it was only momentarily. "When I was out in L.A. A spur of the moment whim. I took some wonderful photographs in Death Valley, by the way. Curiously reminiscent of my series out on the Russian Steppes."

"Any nudes?"

"A few. I engaged the services of a model from UCLA. They draw attention to the landscape."

When everybody started to laugh, Ben Bridgewater held up his hand with a teacher's air of authority. "I'm serious," he said. "You put an unfamiliar object into a space, and it draws attention to the scene in vivid detail. The space becomes a place."

"A place?"

"A place is a space with a fish in it." When his nephew looked at him askance, Ben laughed and hugged him again. "An old photographer's formula."

"How to take a good photograph?"

"Something like that. Substitute 'nude' for 'fish' and you'll get it. How to create a good, lively image. Speaking of which, your father tells me you're illustrating a book of poetry!" Uncle Ben's tone was warm and full of congratulation and enthusiasm. But there was always that element of distance in his warmth that made Bridgewater uncomfortable, a sort of college professor's drilling-the-students style.

"Was," Bridgewater said. The ardor went out of his grip, and he let go of his uncle's arms. "It fell through." Reminded of his professional failure, Bridgewater felt his spirits sink. Damn! Just when he'd started to feel optimistic again! He'd been able to put out of his mind the consciousness of having left the WPCC Graphics Lab two weeks before when Wing Lee, the assistant, had stolen his client, Franklin Wood.

Not exactly "stole." More like picked him up on waivers. Bridgewater remembered it all over again. A freak snowstorm had hit Baltimore the day before, and Wood had called to cancel the meeting they'd scheduled, at which Bridgewater was going to show him his ideas for the cover of his self-published book of poems, *The Collected Works of Franklin Wood*. But then Wood showed up at the WPCC lab despite the cancellation. Although he hadn't been expecting Franklin to show up, Bridgewater was prepared, anyway. He had made several sketches based on the poem that began:

> This year the crabs had lesions
> Marking their bodies like whip-stripes
> Candy-caned on galley slaves.
> Gas puddles, rainbow slick,
> Oases of poison on the water's surface,
> From the motor boats pulling heedless
> Bronze-skinned boys on water skis.

His favorite sketches showed debris and dead fish with enormous accusing sightless eyes in the foreground, partially concealed beneath weeds, a swirl of gas or some chemical in the water in the middle of the sketch, and off in the background, somehow attached to the slick as with an umbilicus, a motorboat dragging along a skier in its wake. He'd made several sketches based on this scene, some with condoms and Clorox bottles, some with dead glassy-eyed carp and crabs. The boys on the skis variously resembled Roman gladiators in chariots or brutal cowboys at a rodeo. In one, the whole scene was in the circular context of a dead fisheye lens. What appealed to Bridgewater about the cover idea was that the sketches looked so serene and idyllic at first glance, but when you focused on the details you saw the decay and the negligence. This was how he conceived Franklin Wood's poetic "vision," so it seemed almost emblematic, as a book cover should.

Thursdays were generally quiet in the graphics lab. Lee Wing and Wing Lee, the lab assistants, were flitting around doing their homework. Bridgewater was patiently explaining to a freshman girl for the fifth time how to save her typeset file on her double density diskette. As he often did, Bridgewater felt like an undiscovered genius laboring thanklessly in obscurity. Just the day before, a Van Gogh had sold for $49 million at an auction in New York. Van Gogh had never sold a painting while he was alive. Bridgewater often basked in the daydream that he, too, would be discovered after he died—if only there were something to "discover."

"It's *this* function key," he said, touching a button on one of the keypads that said "FILE REPLACE." He looked up at Lee Wing standing in the entrance to the typesetting cubicle. She always waited to be noticed before she spoke.

"Mr. Bridgewater," she said, "Mr. Wood is here." As an afterthought, she mumbled, "Peter." Bridgewater wanted her to call him by his first name, but he sensed that she instinctively shied away from the familiarity the first name implied, perhaps intuiting the ravenous lonely guy under the façade of boss. Calling him "Mr. Bridgewater" was like using the formal French *vous* instead of the intimate *tu*. Was she afraid of the demands he might make upon her confidence should she allow him close enough?

"Thank you, Miss Wing," Bridgewater said with mock formality. The suggestion of a smile signaled that she got the joke—but nothing more! A smile as faint as the Xerox of a thought.

"I'll tell him you're back here."

He watched her slim, jeans-clad butt twitch away to the photostat darkroom, a ripening piece of fruit on long, coltish legs, an athletic eroticism implicit in the boyish-feminine movement. Lee probably had pimply boyfriends who groped her in dark corners and took her to movies where they self-consciously worked up the courage halfway through the film to put an arm across her seat. (Or did she have a wildly erotic sex life with one of her professors?)

How different college girls were from the women where Zippy worked. Young women and moms, they walked briskly down corridors on quick-scissoring legs sheathed in nylon, propped up on high-heeled shoes! Though it was true, running shoes were becoming more popular, at least to *get* to work in.

Bridgewater turned at the sound of new leather soles tapping across the linoleum floor with the sharp snap of drumsticks across a snare drum. He saw Franklin's loafers first, then his legs. By the quarter-sized damp spot on his pants, Bridgewater could tell he'd stopped in the men's room on his way in. Like an emblem of the two dark sweat-circles under his arms, the smaller dark circle spread across the fabric of his khaki trousers.

"Think you've got it now, Theresa?" Bridgewater asked the girl at the typesetter. "The FILE REPLACE key saves the new file, replacing what was in the file with what you've added to it."

"Thanks," she said, nodding eagerly, and Bridgewater stood up to shake Franklin Wood's outstretched hand.

"The roads aren't so bad, after all," Franklin explained, smiling apologetically. He wore an old-fashioned undershirt with looping shoulder straps. Immigrant underwear, Mark used to call it, a disparaging reference to their father's choice of undergarment. Bridgewater could see the lines beneath Wood's pink cotton shirt, the arc on his chest. He carried his coat over his arm.

"Well, I've got my sketches right here," Bridgewater said, taking a step toward the small office where the lab personnel kept their coats and belongings.

"Oh, that's all right," Franklin said, stopping him. "I know what I want on the cover of my book. I can just tell you."

"Well, if you'll just let me show you what I've got," Bridgewater said, reluctant to give up on his own ideas without at least showing them first. *Why didn't this asshole say he had "ideas" before? Damn it!*

"No, really," Wood said. "I've thought about it, and I know what I want."

"But—"

Wood raised his hand, palm forward, to silence Bridgewater.

"I want the cover to be . . . interpretive." Franklin chose his words carefully, dragging them out in his Ohio-Kentucky drawl.

"Yes, well, that's exactly what I've—"

Again, Wood's palm pushed the air between them, and Bridgewater stopped talking in mid-sentence.

"I want the cover to show a phoenix rising from its ashes."

"A phoenix rising from its ashes," Bridgewater repeated dully. *A phoenix rising from its ashes*!

"I think that symbolizes the meaning of my poems."

"Excuse me, Franklin, but don't you think that's a little trite? A little bit hackneyed?"

Wood flinched slightly and was silent a moment. "Properly interpreted, it needn't be trite," he said, putting the onus of the hack back onto Bridgewater.

"I don't do comic book covers!" Bridgewater declared with all the fervor of the artiste who won't compromise the integrity of his work, a scene he had played out in his daydreams a thousand times before. ("No! I won't do a Pepsi or a Miller Lite commercial! I don't care how much you're offering me!") "If you want something like that you'll have to get somebody else!" It was Franklin's smug assurance that he could have what he wanted—he was paying for it all himself, after all—that had finally infuriated Bridgewater.

With exaggerated southern politeness, Franklin said, "Well, perhaps you could tell me whose dragons those are out there on the light-table. Perhaps I could make an offer—"

"Wing!" Bridgewater called. Wing Lee drew and painted elaborate posters displaying dragons, fire-breathing sea monsters, green, scaly, red-tongued lizards. While they had been talking, Bridgewater and Wood had moved away from the typesetting cubicles, but Bridgewater noticed that Wing Lee had gone to help Theresa with the typesetting keyboard commands.

"Peter," Wing said, coming over. Near-sighted Wing Lee, the flat-featured Korean work-study student, wore eyeglasses with lenses a third of an inch thick in heavy black frames that were identical to Franklin Wood's. A shock of black hair fell across Wing's forehead, Adolf Hitler-style. He stood at attention, waiting for Bridgewater to speak.

"Wing, I think Mr. Wood here has a proposition for you."

The next day, Bridgewater handed in his resignation. The very thought of the WPCC graphics lab was oppressive to him. He had been there for so long now. He needed a change.

"Sorry to hear it didn't work out," Uncle Ben said, closing what he could see was a sensitive subject. Yet there was a soupçon of disapproval in his voice. "But more important, you're about to become a father!"

"Thanks. That's true," Bridgewater said, looking away. He knew his uncle had him on the ropes, and he tried to change the subject. "So how's everything in A-squared?"

"Oh, fine. Except it looks like the Wolverines won't be going to the Rose Bowl, and that has some people upset. How they worship Bo! But you're the one with the news. Have you got any names picked out yet?"

"Shlomo if it's a boy and Sophie if it's a girl!" Edith piped up from the table.

Ben looked inquiringly at his nephew.

"Those are some relatives of Edith's and Moishe's who died recently."

"I thought the custom was to pick a name that began with the same letter. Steve or Susan, say, would do just as well, wouldn't they?"

"I guess Edith figures, why not go the whole nine yards? But yeah, same Hebrew name, though."

"They're good names," Edith said.

"I really don't know very many women named Sophie these days," Ben mused. "It's an old-fashioned name."

"I don't know what we're going to name the child," Bridgewater said. "We haven't decided yet."

"Oy vey." Edith muttered in a stage whisper so everybody could hear. Her mouth puckered in a look of determination, but she said nothing more.

"You don't know the sex yet, I take it," Ben said, speaking quickly in order to prevent an argument between his nephew and the mother-in-law.

"Not for sure, no. Only the amniocentesis gives definitive proof."

"But there's been a sonogram or something?"

"We honestly don't know the child's sex," Zippy interjected. She had had the amnio, but besides the negative Tay-Sachs report she had kept the results to herself. The secretkeeper!

Bridgewater meanwhile recalled the radiologist pointing to the sonogram and identifying what she called "female sexual characteristics." What looked like labia, no penis in the picture.

Bridgewater thought of saying, "You mean she's got a cunt, doc?" The clinical language of medical personnel.

He recalled the nurse who had taught the preparing-for-parenthood course, too. A chirpy young woman who wore a big blue button on her white lab coat that said:

10
Centimeters
Or Bust!

"It's the custom in the Jewish religion to name a child after a recently deceased relative so that that person's memory will serve as a guide to the new generation!" Edith declared. She was spoiling for a fight. The old ways were not going down on her watch.

"That's Ashkenazic," Bridgewater said. "The Sephardic tradition is to name children after living members of the family, so they'll serve as models or guides."

"We are not Sephardim! We are Ashkenazi!"

"You know there's a 'nazi' in Ashkenazi?" Mark observed.

"I'ze gonna say!" Bambi bubbled.

"Gevalt!"

"I see you brought a Pouilly Fuisse," Mark said, holding up the bottle of wine his brother had put on the table. "I brought a Chablis and a Sauternes."

"The baby's name will either be Shlomo or Sophie," Edith declared.

Nobody wanted to argue with Edith. There was a moment of silence, and then at last Zippy said, "Thanksgiving is always so boring after the meal. There's never anything to do."

"I'ze gonna say," Bambi remarked.

"We could always go to a movie," Mark suggested.

"What's showing?"

Bridgewater rattled off some current titles: "There's Schwarzenegger in *The Running Man*, Bronson in *Death Wish 4*, *Hello Again*, *Made in Heaven*, *Suspect*, *The Princess Bride*, Diane Keaton in *Baby Boom*, *Dirty Dancing*, *Fatal Attraction*, Prince in *Sign O' the Times*, Barbra Streisand in *Nuts*, Dudley Moore in *Like Father Like Son* –"

"Bambi's an actress," Mark said, interrupting the catalog. He hadn't actually cared what was showing.

"Oh yeah? Movies or the stage?"

"Movies."

Bridgewater turned to Bambi. "What have you been in?"

"Nuttin very big," she replied modestly. "You proly never heard'v none ov'm."

"Try me," Bridgewater said, proud of his knowledge of movies and movie lore. "What are some titles?"

"*Big Dicks and Politics*?" Did she blush when she said it, Bridgewater wondered, or was it just that her voice rose in inquiry?

"No, never heard of it. What's it about? Political corruption of the police force or something?"

"Bambi works in a different genre from the tinsel town crap you're used to," Mark said. His voice was defiant. But then Uncle Ben stepped in.

"Well, I suppose we ought to set the table. The turkey's almost done. How's that crab soup coming, Zip?" Always the diplomat, Ben tried to prevent any embarrassing or compromising disclosures from being made. Nudes were one thing; pornography was another. Blue movie titles flashed across Bridgewater's mind. He'd seen them advertised at the Little X on Howard Street, where he often caught the bus. *Miami Spice*, *First Time at Cherry High*, *Peeping Tom*, *Hot Flashes*, *Debbie Does Dallas*, *Manhattan Mistress*, *Little French Maid*, *V, the Hot One*. . . .

When they were all seated at the dining table, Bridgewater noticed that he was the only man who wasn't wearing a tie. Moishe wore an old-fashioned brown bow tie with white polka dots; Frank and Ben wore solid color neckties, red and navy blue, respectively; Mark had on a bright pink and blue-flowered job. Bridgewater had planned to wear a tie, but that morning, as he sucked in his neck to button the collar, the button crumbled in his fingers, and he did not bother to change his shirt. More and more often lately, he had noted, his collar and cuff buttons crumbled into dust when he tried to push them through the buttonholes. Lately, too, he had been waking up at 4:00 a.m. with an unpleasant taste in his mouth: the foulness of human breath intensified by hours of closed-mouth stagnancy, like a backwoods swamp; he had even considered using mouthwash.

Bridgewater noticed that Mark's cuffs were fastened with gold cufflinks at the inner of the two available buttonholes, so that the cuff was tight across his wrist. He noticed, too, the diamond-studded wristwatch. When had Mark started wearing jewelry?

Bridgewater observed the men, mainly, the group to which he felt he ought to belong; the three women all seemed individual and unrelated—the old lady, the bimbo, and Zippy, the pregnant woman; they were not necessarily representatives of one group, the way the men were, just because they all had cunts and wore makeup.

Three balding heads and two full of hair. The brothers Bridgewater senior had lost none of theirs to speak of, while the junior Bridgewater brothers, Mark and Peter, were thinning on top. The gene for baldness had come from his mother's side, the Dutch-German strain of their genetic makeup. Their maternal grandfather had been sleek-headed. But where the Bridgewater grandfather had lost his marbles to Alzheimer's, Grandfather Kleinpoppen had been sharp up until his death. Moishe's hair, too, combed straight back, was shot through with streaks of scalp. It began about a quarter of the way up his skull. What hair he had he combed straight back. Black kinky ridges that had lost their vitality now rippled back in weak waves.

"Do you have any objections to crab soup?" Uncle Ben asked Edith, ladling out a bowl for her.

"We only keep kosher at home," Moishe said. "We'd starve if we tried to everywhere."

"But we're good Jews anyway," Edith said, accepting a bowl of soup. "And we're going to give the child, our first grandchild, a good, proper Jewish name."

"Probably not much of a Jewish community in Potawatomi Rapids," Ben observed.

"There's a shul," Moishe said, "a small one."

"Shlomo if it's a boy and Sophie if it's a girl," Edith continued, adamant. "The bris will be in Baltimore if it's a boy, but if it's a girl, she'll be named in our shul," she further stipulated.

"Salisbury, Sampson, Sanborn, Sander, Sawyer, Saxon, Sebastian, Shelby, Sherlock, Sylvester," Bridgewater speculated aloud, partly to establish authority over the naming, partly for the fun of needling Edith.

"Boys' names beginning with 'S'?" Ben asked, smiling.

"I'ze gonna say!" Bambi blurted.

"Sabrina, Sasha, Sarah, Sharon, Sybil, Stacy, Stella, Stephanie."

"Shlomo or Sophie."

"Oh, Mom!" Zippy implored.

"You can give him or her half a dozen names if you want," Mark observed. "Like that lady in England who named her child something like fifty or a hundred names."

"Or we could just hang fire until the baby's five years old and has to go to school," Bridgewater said, remembering the joke about the parents whose indecision about naming their twins resulted in a trip to the barnyard the morning they had to enroll in school, with the father calling his sons whatever he happened to see first. The punchline came when Wagonwheel, being led to the principal's office for the impertinence of insisting his name was Wagonwheel, turned to his brother and said, "You'd better come, too, Chickenshit; they won't believe you, either."

"Hang fire," Frank said. He plucked a carrot from the relish tray and bit into it. "That's an interesting expression. Where does it come from?"

"It derives from gunnery," Uncle Ben explained. He was a first-class pedant. "When a gun is slow in firing the charge. Hang fire. You see the phrase in Henry James stories; it's probably of nineteenth century coinage. But you also see it used in Walker Percy's novels. It sounds like a Southernism. Or a Britishism."

"The Rolling Stones have a song on their *Tattoo You* album called 'Hang Fire,'" Bridgewater said. He glanced over at Zippy to see if the allusion to Mick Jagger meant anything to her, but she did not react.

"Oy vey," Edith muttered.

As Frank carved the turkey and Zippy scooped stuffing and broccoli and potatoes onto the plates, Ben launched into a non-stop dissertation to avert a scene, put off the showdown until after the day of giving thanks. His conversation ranged from international politics to the Russian Revolution, from Kant and Hegel to Kierkegaard and Marx and Lenin and Stalin, from the rejection of the Supreme Court nominee, Bork, to nuclear disarmament and Gorbachev's *glasnost* policy and the rehabilitation of Nikolai Bukharin, the Communist theoretician disgraced and executed by Stalin in 1938, all peppered with tales of his own travels to the Soviet Union; from the revision of Soviet history to the broad span of Russian culture to Dostoyevski and Tolstoy, and from Tolstoy to Rimbaud and writers/poets who simply stopped writing in the middle of their careers, Tolstoy to become a reformer, Rimbaud to become a slavetrader and gunrunner; he mentioned J.D. Salinger. The mention of Salinger brought the recollection of a friend in Ann Arbor who had known Salinger and was now hobnobbing with the Nobel prize-winning chemist Crum out in Los Angeles.

At the mention of the friend from Ann Arbor, Bridgewater stopped him a moment to ask about the friend who had driven them to the baseball game in Detroit the day Marilyn Monroe died. Cecilia Nestorick's image flitted across Bridgewater's mind, like a ballerina pirouetting across the stage.

"Vern Baker? You remember that? You and Mark were just little boys! Vern's retired now. Lives in Tucson. He just called me last week, in fact." Then he was off again, talking about the miracles of modern communication, the speed with which information travels; how we not only know about explosions in the Persian Gulf the same day they happen but we even get an exhaustive list of injury statistics.

"And remember the story last month about the 18-month old kid in Midland, Texas, who fell down the well, how the whole country held its breath while the drama unfolded? It was the lead story on the evening news. It reminds me of Woody Allen's movie *Radio Days*, where everybody huddles around the radio listening to on-the-scene accounts of a little girl who fell into a well in Pennsylvania. But this was in Texas, on the national television news broadcast, no less." And then he went on about the climate in desert areas, about Vern Baker's observations of life in Arizona, about retirement communities in Florida, about the greenhouse effect. The depletion of the ozone layer, the rape of the rain forests, the effects these events had on global climates, about summer weather and its effects on one's disposition, mobility and sociability, reminiscences of dust storms he'd been in during one hot Egyptian summer, humid summers in New Orleans and Bangkok.

"Frank tells me you had the 17-year cicadas out here this summer," Ben said, and then a new idea occurred to him. "Do you recall Aristotle's example of a maxim as part of an enthymeme? It goes, 'Insolence is better avoided, lest cicadas chirp on the ground.' He meant that insolence can provoke an enemy to mass destruction; the cicadas—or cicalas, as he called them—would have to chirp from the ground because the enemy destroyed all the trees—and razed all the buildings and raped all the women and destroyed all the villages; your imagination fills in all the blanks, you see."

"What's a—a—" Bambi said.

"An enthymeme? A syllogism with one of its premises missing. A rhetorical device that Aristotle talks about in his *Rhetoric* and *Poetics*. Most effective for purposes of persuasion; you don't spoon feed the logic, you see; you spark the imagination."

"I wasn't here for the cicadas," Zippy said.

"Ah, yes, you were in Barbados," Ben said affably, as if her abrupt departure had been planned all along. Keen to the awkward pitfalls all around him, Ben artfully dodged the embarrassment of pregnant pauses and spoke easily without losing a beat. "A wonderful place to spend the summer! Of course, the winter months might be even nicer. With whom did you stay, by the way?"

"A friend from college named Liz McEver." Zippy explained that Liz's father and mother were divorced. Her mother lived in Topsfield, Massachusetts, and her father lived in Barbados. Liz chose the warmer climate when she graduated from Brandeis, and now she had something to do with island tourism.

Bridgewater had not been sure how to react to the way everybody chose to ignore the fact of Zippy's desertion after she returned, as if no betrayal had occurred, no breach of faith, as if nothing out of the ordinary had happened. Not that he wanted Zippy tried, sentenced, hanged and quartered, but he had thought, at first, that there should at least be some acknowledgement. But now he was starting to believe that the tactful, tacit forgiveness was best, after all.

Frank had warmly accepted Zippy back, as he always had, without reservations, and Mark had basically ignored her, as he had always done; no change in behavior there. Bridgewater and Mark had always chosen to ignore each other's girlfriends. These women had always been merely something in the way, something a little embarrassing. Each brother assumed that the only reason the other pursued these girls was for sexual gratification. If you let a girl assume any more importance than that it meant you were "pussywhipped." Bridgewater recognized that attitude in his assessment of Bambi. What else did Mark see in her?

They all had seconds on turkey and stuffing, and Ben paused in his rambling to have some food. His plate had not been touched. During the pause, Mark brought the conversation back to the vacancy on the Supreme Court and Douglas Ginsburg's disqualification on the grounds of his use of marijuana.

"There's nothing wrong with marijuana," he declared. "No human being has ever died from an overdose. It just increases your appetite and makes you feel happy."

"I'ze gonna say," Bambi agreed.

Looking at Mark while his brother tried to appear casual, fondling under Bambi's dress beneath the table, Bridgewater speculated that Bambi filled the gap left by Mark's failed stock market investment plans. He had certainly taken a beating; his investments had all been in "growth" companies that failed when the market crashed in October. Bridgewater counted his blessings that he had not gone in with Mark on his investment schemes. But in lieu of the power the money would have brought, he now had the bombshell. Sex equates to power, and Bambi was the very incarnation of sex. The *sine qua non* of tits and ass. Mark had met her down in Fort Lauderdale in the spring. A Baltimore girl, she had been making a film down in Florida about a wild college beach party when he met her, Peter learned later.

"I'm just glad Ginsburg wasn't nominated," Ben said, changing the subject. It seemed less controversial ground than drugs. "He didn't have enough experience. All we knew about him was that he had a conservative, free-market approach to regulatory issues and anti-trust law."

"Nothing wrong with that," Moishe said.

"We haven't had a Jew on the Court since Abe Fortas," Edith said.

"The fact that he's Jewish is irrelevant," Moishe said. "But there will be those who condemn Jews because this man smoked pot!"

"My point exactly!" Mark said. "And there's nothing wrong with it!"

"I'ze gonna say."

"Anti-Semitism is on the rise in the Netherlands and throughout Europe; incidents of anti-Semitism in Amsterdam are at their highest since the Nazis; vitriolic anti-Semitic attacks are occurring in Japan; in the Soviet Union the government-run press attacks Israel daily, equating Zionism with racism, attacking Israel for trampling the rights of Arabs, for supporting Somosa in Nicaragua—"

"Who *hasn't* smoked pot? Babbitt and Gore came out saying they'd tried it; Senator Simon of Illinois and Jesse Jackson say they haven't, but—"

"Jesse Jackson! Oy vey!" Edith said. "Talk about an anti-Semite!"

"Oh, I don't think Jesse's anti-Semitic," Frank said, speaking as a politician gauging another politician's sentiments.

"Not anti-Semitic!" Moishe cried. "He has his picture taken with Arafat and Louis Farrakhan, Halfass Al-Assad. He makes remarks about 'hymies'! What more do you want? Swastikas on an armband?"

"Just a slip of the tongue. He's like Mimi DiPietro, our loose-tongued city councilman. Besides, don't judge the man on one issue alone."

"Well to me it's the single most important issue. Just like the Holocaust was the century's worst tragedy."

"They pooh-poohed Hitler, too, remember! Oy vey!"

"If you want to see real violence, just take a look at Haiti," Frank said. "Or take a look at South Korea."

"That guy Chun Doo Hwan makes me think of a rock-and-roll refrain," Bridgewater said. "Chun-chun-chun-chun-do-hwan, chun-chun-chun-chun-do-hwan," he crooned to the tune of "Sweet Talkin' Guy." "You know, the doo-wop-diddy background vocals."

Bambi laughed. "I'ze gonna say!" she blurted. She had a sort of put-on sweetness, but Bridgewater sensed that she could be as mean as a yard dog if you scratched beneath the surface. Her enormous tits were impossible to ignore, packed into the décolletage (Delores del Rio in *Play Me Again*, showing at the Little X along with *Hot Pursuit*). Bridgewater had noticed Moishe's eyes flitting around them like sparrows pecking at birdseed, lighting momentarily on the cleavage as though coming to rest on a twig. She turned to Bridgewater now and repeated her earlier comment that she had been charmed by the stories Mark had told her about their cats. Bridgewater could not recall any memorable incidents involving the cats other than the time Mark had given Fluffy some LSD, and he just smiled.

"I wonder how Ozzie's doing," he said.

"Ozzie?"

"Our cat." Bridgewater removed a photograph from his wallet and showed Bambi. The cat was swatting a cockroach that was walking across the mirror on the dresser, but from the photograph you would have thought he was trying to interact with the cat in the reflection.

"A pitcher!" Bambi exclaimed. "Aww. Idn he cute?"

"Ozzie's your cat?" Uncle Ben asked, turning the conversational spotlight onto a neutral topic. Household pets. Nothing controversial there. "As in 'Ozzie and Harriet'?"

"Short for Azazel," Bridgewater said. "Zippy found him in the alley behind our apartment and brought him home. He's black with white paws."

"Azazel," Ben said. "You know who Azazel was, don't you?"

"The scapegoat."

"Azazel was the standard-bearer of the rebellious angels in Milton's *Paradise Lost*," Uncle Ben said. "In Islamic literature, Azazel was a djinn. A spirit."

"But the reason Zippy chose the name—"

The mention of choosing names reminded Edith of her fixed idea, and again she announced that the baby would be named either Shlomo or Sophie.

"The center will not hold," Uncle Ben muttered, and it was as if he were throwing in the towel; he would no longer try to be the mediator, the peacemaker.

"You got a lisince fer yer cat?" Bambi asked.

"Well, he never goes out."

"It's a twenny-figh dollar fine in Balmer naow if they catch yer cat without his lisince."

"Well, Ozzie never goes out." Bridgewater shrugged, looking at Bambi's tits. *Crazy with the Heat, Desperate Women.*

"Better not. It's a twenny-figh dollar fine," Bambi cautioned again.

"Well, does anybody want dessert?" Frank said. He and Zippy began to clear the dishes, and Ben went into the kitchen to get the pie.

"Anybody want tea?" he called.

When Frank came back into the room, Bambi, who had been sitting at his left at the head of the table, got up and presented him with a box of candy, a Whitman Sampler. She pressed her tits against his shoulder and kissed him on the forehead, and then she mussed his hair up a little bit.

"Wow, you can do that again, Bam," Frank said with boyish candor. Bambi did not blush, and Mark glanced over at Bridgewater with a look that expressed his disgust with their father.

Bambi sat down again. She opened the Whitman Sampler and selected a piece of chocolate and began to gnaw at it while they waited for Ben to bring in the tea and dessert.

When they were all seated with their pie and tea in front of them, Moishe confessed that he had always wanted a son but had gotten two daughters instead, and then Edith had had a hysterectomy.

"You'd never want sons, Mo," Frank said. "Sons are always in competition with you, and they want to make you out to be some kind of failure. A daughter will love you if you treat her right. She'll want to marry somebody just like her dad."

"I've never thought you were a failure," Bridgewater said, wondering at his father's insight. Then again, Oedipal complexes are generally taken for granted these days.

"Well, you know what I mean," Frank said.

"What *do* you mean?"

"I had you figured for a failure long ago, Dad," Mark said, "but when you're judging from a level of success like I've reached, who *isn't* a failure?"

Frank howled with laughter. "That's my boy!"

"Well, from somebody who's had no children at all, I find it interesting that you regret having had daughters instead of sons," Ben said to Moishe.

"I didn't say I *regretted* having daughters; I just said that I—"

"He just meant that he wants *Zippy* to have a boy," Edith interrupted. "So he can name him Shlomo."

"Exactly who was Shlomo?"

"Moishe's father. May he rest in peace."

But Moishe was thinking of something else. "My daughter, Rachael," he said, shaking his head. "The apple of my eye. She recently told us she's involved with—with an unacceptable man."

"Oy vey! Don't talk about it, Moishe!"

The subject was obviously painful for the Feldmans and very personal, and nobody asked any questions. Finally, Uncle Ben broke the silence before it became too embarrassing. He evidently hadn't given up on holding that center together.

"Wasn't she a student at Brandeis, your daughter?"

"Years ago, when these two got married. Since then she's been to graduate school and working in a bank in Kalamazoo for six years."

"You went to Brandeis, too, didn't you, Zippy?"

Zippy nodded but did not enter the conversation. They were on shaky ground, and she did not want to be dragged into the ancient family dispute, a tribal taboo that was around even before she was born.

"Where is Rachael having Thanksgiving, anyway? Kalamazoo?" Even as he said it, Bridgewater saw, his uncle knew he'd stepped on a landmine.

"Probably with that Docina," Edith hissed. "'Dody'." She spoke the little pet name with fine sarcasm. Bridgewater could hear the mimicry in her voice and supposed it was Rachael she was putting down.

All eyes turned to Zippy, but she wasn't saying anything. The secretkeeper. Rachael had indeed called Zippy a few days earlier and confided that she was upset with their parents. But if Rachael had told Zippy what she was doing for Thanksgiving, Zippy hadn't told her husband. Or anybody. She'd have made a wonderful spy, Bridgewater thought, the country's secrets safe with her.

After another awkward pause, Ben changed the subject. Uncle Ben to the rescue.

"Do you have any brothers?" he asked Moishe.

"No," Edith said.

"Yes," Moishe said.

Moishe's older brother, Sidney, a politician in New Jersey, convicted of embezzling $250,000 from the state teachers' pension fund, had been out on appeal when he faked his death in an airline disaster. He had forged documents proving he was on board a flight that crashed near Philadelphia, slipped in fake identity records. Now he was living in Tel Aviv and running a cigar store on Dizengoff Street under the name of Seth Friedman. It was a family secret, the skeleton in the closet.

"He's dead," Edith explained. "Died in a plane crash a few years ago."

"I'm sorry to hear that. What was his name?"

"Sidney."

"Ah!" Uncle Ben said. A name that began with an "S". A recently deceased relative. He looked over at Bridgewater and then back to Moishe, aware that the subject was not exactly a comfortable one for the Feldmans. "Was he older or younger?"

"Younger."

"Have any others?"

Moishe shook his head.

"Two brothers! Just like Frank and me and Peter and Mark. Saul Bellow often has his protagonist as the younger of two brothers, the older of whom is always sort of ruthless and unscrupulous, while the younger is sentimental, full of family feeling, drenched in dreams."

At the mention of Saul Bellow, Bridgewater's hand jerked, and he spilled hot tea in his lap.

"This lapsang souchong smells like pipe tobacco!" Zippy said, making a face at her own cup of tea. She noticed her husband's awkwardness but did not attribute any special significance to it. She did offer him her napkin, though.

"What Saul Bellow stories are you thinking of?" Bridgewater asked casually, dabbing at the stain on his pants.

"Oh, let's see. *Humboldt's Gift*, *Augie March*. There must be some others. I'm sure there are. I'd have to think about it. The younger brother always has a tender heart for members of his family, and the older brother can rarely even remember them. Maybe the short story 'Him with His Foot in His Mouth' too. I think there's a callous older brother in that one, too." He shook his head. "Do you ever wish you knew somebody who was an expert in some arcane field and you could just call them up and ask? Anyway, that's my impression of Saul Bellow, but I'm no expert."

"The younger son is usually the more loyal one," Frank said.

"You mean in Bellow? I think you're right." Ben looked dubiously at his brother, sure Frank had never read Saul Bellow.

"I just mean in general."

Bridgewater watched Ben turn to Moishe. Had Ben, too, been the favorite son? Had Frank subconsciously been trying all those years to reproduce the same familiar set of circumstances from his own childhood? The thought had occurred to Bridgewater before, but never in quite those terms. Usually he thought in terms of the Jacob and Esau archetypes.

"You don't want your grandchild named for your brother?"

"It's more complicated than that."

"I see," Ben said, plainly signifying that he didn't.

"Sid might still be alive," Edith confessed.

"They weren't able to identify his remains?"

"Not positively. The plane just exploded."

"Nobody's heard from him in years," Edith added.

"You're still holding out hope, though."

"Well, there weren't any survivors."

"I guess without the definitive evidence, though, it's hard to accept the fact," Ben murmured, consoling the Feldmans but plainly mystified.

Why didn't they just tell him, Bridgewater wondered. What would happen if he just spelled it out for Ben right here, cleared the air? But he knew he couldn't. It was a secret. Life is full of secrets to be kept, confidences, classified information, mysteries.

"Well," he said, pushing away from the table. "What say we catch the news on TV? That was a sensational meal. You still want to go to the movies, Zippy?" He looked at Bambi, leaning over to stand up from the table, and he thought, *Deep Throat*, *The Devil in Miss Jones*. How he would like to do a painting of her, or at least a cartoon sketch. *Big Mama Goes to Work*. A B-Girl flirting with a lounge lizard in some titty bar, the bartender in the background, bored, washing glasses.

"Gazookis has a good idea there!" Moishe declared, relieved. "Let's see if the Lions pulled it out."

The insipid cheery theme music of the local news show had just begun to fade when Bridgewater turned on the television, and the pretty blond anchorwoman and the chubby, bespectacled black anchorman wished the television audience a happy Thanksgiving Day. They traded silly jokes about turkeys before the commercial break, and then after they came back on, they reported the usual stuff about parades and football games. The Lions had lost to Kansas City. Then, just before another commercial break, the pretty blonde's face assumed a serious expression, and she announced the tragic murder-suicide of a brother and sister in a Pimlico apartment just after midnight the night before. Details next. Then the screen cut to an advertisement for a local Chevrolet dealership. Bridgewater had an uncanny feeling about the news story. He *knew* it would be about Cecilia and Roger Nestorick. Zippy noticed that he looked agitated, and she asked if he felt all right. Meanwhile, Moishe was sounding off about the Detroit Lions.

"The year the Packers lost only one game, back during Lombardi's coaching days? The Lions. The Lions beat 'em on Thanksgiving Day. After that, Green Bay called it quits on being the annual opponent. Now they play a different team every year. The Lions were just incredible on Thanksgiving. You couldn't touch them. Couldn't come close." His voice took on the elegiac tone reserved for great encounters between titans—Frazier and Ali, the Yankees and the Dodgers, the Celtics and the Lakers. But then his tone sank into disgust. "Now they can't even beat the Kansas City Chiefs!

"The Lions used to have Earl Morall, and they used him as their back-up quarterback! A second-stringer! You understand? They used some bozo named Milton Plum instead as the starting quarterback. Milt Plum! Gazookis here could throw better than Plum! Then they traded Morall to the Colts, and you know what he did for Baltimore. I don't know. I had high hopes for them when they got this fella Long from Iowa, but just look at them today. Pathetic!" He shook his head and took a sip of tea. The news came on again, but Moishe was still on his soapbox.

"Now the Colts aren't doing so bad in Indianapolis. Not with Eric Dickerson and this guy Trudeau. They might even make the playoffs. But the Lions—" Bridgewater turned and shushed him.

"A brother and sister were found dead in a Pimlico apartment this morning in what police think was a murder-suicide. Roger Nestorick, out on bond pending a re-trial for sexual misconduct involving teenage boys and girls a year ago, and his sister, Cecilia, were found by their mother, Mrs. Betty Nestorick, shot to death. She had gone over to the apartment to drive them to the Nestorick home in Timonium for Thanksgiving dinner. Cecilia Nestorick was three-months pregnant. Sources speculate that the baby she was carrying was her brother's."

"Oy vey!"

"I'ze gonna say!"

"Isn't he the same guy—" Frank began, but Mark cut him off.

"There were stories about him with dogs and cats!" He thought it was funny, but Uncle Ben looked sick. His voice hollow with horror, Ben said:

"Bestialism?"

"If that's what you call it. You know, when men were men and sheep were nervous." Mark laughed again.

"Oh, that is really sick," Edith said. "I see the hand of God in this. This is like Sodom and Gomorrah."

"I'ze gonna say!" Bambi bit into another chocolate. She had brought the Whitman Sampler with her into the sunken den and placed it on a coffee table beside her.

Zippy, meanwhile, had been looking at her husband with a solemn, shocked expression on her face. But Bridgewater was too absorbed in his own shock to pay any attention to her.

"Talk about a close-knit family," Mark said as the story ended. "The family that lays together stays together. Lies together, dies together."

"Oy vey!"

"I'ze gonna say!"

The reporter covering the story said that since last summer Roger had been periodically released into the care of his parents and sister as a part of his rehabilitation program. He'd been performing community service work while living in a halfway house in Glen Burnie. Since October, Ms. Nestorick, a graduate student at Johns Hopkins and a substitute teacher in the Baltimore City school system, had been living in the Pimlico apartment. Neighbors had reported suspicious behavior during a visit from Roger earlier in November. Their mother had been actively soliciting donations to the American Mental Health Fund since her son's trial last year. The AMHF, the reporter noted, was founded by John Hinckley, Sr., father of the young man who attempted to assassinate President Reagan.

"Jeez," Uncle Ben said. "What's the world coming to? This even tops the child-abuse story in New York. What was the guy's name? Steinberg? The tabloids referred to the child as 'Torture Tot'. They made it into a real circus."

"Oy vey! The coming of the messiah is at hand, I can tell it! This is God's work. The end is coming, I just know it!"

Bridgewater sat in his armchair but felt as if he were floating, thinking numbly of the signs on city buses with the grainy black and white mug shots of missing children. HELP FIND MARYLAND'S MISSING CHILDREN. A "Child Safety Tip" always followed. It changed periodically. The one that had been up for several months now said, "Develop a family password only you and your child know. Teach your child not to go with anyone who does not know the password; guessing is not allowed." Talk about a circus! That was advice right out of a Bazooka bubblegum wrapper.

Funny, the things you thought about when you were in a state of shock. Why had he thought of that sign on the bus? Oh yes, "Torture Tot."

The next news story was about a court case in which a tobacco company was being sued for causing the death of a man from emphysema and lung cancer. The man's wife was suing the tobacco company. She was shown weeping and grieving for the way cigarettes had ruined her life; she wanted revenge. An eye for an eye, a lung for a lung. The reporter also interviewed one of those glib, duplicitous creeps who work for tobacco companies. Spokesmen. The ones who insist there is no medical evidence linking cigarettes and lung cancer. Did anybody actually believe what he was saying? In which level of Hell would Dante put somebody like that?

Zippy stood up in the middle of the story and said she wanted Bridgewater to take her home. Her abrupt announcement took everybody by surprise. Even Bridgewater did not understand her at first. But then, like everybody else, he assumed her condition had tired her out.

"Sure you don't want to take a peek at my electric trains?" Frank asked.

"*I* sure do," Mark said, winking broadly at his brother. "That's the main reason we came here!"

"I'ze gonna say," Bambi agreed.

But Zippy and Bridgewater got the jackets they'd brought in case the weather turned cooler, and they said goodbye.

Zippy and Bridgewater prepared for bed as soon as they got home, even though it was still early. They took turns in the bathroom and avoided each other's eyes until they were in bed and the lights were out.

"She was the one who modeled for you, wasn't she?" Zippy said in the dark. Her voice was sad and dull; she was not accusing him, only confirming a fact.

"While you were in Barbados," Bridgewater said bitterly. "What a marvelous place to spend the summer!" he mimicked his uncle.

"I know I'm not blameless! I just wish—! Oh, I just hope things will be different now, Peter! I just hope, everything will turn out better!"

Bridgewater did not reply. He reached over and stroked his wife's arm. Eventually, Zippy turned over on her side, away from him, and began to breathe evenly. Bridgewater spooned her loosely, her ass fitting snugly into his lap, and he reached his arm around her swollen, pregnant belly.

He lay quietly, hugging his wife, wondering if the child Cecilia had been carrying were really Roger's or if it had been his. He felt movement in Zippy's belly and tried to discern body parts in the pulsing. A hand or a foot or the contour of a head.

Bridgewater wished passionately then, as if making a prayer to a God he did not really believe in, that fatherhood would bring a sense of belonging to him, a feeling of family. He knew he was not a man with a strong will, one who could face down circumstances, dominate his fate. He only wanted to fit in somehow, to *belong*! Oh, how passionately he longed for it, how fervently he wished to belong!

Trust

Dreamers

The delivery had gone pretty easily. Only three hours of active labor and just twenty minutes of pushing. Of course, "easy" is a relative term; the pains of labor and birth were unimaginable torture; with each wave, Zippy had been sure she would be unable to endure it any longer; she whimpered like an injured dog. Peter had helped her through the contractions with a rolling pin, which he pressed down her back. The sight of the tiny blue crying infant almost erased the pain—at least gave it meaning.

"It's got a full head of hair," the doctor commented as the baby progressed down the birth canal and the top of its head pressed through the gap between her legs. He performed an episiotomy to widen the opening, an incision that would be sore for weeks afterward; the stitches in her perineum would itch worse than the hemorrhoids she had developed during pregnancy.

Peter watched the baby emerge, fascinated. He had promised not to take any pictures of the birth, but he stared as if etching the image indelibly into his brain. A painting: *Deliverance.* Zippy pushed and pushed with the effort of the terminally constipated trying to take a shit. At last she squeezed her vaginal muscles, and the baby came squalling out into the doctor's hands.

"It's a girl," the doctor said. Zippy had known it all along, of course. Susanna.

Everybody said she was a gorgeous child, and with pride Zippy could tell from their voices that they really thought so. The pursed little O of a mouth, the closed eyes, the well-shaped nose, the film of hair all over her skull: a delight to behold. A bumpersticker: I Saw Delight.

Peter had taken pictures within fifteen minutes of her birth. In a burst of enthusiasm, he took roll after roll of photographs of their daughter those first days in the hospital. These hemorrhages of excitement weakened her husband, Zippy reflected; it was the sort of openness that made him vulnerable to doubt and bred suspicion and fears of betrayal, of not being dealt with honestly. Zippy knew that he respected her privacy, but he also thought she was "secretive." Talk about secretive! He had not breathed a word to her about his involvement with that woman whose brother had killed her and then committed suicide. He admitted that she had modeled for him, and that was all. Well, maybe that *was* all. But methinks the lady doth talk too *little*, to cite Shakespeare, Zippy reflected.

Not only had the birth been relatively easy, but Susanna had come at a civilized hour. No waking up at three in the morning with frantic telephone calls to groggy obstetricians and tardy taxicabs for the Bridgewaters. Susanna was born late on a Sunday afternoon, a December dusk just settling over the city, in time to watch the evening news. Lawmakers reach tentative Contra aid agreement. U.S. warships escort Danish ship through the Persian Gulf. Palestinian youths riot in East Jerusalem. Gary Kasparov keeps his world chess title.

Peter left her around nine o'clock to call their families, and Zippy, exhausted but pleased, tried to sleep, looking forward a little apprehensively to assuming the role of motherhood the next day.

But overnight Zippy developed a fever, and although the doctors suspected that she had a non-contagious urinary tract infection, she was not allowed to see the newborn until they were sure. In the meantime, she lay in bed hooked up to an IV contraption that monitored the flow of antibiotics into her veins. The tubes were attached to a big aluminum frame that resembled a coatrack; it made a shrill beeping noise, like a busy signal, when it ran out of medication.

Peter stayed at home from work the first day to care for the baby. Shrouded in a hospital gown, he gave the infant her bottle of formula every four hours in the nursery. The next day he came in after work to give Susanna her bottle again, and he reported glowingly how beautiful she was, almost as if he couldn't believe it: the cynical man of the world reduced to a blob of sentimental putty. His demeanor made Zippy feel wistful and yearn for the same. He had freckled his shirt and tie with spaghetti sauce spots, she noticed, pale red tomato stains that revealed the hasty hurryup manner with which he fed himself in her absence, impatient to be with his family. Convenience foods consumed before they were even cooked. Tuna helper, canned spaghetti, frozen dinners, pot pies, pizza and Chinese takeout.

Two weeks before Susanna was born, Peter had gotten a job as graphics coordinator in the marketing department at Maryputa, a high tech firm out in Hunt Valley. He seemed to like the company; his job amused him, teased his imagination; he swung between the charm and the challenge. In small gusts of enthusiasm he made up quirky little slogans, probably inspired by his projects at work, the pithy little tag lines meant to lure corporate customers. Peter jotted down things like: "Poetry, fiction, drug addiction." Or, "Pastoral, bucolic, alcoholic." "Philosopher, king, gambling ring." "Poet, thinker, problem drinker."

When Peter was not in the hospital, Zippy lay in bed vaguely watching talkshows on television and old daytime reruns of once-popular sitcoms, alternately shivering and sweating as the fever came and went. At times she almost forgot why she was in the hospital at all. She was allowed to walk with her cumbersome coatrack to the nursery window and look in at the swaddled babies in their bassinets, as though she were at an aquarium looking at fish in a glass tank. The effort exhausted her. It was like a hideous nightmare; Peter likened it to a punishment in Hell as imagined by Dante.

The third night, after Peter had gone home, as Zippy lay in bed feeling sorry for herself, a predictable Christmas variety show flickering on the television screen, complete with canned laughter and schmaltzy solemnity at "appropriate" moments, Mrs. Fitch, the night nurse, came in to check the antibiotics and to take her temperature. She was a round, jolly, doughy woman in her fifties who made Zippy think of a farmer's wife. Zippy smiled at her wanly as she bustled into the room.

"Still can't see the baby, can you. Oh! I feel for you, dear!" Mrs. Fitch said, looking at the dials and meters on the IV rack, jotting down numbers on a pad. Zippy did not say anything.

"I remember when Tiger was born and they wouldn't let me see him, either! Oh, was I disappointed! Tiger was such a beautiful baby, too. He looks just like his dad, now! He didn't when he was born, but he does now. Now, Marianne, she looks more like my side of the family. Right from the start, people'd say, that child's a McKenna! Open up your mouth and let me take your temperature. There, that's it.

"Yes, she looked just like a McKenna, everybody said. Right down to the dimple in the chin, the spit and image of a McKenna! But Tiger didn't look like either one of us at first!" She laughed, looking at her wristwatch. "We thought somebody must have given us the wrong baby! He was born at Good Samaritan; Marianne was born at Sinai. She looked just like a McKenna, right from the first, I'll swear. But Tiger! Tiger didn't look like nobody we knew, but we was glad to have him because he was so beautiful, and they wouldn't let me see him! Oh, how I suffered! But now he's grown up to be the spit and image of his dad. Looks just exactly like his father, you can't hardly tell the difference."

Zippy murmured some vague acknowledgement of the nurse's efforts to cheer her, meanwhile wondering at the logic of her sentences. Was she saying the Fitches were ugly people? Zippy felt a tolerant, grudging gratitude toward Mrs. Fitch, but she really wanted to be left alone. She smiled wanly again, a signal, she thought, that the conversation was over and Mrs. Fitch could return to her other duties. But Mrs. Fitch evidently took the sign differently. Or maybe she just didn't have anything else to do.

"Say," she said, "would you like to look at some pictures of Tiger and Marianne? I've got an album right out here at the nurses' station! I'll be right back." Before Zippy could even reply, Mrs. Fitch sailed out the door to retrieve the photo album.

Damn! Zippy thought. She felt trapped. This simply wasn't fair! She couldn't see her baby; she was a prisoner in a hospital bed; she was sore between her legs as well as feverish all over; she could not even move around without lugging a coatrack with her, and now she had to endure this boring, well-meaning old crone's family photo album! She wanted to weep.

"This was Tiger when he was three years old," Mrs. Fitch was saying, even as she came back into the room. "You wouldn't hardly believe he weighed practically two hundred pounds now to look at him back then. Was he handsome! Just look!" She brought the brown imitation leather photo album over to Zippy and began pointing out pictures. The plastic pages made a sticky peeling-off noise as she turned the pages with dreamy reverence. There was Tiger when he was three years old. Tiger on the little league ball team. Tiger at his high school graduation. Tiger just before he went into the service. Tiger and his fiancée. Marianne missing her two front teeth. Marianne on her first two-wheeler. Marianne at *her* high school graduation. Marianne at the family reunion last summer. ("Can't you just see the McKenna in her? Just compare her with her uncle Dale or my sister, Midge! Don't you see it? The scrunched up eyes? The round cheeks?")

Mrs. Fitch elaborated on the circumstances in which each photograph was taken and expounded on the personalities not only of Tiger and Marianne but of every aunt and uncle and cousin and grandparent featured in the album. Her voice took on the fondness of memory, and her eyes glazed over as if she were in a trance, a waking dream.

The timelessness of Mrs. Fitch's tone had the soporific effect of a lullaby, and though she tried to stay awake, Zippy was unable to remain conscious for long. She slumped over onto her pillow, asleep.

Zippy dreamed she was at home, in Potawatomi Rapids, in her parents' house. She was fast asleep up in her room in the third floor garret. Across the hall, her sister Rachael was asleep in her room, the only other room on the third floor, a mirror image of Zippy's room, its north-sloping ceiling symmetrical with the south-sloping ceiling of Zippy's room. Their mother was calling up the stairs to them to get up. They were going to be late for school. In her dream, Zippy felt that she was being dreamed asleep by her sister Rachael, a sort of captive of her younger sister's unconsciousness. When Rachael awoke, she, too, would be able to rise. Meanwhile, Edith's voice was becoming more and more impatient, more and more insistent, more and more urgent. It was starting to sound like a police siren.

"Wake up, Zipporah!" she called up the stairs. "Wake up, Rachael! Gevalt! You have to get up now! Hurry, Zipporah! Hurry, Rachael! Wake up! Wake up!"

Faster than a Man Can Walk

Moishe told Rachael that if she married Docina he would disown her. He said that he only had her best interests in mind, but she knew his reaction was more visceral than rational, that it tapped into deep wells of prejudice and fear. This hurt her because she had always depended on her father to be reasonable. Her mother, Edith, she knew, could never be reasoned with, but she expected this from her mother. Edith was stubborn and conservative, the classic Jewish mother. But her father was a different matter.

"I only know she'll be unhappy if she marries him," Moishe said to Zippy and Bridgewater when he and Edith came to look at the new baby in January. "He's a nice enough fellow, I suppose, kind and all that, but he's stupid. What does she have in common with him? What does she see in him? It's just an infatuation. Rachael scored 800 on both the verbal and math exams when she took the SAT; she graduated Phi Beta Kappa from Brandeis; she has a Master's degree in Economics from the University of Illinois and an MBA; she's the assistant manager of one of the biggest banks in Michigan." He shrugged helplessly. "And Dody? He plays basketball."

Dody was one of the coaches for a high school basketball team in Kalamazoo, and he taught a couple of sections of Physical Education and Geography, and he oversaw a study hall as well. Both Moishe and Edith were appalled by Dody's ghetto English. He said "libary" instead of "library," "troof" instead of "truth," "axed" instead of "asked." Prudish Moishe was also horrified by the vision of the black buck *shtupping* his daughter. Mentally, he slammed the door on this unwelcome image.

"If Rachael marries this Dody I will sit shiva for her," Edith said, write her off as dead. It was not that he was black that troubled her but that he was a goy; he was not Jewish. He could be green for all she cared, she said, and yet, in her Yiddish, she often spoke of *schvartzes* with a pitying contempt. Similarly, she spoke with bitterness about Germans, Palestinians and Arabs in general. But these prejudices were rooted in history. Where did the anti-black sentiment come from?

In less than a year, Rachael would be thirty. She wanted a family. The birth of her niece made her realize how much she wanted this: it seemed to represent progress, maturity, adulthood, independence. She had been involved with Dody for seven years now, ever since she was a graduate student in Urbana. There was nothing about him for which she was not already prepared. Their relationship was stalled. They had to make a move.

Her sister Zippy advised her to continue with Docina as she was. They maintained separate apartments in Kalamazoo and spent weekends together. Why did they have to get married? But this was easy for Zippy to say, Rachael thought. She already had a family, a home. She didn't know what it felt like to return to an empty apartment night after night.

"If you want to maintain relations with Mom and Dad, you'd better not marry him, Rache," Zippy warned.

"But I can't spend the rest of my life pleasing Mom and Dad! I have to think about myself before it's too late!"

"Too late for what?"

"Maybe I'd like to start a family," she said. Saying the words aloud put them in doubt. Already she felt defeated.

Zippy did not have a reply to this. She never did. What could she say? *With Dody Brown?* She did not want to take her parents' side, but she did not see why Rachael had to have a baby, either. Not that she wanted to deny her sister motherhood, but Rachael was aware of the difficulties she had with her parents about Peter, and he had converted. Docina did not want to be a black Jew: the distaste was two-sided, even though he loved Rachael with dog-like devotion. Rachael knew about the Tay-Sachs gene and the abortions, too; something like that could just as easily happen to her. They both knew about the mess with their cousin, Sandy, Sid's daughter, who was getting a divorce from her goy husband, Brad Reynolds. Brad had dumped Sandy for a shikse. If it was Dody Rachael cared about, she could still have him without alienating their parents, Zippy thought. She could live with him; she did not have to marry him. Maybe their parents *were* bigots; maybe Zionism *was* racism, but Rachael did not have to flaunt it in their faces. They were too old to change. Then again, it *was* Rachael's life, and Dody *was* a good man, and they really *did* seem happy together.

"Maybe Mom and Dad are right," Rachael said after a pause. She had always been their parents' favorite daughter, and the thought of losing that, of relinquishing their parents' love (especially Moishe's) unsettled her. The fact that she lived so near—Kalamazoo was about a two-hour drive from Potawatomi Rapids—indicated how important her parents' approval was to her. She had felt so far away from them in Boston; even Chicago and Urbana had seemed distant. She regarded Potawatomi Rapids as her retreat, reserved for a sort of Buddhistic contemplation, just her and the elements—earth, wind, sun and lake. Yet she hated herself for being a slave to their likes and dislikes. Indeed, Rachael did not really feel as though she *had* a "home," despite her affection for Potawatomi Rapids. She did not even have a perspective. She was only held in suspense, her fate determined by others, a *captive* of fate. She did have Dody, but possession of Dody entailed restriction elsewhere—privation, banishment, dispossession. If only they would accept him! Once they got to know him they would love him! But of course, they wouldn't get to know him.

An exchange she overheard one day on her lunch break in a fast-food restaurant seemed to capture her ambivalence and hold it like an emblem. She had driven carefully through the slushy, snow-packed streets of Kalamazoo to the Burger King, wrapped snugly in her warm, violet, full-length down coat, and once inside ordered a sandwich and a drink. Mentally preoccupied with her work, she took her food to a booth where she unfolded her *Chicago Tribune* with the expectation of eating a quick lunch and going back to the bank to resume work on the quarterly reports. In the booth ahead of hers—they shared a cushioned backboard—a wrinkled old guy was haranguing his companion, a younger fellow with oily dark hair parted down the middle. The older man was trying to sell the younger man a used car. They evidently knew each other, may even have been related. Rachael could see a resemblance in the fleshy, freckled span across the nose and upper cheeks. An uncle and a nephew, perhaps. Nor was this the first time the transaction had been discussed, she could see. In her former capacity as a loan officer, Rachael had been interested in the details of such deals and could gauge their progress with fine accuracy. She had arranged the financing for car loans for many a college student at Western Michigan and Kalamazoo College. She eavesdropped on the two men while feigning an interest in the news—but it was just more of the same stuff about the presidential primaries, and she got enough of that on television. Super Tuesday! Government and politics were equated with a professional football game! What next? The economy identified with the state lottery? Lincoln's and Washington's birthdays had already been lumped together to form one consumer holiday. But Presidents' Day sales and Super Tuesday could never relieve the bleakness of a Michigan winter.

The wizened older fellow sat facing her across the two tables. Crows' feet spread from the corners of his eyes and mouth (as they would on the nephew in twenty or thirty years), as if he had squinted for focus so long appraising animals and objects. A horse trader. He reminded her of her father in that respect: sizing up the world to cut it down to size; Moishe's ever-moving eyes were like scythes mowing a field of hay. The man leaned across the Formica tabletop and spoke in a low urgent whisper to his companion. Rachael did not catch the words, though she strained her ears while nibbling at her Whopper.

Finally, the younger man pulled back, almost seduced by the older, but freeing himself at last, like a man escaping the tangle of an octopus's writhing tentacles.

"What do I want a piece of junk like that for, anyway?" he said. "It ain't gonna take me nowhere I want to go!"

"But it'll go faster than a man can walk, and you'll be wantin' to go somewhere. Ever'body does. 'Specially you hot-blooded youngens these days. Think about it, Lonnie. Don't decide just yet. It'll go faster'n a man can walk, and it's a whole lot more comftable, too."

"I ain't wanna go noplace."

The old man laughed. "You get Patty in trouble, you gonna wish you had a way out."

Then they both got up to leave. They collected their empty styrofoam containers and paper bags, put on their coats and went toward the door. The old fellow, stooped, walked more slowly than his nephew (son? neighbor?) did.

Faster than a man can walk. Walk—don't run—to the nearest exit. Nobody talks, everybody walks. Getting away. Fleeing. Escape. Out of context, perhaps the phrase was meaningless, its power linked to the image of the two relatives locked in a tense struggle of wills over a minor business transaction. But somehow the phrase stuck in Rachael's mind. Like the punchline of a joke or the title of a rock and roll song, the refrain. She improvised lyrics:

> Shit or get off the pot.
> Either you're with us or you're not.
> Do something, don't just talk.
> Faster than a man can walk.

Either you're for or against.
No sitting on a fence.
Don't just stand there and gawk.
Faster than a man can walk.

"Maybe Mom and Dad are right," Rachael conceded to Zippy on the phone that night. "I want more than just to live with him. That's just playing house. If I break up with Dody I can probably find an eligible man in a year or two. Maybe less. There's somebody at the bank who asked me out, a Jewish man, but he's kind of boring. But I don't want to go out with him just to please Mom and Dad! I want somebody I like and who I can share a life with; that's the main thing, not if he's Jewish or not."

"But if you like Dody there's no reason to break up with him just because you can't marry him."

"Zippy! I'm going to do something! I can't stand this! Dody and I are going to have to come to terms with this somehow, even if it means we have to stop seeing each other! I can't take this—this *suspense* any longer!"

"But Mom and Dad *aren't* right, Rachael! Not completely! Dody's a fine man, you know that."

"It's the thought of throwing away all we've shared together for the past seven years that tears me up," Rachael sobbed, consoled by her sister's support.

"Well, just don't do anything rash. Don't do anything you'll regret. Don't do anything you can't reverse if you have to." Zippy tried to cover all the possibilities before she rang off.

Two nights later, Rachael called her sister in Baltimore. She said she and Docina had talked it over and reached a solution. They had decided not to break up after all. They would stay together and see how their relationship developed. If it seemed to be going all right, they might rent an apartment together, maybe even buy a house. She sounded relieved—a real breakthrough—but it was the same decision she and Dody had been making for the past seven years.

Daddy Dreams

Hugging his bundle to his chest, Bridgewater hurried across the street from the Remington rowhouse to his Toyota like a soldier in a war zone. He opened the door on the passenger's side, reached over and stuck the key into the ignition, climbed into the rear of the two-door Tercel and then snapped Susanna into the car seat, facing the back windshield; he pushed himself back out of the rear seat like some sort of shellfish, climbed back out of the passenger door to run around to the driver's side, flipped the doorlock and slammed the door, and only then did the shrill buzzing stop, only then did he realize he had vaguely, unconsciously, associated the noise with his own urgency to get moving; only then did Bridgewater realize that he had locked the car with the keys in the ignition. With the baby inside!

Why hadn't he paid attention to the car's warning signal? He wanted to kick himself! His head started to throb as waves of panic rolled over him. All this haste to get to Social Security to pick Zippy up, and look what it had gotten him! Now he had *really* fucked up. Now he *would* be late!

With a sudden lucid calmness, Bridgewater realized he had just done one of those stupid things he had been fearing he would do for the past twelve weeks since the baby was born. He had had visions—nightmares!—of tripping while holding the baby, watching her fly from his arms, visions of stumbling down the stairs and dropping her as he instinctively grabbed for the railing to support himself (damned reflexes!), of slipping on a patch of ice and crushing her beneath him, of banging her head against doorjambs as he walked into a room, cradling her in his arms. All it took was one fatal mistake! And now he'd made one.

He looked through the rear windshield at his daughter, slumped over asleep. Like a tiny victim strapped into an electric chair, he thought with dismay. How she struggled when he snapped her in, waving her little arms and legs about, as ineffectual as a trapped insect. So helpless, so dependent on him, the way a small animal depends on its owner.

All at once he had a feeling of déjà vu, as if he'd been through this before—or was it only in his dreams? Carelessly locking Susanna in the car. Committing one of those idiotic mistakes that had lurked in his consciousness for the past three months like a viper waiting to strike, was like suddenly remembering he'd forgotten something, some idea, and then desperately trying to recall it, as if his life depended on it, and not being able to do so, unsure if what he was trying to recall was just a random thought or a crucial decision. *This* was crucial, though, no doubt about it. Not to mention negligent and irresponsible, something for which his Daddy license should rightfully be revoked! If only he didn't have so much on his mind! Work, the baby, picking up Zippy, his sister-in-law's frequent despairing calls from Kalamazoo. Rachael's indecision was infectious. Then there was the overwhelming thought of Cecilia Nestorick and her baby, a thought so perilous to think about he evicted it from his mind the moment he caught himself thinking about it. Bridgewater felt his despair creeping over him. Maybe he was being punished. Maybe he was just being tested.

Yes, he was Dad and he had better act like Dad. Mature, responsible, in control. Besides, he was not the kind of guy who broke his hands slugging a wall out of anger or frustration. Resolutely, Bridgewater walked back to Mrs. McCoy's and knocked on her door to use her phone. It was a hassle, but he'd gotten himself into this mess and he would have to get himself out. He'd call the auto club and get them to come open the car door.

Then he remembered that Mrs. McCoy's family did not have a telephone. They had a twenty-five inch color television set, but they did not have a telephone! Where were their priorities? One eye glued to host Bob Eubanks on *The Newlywed Game* when Bridgewater and Zippy interviewed her, Mrs. McCoy had promised to have a telephone within two weeks. Bridgewater had watched as the briefest, most elusive smile turned the thin, bloodless lips on Marlene McCoy's serene, meaty, impassive face when the husband of couple number one said he and his wife had first made whoopee in the backseat of his Mustang. The Bridgewaters were desperate—Zippy was returning to work the next Monday—and reluctantly Bridgewater had agreed; after all, she'd been referred by some social services outfit or other, hadn't she? Bridgewater was skeptical of these organizations he'd never even heard of. Oh, *why* hadn't he trusted his original instincts? He felt his patience crumble and then reminded himself he had to rescue his daughter, and he went to the door. Maybe Marlene would have a suggestion. Just then, Dolly, Mrs. McCoy's six-foot, carrot-haired, thirteen-year-old daughter, came to the door, on her way out.

"Gotta use a phone!" Bridgewater called from the sidewalk. "Where can I get a phone?" He glanced back at the Tercel. "I locked my keys in the car!"

"With the baby inside?" Dolly could hardly believe it. And Bridgewater had worried about *Mrs. McCoy's* competence to care for children, had had doubts about Dolly, too. He felt sheepish.

"Triple-A can get her out. She'll be okay if we can get to her soon. She's asleep. There's no need to worry. We just need to locate a telephone."

"Look! She's cryin'!" Dolly said, aiming a long arm at the car, the limp pointing finger like a fishhook yanking at the flounder that was Bridgewater's conscience.

He rushed over to the car and looked in through the rear window at his daughter's face. The tender flesh had crumpled into pink, wrinkled misery, the lower lip stiff, jutting out, the eyes scrunched up. Such misery! Real tears stained her cheeks. He could hear her rhythmic, honking cry muffled through the steel and glass. What a pair of lungs the kid had! He peered through his peering reflection at Susanna, hunkered over, her little arms waving against the black vinyl straps, her gaping toothless mouth wide open, like a baby bird blindly stretching its neck forward for food. Too tiny to know who was responsible, he thought, too young to understand guilt.

"Susanna, honey, it'll be okay," he said in a soothing, quiet voice. He knew she could not hear him, and he felt all the more ineffectual.

"Mr. Hayes! Hey! Mr. Hayes!" Dolly called. Bridgewater looked around and saw the tall girl hailing a police car. They regularly swarmed the streets of the neighborhood. Dolly evidently knew this policeman. The cruiser idled up to the curb behind a rusty, snotgreen Chevy with a bumpersticker on the back that read:

I BRAKE FOR BEER

A burly police officer looked inquiringly out his window.

"Officer," Bridgewater said, stepping over to the rolled-down window and looking in. "I've locked my baby and my car keys inside my car." He shrugged helplessly, embarrassed, and gestured toward the

Toyota. The cop car's engine stopped, and Hayes climbed out. He looked over at Dolly, who nodded grimly.

"Lucky I came along when I did," Hayes chuckled, with just the trace of a sneer for the bumbling Bridgewater. An Elvis Presley smirk momentarily warped his rubbery lips. He went around to the trunk of his car and removed a long, wire lock opener and then walked over to Bridgewater's car. Susanna was still crying inside, but she seemed to have tired herself out to a whimper.

"Don't you worry, Little-little," Hayes cooed to her. "I'll get you out." He turned to Bridgewater. "Have you got any ID, sir? Can you prove this is your car?"

Bridgewater resented the protective savior attitude, but he knew he had it coming. He knew it was his punishment. He flipped open his wallet, showed his driver's license. "The registration's in the glove compartment."

Hayes fiddled around with the wire a few moments and finally got the door open. They were greeted by Susanna's piercing cry. Her second wind. Bridgewater immediately dove into the rear seat, as much to get away from Dolly's accusing glare and Hayes' smug self-assurance as to calm his daughter. He was gratified by the way Susanna stopped howling as soon as he touched her and cooed at her, reassured by the familiar contact. He left her buckled into her car seat, removed the keys from the ignition, and got the registration from the glove compartment. He showed it to Hayes, but the policeman only gave it a cursory glance.

"Thanks a lot," Bridgewater said. "You have no idea how relieved I am!"

Hayes let out a single sharp bark of laughter before returning to his car. "Oh, I've got some idea."

"Thanks again!" Bridgewater called as Hayes got into the cop car and started the engine. He watched Hayes drive off like the Lone Ranger and then turned to Dolly. She seemed to be concealing a smile. Her amusement further embarrassed Bridgewater. He raised his hand in a lame farewell.

"See you tomorrow," he muttered, and he got into the car. "With luck, we can still make Social Security in time, honeypie," he said to Susanna, glancing at his watch and starting the engine. But he knew it didn't really matter if he were early, late, or right on time.

A Name for Everything

It hardly seemed fair to Peter Bridgewater that he and his family had to leave Baltimore just as the dogwoods were blossoming to go out to his parents-in-law's place in Potawatomi Rapids, in bare, bleak Michigan, still in the grips of winter. Why did they have to leave just as Baltimore was budding with the thousands of sounds and odors that marked the end of winter, so elusive and evanescent, many of them, they did not even have names? Passover. He and Zippy were April Fools indeed, he thought, looking at the calendar. He placed a full dish of dry cat food on the floor for Ozzie before taking the suitcases out to the car. Meant to last three days, the food would surely be devoured by evening. The poor guy didn't know what was going to happen. In the study, now converted to a nursery, Susanna wriggled on the changing table while Zippy changed her diaper.

But it would only be for a weekend, Bridgewater consoled himself, and when they got back the dogwoods would still be in bloom. Bolton Hill and Charles Village would still glow at night under the streetlamps with their ghostly luminescence, and the sweet, cloying odor would still perfume the air.

Besides, the weekend would be busy and would pass quickly, what with the two seders tonight and tomorrow and the baby-naming ceremony on Saturday. They'd come back to Baltimore Sunday in order to go to work on Monday.

Unemployment, medicare, online welfare. The slogan of the marketing strategy at Maryputa where he worked as graphics coordinator slouched across his mind, the eleven syllables sauntering by like a football team leaving the field. Maryputa developed computerized welfare and unemployment disbursement systems. ("Secure and reliable, Maryputa can save state agencies millions of dollars in administrative costs and losses from fraud and mismanagement.") The name of the company was an abbreviation of "Maryland" and "computer," he was told, though it sounded blasphemous to Bridgewater, especially on this holy weekend. But for now, he could put work out of his mind. Unemployment, medicare, online welfare.

At the airport, after they'd left the Toyota in satellite parking, took the shuttle bus to the terminal, passed through the metal detectors and gotten their seat assignments, carrying luggage and the baby, Bridgewater realized that they would be first to board the aircraft. People with small children and those needing assistance came first! One less hassle. A small stroke of good fortune. Once they were on the plane with their luggage stored overhead, Zippy whipped out a tit for Susanna to suckle when they left the ground, tricking her into swallowing so her ears wouldn't hurt when they took off.

During the flight, Bridgewater read the newspaper. The Contras and the Sandinistas were trying to come to an agreement. In Panama, Noriega was refusing to leave office. Palestinians and Israelis were fighting on the West Bank and Gaza. Jesse Jackson was doing well in the Democratic caucuses in Michigan. Zippy's parents would take this as a personal threat.

The item that caught Bridgewater's attention, however, was a story on the extent of damage caused by the cicadas last summer. It was just now becoming apparent as Spring commenced. Nurseries, orchards, even suburbanites with backyards were calling state and county government horticultural officials with reports of damage to fruit trees, shrubs and hardwoods. Small trees, like young oaks and maples, rhododendrons, dogwoods, cherry, apple, peach and plum trees had all suffered from the cicadas' onslaught. The cicadas made slits in the bark on the underside of twigs and branches, and the female cicadas laid eggs there by the hundreds. Larger trees were able to survive. For them it was more like a natural pruning process, and you could even say the cicadas spurred more vigorous growth in these trees, but the smaller ones struggled to survive. They were deformed. One nursery reported losing ninety-five percent of its northern red oaks, saplings that the state of Maryland planted along its highways.

In Detroit, changing planes for Grand Rapids, their airport luck did not hold out. They had to walk down endless corridors to get to the commuter flight in a distant terminal, lugging unwieldy bags and a baby. They arrived at the check-in desk, sweaty and grumpy, and got their seat assignments.

"Have a Happy Easter!" the airline employee bubbled, "but I guess the little one's still too young for chocolate bunnies."

"You, too," Zippy said automatically.

"Today's Good Friday, isn't it?" Bridgewater said.

At last they made it to Grand Rapids, and there was Rachael to meet them, diminutive, dark-eyed, bright-faced Rachael with her short dark hair curling around her face and neck in a new perm. Big tits bubbling into her white cashmere sweater. She was waiting in the lounge with Docina Brown, a tall, lean, muscular man with a warm toothy smile and smooth, taut cheeks of a light cocoa color, the planes of which slanted down a long, lupine jaw to a sharp jutting chin. There were acne scars on his forehead, but nobody would deny that he was a handsome man. The urge to paint, always growing dimmer in Bridgewater, especially since he'd become a father, jabbed into his consciousness with a faint glowing urgency that soon died. *The Doomed Couple*. Some sort of racist symbolism in the background. A lynching? A burning cross? A swastika? Or was that too heavy-handed, too much of a message piece?

Dody stood and extended his hand to Bridgewater, and Zippy had to stand up on her tiptoes to kiss him. Though a tall man, he'd been too short and a step too slow to make the Illini basketball team. The public intimacy of Zippy's kiss seemed to embarrass him, and seeing that bald *human* reaction, Bridgewater had to wonder at his parents-in-law's fear of the man. This was the first time Bridgewater had met him.

Rachael fussed over her niece, whom she had never seen before, and she and Zippy huddled together and talked about the baby and about their parents.

"Your team do okay this year?" Bridgewater asked Dody.

He made a face. "We got eliminated in the regionals by a team from Battle Creek. We a better team than they was, too."

"Battle Creek had a good game?"

"They shot seveny percent fum na field, niney percent fum na line."

"Wow. Sounds like what Villanova did to Georgetown a few years ago."

They talked about the NCAA finals. Dody liked the looks of Arizona. Then the women included them in their conversation.

"Wouldn't you like to have one of these, Dody?" Rachael asked, hugging Susanna. The question embarrassed him, but everybody was looking at the baby, and nobody noticed.

"She cute, ain't she?" Dody stuck a finger out to Susanna, who grabbed it with her whole hand and looked at him with huge blank blue eyes. Dody had big hands, Bridgewater noticed, but still not large enough to handle a basketball as dexterously as the pros.

"Ain't she cute?" he said to Susanna. "Huh? Ain't you cute now? Where'd you get them eyes, anyway? Huh? Where'd you get them eyes at?" Dody looked up at Bridgewater.

"She's got my eyes, but they may change to brown. You can see gold shafts in them sometimes, like marbles."

"They pretty."

"Mom and Dad really wish they'd turn brown," Zippy said. "Our genes. You can tell the blue eyes disappoint them."

"If we had a baby, its eyes would be brown," Rachael said to Dody.

"So would his skin." He tried to joke, but his voice was too heavy with irony. He was well aware of the Feldmans' opposition to him and the emotional conflict this caused for Rachael.

Bridgewater and Zippy collected their belongings and went out to the parking lot. Bridgewater shook hands again with Dody, and then Dody and Rachael embraced. Dody got into his car, and everybody else piled into Rachael's. The separation had a special poignance for them all. Bridgewater felt depressed. Rachael was sniffling, fighting back the tears.

"Have a good weekend," Dody said, smiling.

"Happy Easter," Bridgewater said.

"Oh yeah, that's this weekend, too," Zippy said, reminded again.

"Dody drove up from Kalamazoo with me just to meet you," Rachael said. "Wasn't that sweet of him? He's such a doll."

"Today's Good Friday," Bridgewater said.

In Potawatomi Rapids the trees were all bare. No flowers had blossomed yet, not even early crocuses. Though not a gardener himself, Bridgewater was pleased by the sight of trumpeting yellow daffodils in the garden in front of their apartment. The landlord's wife had planted them. Traces of snow veined and pockmarked the ground in Potawatomi Rapids; in dark shadowed ditches and under bushes where the sun never shone the dirty snow smiled its bum's crazy grin. Another late season snowstorm was always a possibility this far north.

They drove through the town to get to Moishe's and Edith's. There was one movie theater in Potawatomi Rapids, on the main commercial drag, Superior Street. The Bijou. Black letters on the protruding triangular art deco marquee advertised:

G O D
M O R N I N G,
V I E T N A M

"Maybe they only had two O's," Bridgewater said as they drove past in the car they'd rented in Grand Rapids.

"Some juvenile delinquent probably stole the other one."

"Maybe they're just illiterate."

"But everybody knows what G-O-D spells," Zippy said.

"Trouble." Mentally, Bridgewater reviewed the current movies in Baltimore. Not that he and Zippy went to the movies once the baby was born, but he liked to keep abreast of the titles. *Police Academy 5, Johnny Be Good, Biloxi Blues, Beetlejuice, D.O.A., Vice Versa, Masquerade.* A bunch of forgettable crap. *Bright Lights, Big City* was just opening in Baltimore that day. Good novel but all the movie reviews were negative. At the Little X porn theater they were showing *L'Amour, New Wave Hookers*, and *Surrender to Paradise*.

"It's an even bet whether Dolly McCoy knows how to spell 'good' or 'God'," Bridgewater said.

"Dolly McCoy?"

"Our babysitter's daughter. She never goes to school. She may not even know how to spell her own name."

"You're coming to the baby-naming tomorrow, aren't you, Rach?" Zippy asked.

"Mom wants to go to the shul this evening, too."

"Well, we ought to meet the rabbi, I suppose," Zippy said, resigned. "I'm glad she arranged this. The way she carried on about the names Shlomo and Sophie last Thanksgiving, I'm surprised she forgave us."

"So I heard. That even made *my* knees shake. What's Susanna's Hebrew name, anyway?"

"Shoshonah. Shoshonah Golda."

"That's pretty."

"Susanna's kind of like our hostage," Bridgewater observed. "If Edith wants to see the baby she'll cooperate. We have her under our thumb."

"Don't count on it."

Outside of town they passed farmhouses and fields, empty and muddy now, though in another month the grass would be tall. They passed a single brown-and-white mottled cow standing in the mouth of a barn. Its huge brown eyes looked forlornly out at the bare mud. I know how you feel! They passed Detweiler's, the general store. Paunchy, gray-haired Ernie Detweiler was filling a final car with gas. No self-service pumps for Ernie.

"So what about you and Dody?" Bridgewater asked.

Rachael, driving, bit her lip, and her eyes filmed over. She had to blink to clear them. Zippy sat in the back, nursing the baby.

"We've been talking about getting a house," Rachael said. "We've also decided to see other people. Maybe. For a while."

"Oh yeah?" Bridgewater waited for her to go on, but she didn't say anything more, and he thought it tactful not to pursue the conversation. He told her about his new job. Then the lake came into view. They were almost there.

Bridgewater looked out the car at the ribbed sky over the lake. Patches of light came through the wickerwork of clouds. Jacob's Ladder. A mixed blessing, like a stolen birthright. Would it rain? Snow? Would the clouds blow away? The red, sun-laned water was calm; the reddening sun hung on the horizon, visible through a break in the clouds; it branded the lake with an orange stripe. A postcard image. Visit Peaceful Potawatomi Rapids. At night, the glittering moonlanes were spectacular. Silver and yellow and blue on the sparkling lake. Greetings from Beautiful Potawatomi Rapids.

The picture postcard scenes of Potawatomi Rapids were vivid in Bridgewater's mind, but then, nothing was as vivid as the *word,* "vivid," its two needlepoint v's digging sharply into the mind, carving, whittling, etching a picture of itself in ever-changing detail: the individual scales of a fish he once caught with his brother Mark (Bridgewater disliked fishing, and with a sort of fascinated horror, the appearance of the 15-inch trout stuck in his mind, the gaping livid mouth, the dead eyes, the sharp, silvery, translucent fins); the distinctive odor of his first-grade classroom; the feel of construction paper in grade school as he rubbed his tender child's hands across the rough surface; the sound of his mother's voice, dead now all these years; many, many fugitive detailed images had been vividly gouged into his memory, tattooed with the needles of the senses.

They turned off the pavement down a gravel road. At the corner, a long row of tin mailboxes stood on wooden poles, some with red flags raised. They turned abruptly down a rutted drive with a mane of dead weeds flattened on the hump and bounced down to the Feldmans' lakeside home. The bumpy ride delighted the baby.

Moishe and Edith were both in the kitchen when they carried their belongings into the house. Edith had two separate kitchens, one reserved only for Pesach. Both were equipped with stove, refrigerator, two sinks and several surfaces to keep fleishiche, milcheche and parvah foods separate. (Bridgewater loved that word, "fleishiche," to signify meat because it sounded so much like "flesh" and gave him pause about what he was actually eating when he ate meat. "Milcheche" signified dairy products, which were always kept separate from meat, but he could never understand why fish was classified as milcheche; of course, the parvah foods, the grains and vegetables, could be mixed with anything, the eternally neutral Switzerland of foodstuffs.) Bridgewater could not decide if his mother-in-law was simply conscientious or a fanatic; there must be a name for a category in between, but Bridgewater did not know it. Certainly both Moishe and Edith were zealous Zionists, but there was something admirable in the punctiliousness of Edith's observance of the laws of kashruth. Her kitchen religion, Bridgewater sometimes thought derisively.

"Where's my baby?" Edith cried, a shrill bird swooping into the foyer to greet them. "Ketzulah!" she cried, grabbing the baby from her daughter. Yiddish for 'little kitten.' That made Zippy the mother cat, Bridgewater thought, smiling.

Cooing and warbling over her prize, she led them into the kitchen where Moishe was tending to the evening feast. He kissed his daughter and granddaughter and shook Bridgewater's hand.

"We'd better get going," he said, nodding toward the clock. Actually, there were three clocks in the Feldmans' kitchen, all with different times, a few minutes apart. One said 5:21, and the others said 5:15 and 5:27. The white electric one was the one Edith used to determine when to light the Shabbos candles.

"It's already twenty past. Services are at six."

Bridgewater looked at Edith's Tzivos Hashem calendar hanging from a nail by the door. It said candles must be lit at 6:02 this first night of Passover. Of course, Michigan was at the far western end of the eastern time zone, and the sun would still be red on the horizon at six o'clock, a drop of blood staining the sky. The Tzivos Hashem calendar also said you were allowed to eat chometz only until 9:48 that morning. Bridgewater had had a turkey sandwich on rye at noon and some chips from a bag Dody had at the Grand Rapids airport. Tzivos Hashem. Army of God. Sounded like the Hezbollah. But while that was an Iranian-backed Shi'ite militia in Lebanon, Tzivos Hashem was an organization for Jewish children. Still, it sounded a little frightening to Bridgewater. Army of God. Like brainwashing. Bridgewater wondered whether Edith would unilaterally sign Susanna up for summer Hebrew camp in a few years. She'd pass it off as a gift.

"Yes, we'd better go," Edith agreed. "It'll be a short service. The rabbi will let everybody go home to prepare for the seder. We'll light candles when we get home. Come on, Ketzulah. Let's go meet the rabbi."

Temple Beth Chaim was a quaint little synagogue tucked away on a residential back street in Potawatomi Rapids. Formerly a Methodist Church, it had been converted to a synagogue in the 1960's. Bridgewater and Zippy had been married in Muskegon, even though this shul had been available at the time. Edith had not gotten along with the rabbi who was leading the congregation then, five years earlier. But she liked the current one. Rabbi Joshua Marx was a solemn man in his late forties, Bridgewater guessed, with a long salt and pepper beard and forelocks in the Orthodox style and thick hornrim glasses that he wore at an angle as if for reading. He had the fatherly smile of a spiritual leader and a firm, dry handshake.

"Pinchas and Zipporah, I've been anxious to meet you," he said calling Bridgewater by his chosen Hebrew name. "Shoshonah's Bubbe has told me so much about you."

"What's Mom said? Anything good?"

The rabbi laughed at Zippy's remark. He pinched the baby's cheek.

There were eight men present, and they were only able to field a minyan by counting Edith and Zippy. Edith silently objected. but what could she do? She liked the rabbi, and she knew he felt the same way she did; he was only giving in to the necessities of the situation to include women in the minyan. The others were all bent, feeble-looking old men with wrinkles. They wished the Feldmans a "Good yom tov" and "Good Shabbos" as they entered the sanctuary.

The congregation chanted the evening prayers, and Rabbi Marx made a few observations on the theme of liberation that was central to Pesach, its relevance today, the identification Jews still feel with the ancient Hebrews who escaped bondage in Egypt. Consulting a notebook, the rabbi discussed upcoming events, noting the Bridgewaters' baby-naming the next day, and then, wishing everybody a good yom tov, he ended the service. Edith lingered behind to finalize some details about the kiddush that would follow the baby-naming ceremony the next day.

They drove home by way of Superior Street, and Bridgewater noted that the extra O had been put back into GOOD MORNING, VIETNAM on the Bijou marquee.

Back at the Feldmans' they lit Shabbos candles and then made final preparations for the seder. The turkey, their "pascal lamb" for the evening, had already been baked and basted and was warming in the oven. Bridgewater set the table while Edith combined apples, nuts, wine and cinnamon to make the charoseth. The sisters, who had dressed hastily for the synagogue service, spent more time preparing themselves for the festive occasion, dressing and putting on makeup. Finally, Moishe prepared the seder plate, a cushion was placed on his chair, as was the custom, and the seder began.

Everybody had a Haggadah, and they took turns around the table reading passages, the re-enactment of the exodus from Egypt, the ten plagues, the parting of the Red Sea and so forth. As the youngest present, barring Susanna, who was asleep in the living room in a makeshift crib, Rachael asked the four questions (the *fier kashes*, as Edith called them), chanting the Hebrew words to the familiar tune. "*Mah nishtanah*. . . ." ("Why is tonight different from all other nights?") They read about the four sons—the wise one, the obstinate one, the slow one, and the one incapable of understanding—and their orientation to Pesach; how they are each dealt with in turn to enlighten them about the significance of Passover. The components of the seder plate were named—the matzoh, the mahror, the karpas, the shankbone, the egg and the charoseth—and their significance explained. They read about the ten plagues and the talmudic extrapolation of their meaning by Rabbi Akiba, Ben Zoma, et al. They sang "Dayenu" and recited the gifts of God to His people.

When they reached the part about somebody rising up in every generation to strike down the Jews, Edith sounded off. They'd already had the first cup of wine, and she was feeling festive anyway, free to speak her mind. The Germans, the PLO, Jordan and all the Arabs got a piece of it.

Edith referred to the West Bank territories by their Biblical names, Judea and Samaria. As far as she was concerned, this land was given to the Jews by God, part of the Covenant, the very borders named in Numbers. What to do with the Palestinians who were already there?

"Let the Arabs take them! They're theirs, not ours! If they won't take them, then put them on a ship and send them out into the Mediterranean!"

To Bridgewater, this sounded like the Chicago cabdriver who'd taken him from O'Hare to the Loop ten years back who, commenting on racial problems, said, "They oughta take all the niggers and ship 'em back to Africa!"

"You sound like Kahane," he said, aiming for levity in his abashment, trying to jolly her out of her combativeness. He did not want to argue with her because she felt so strongly about Israel and he could never change her mind anyway. Besides, she might make life hell for him while he was here at her house.

"It's the Arab strategy to leave the Palestinians there in Israel," Moishe said, agreeing with his wife and ignoring Bridgewater. "Like a festering wound. They won't go away." The prospect of confrontation put a sinister bloom on Moishe's manner; like a flower unfolding he seemed to expand, and color entered his cheeks, putting a glowing, waxy, tannish-pink complexion into his weather-worn cheeks; it highlighted the Oriental slant of his eyes. He was a powerful, stocky man whose rippling dark hair had flattened and thinned over the years so that it resembled a frayed yarmulke now on the crown of his skull, with fringes sticking out, spider-like, to the edges of his skull. His eyes, slits now, darted about the room.

"It's the press who's responsible for all this meshugas," Edith said. "Stick a camera in the direction of one of those Arabs and he starts throwing rocks."

"They call it the 'Israeli-occupied West Bank,' as if we didn't win it fair and square from Jordan when the Arabs attacked us in 1967, the bastards."

"Took it *back* from Jordan in 1967! The Arabs stole Judea and Samaria in 1948, even though it was ours by rights!"

"That's right! The League of Nations mandated a Jewish National Home in 1922! Everything *west* of the Jordan! But Transjordan took it from us in 1948, and we took it back in 1967, and now everybody says we have to give it to the Palestinians, and I say NO!" Moishe pounded the table with his fist, and wine spilled from the cups. Just the tiniest bit alarmed, Bridgewater wondered what they were commemorating at the Passover seder, the Escape from Egypt or the Six-Day War.

"We gave Sinai back to Egypt after we won that. Now the Arabs want more. They won't be satisfied until they've wiped us out."

"And the media goes right along with them."

"Too bad they didn't do the same thing to Hitler, hound him the same way. Then maybe six million wouldn't have died."

"They make Israel out to be some kind of Hitler now. The press!"

"And yet it's the PLO who pass out leaflets that say things like, 'Jewish Blood Is Fair Game' and 'Go Back to Germany.' Oy vey!"

"Just wait till Jesse Jackson gets elected," Moishe said with exaggerated dismay at the improbable event.

"Oy vey!" Edith cried. "He'll have Arafat here as an honored guest of state!"

"And Louis Farrakhan will be his Secretary of State! Then we'll have Nazi Germany all over again, right here in the United States!"

"Intermarriage will be Hitler's final victory," Edith said quietly. "That's how the Jews will be wiped out, through assimilation." She avoided looking at Bridgewater, speaking to a point on the wall above Moishe's head. They'd always been a little dubious about his conversion, suspicious about people just "becoming" Jewish. On the other hand, he wasn't exactly a gentile now, either. They couldn't quite find the right word for the situation and felt a little uncomfortable about it, skeptical about the moral alchemy conversion implied, especially as it had been a Conservative conversion, not recognized as valid in Israel.

"How's Sandy doing, Mom?" Zippy asked.

"She's depressed! She calls her mother from Los Angeles and says she's depressed. She says she's thinking about committing suicide, God forbid. But when Brenda offers to come out, she says no, her therapist is against it!"

"Does Uncle Sid know anything about this?"

"Sid! Who knows what Sid knows!" Moishe exclaimed. Sid was still living in Tel Aviv under an assumed name. Though the authorities assumed he was dead, he was still wanted in New Jersey for extortion and embezzlement.

"This is God's judgement and punishment," Edith said, referring to Sandy's depression. "The fourth commandment says thou shalt honor thy father and thy mother. It does not say thou shalt honor thy therapist." Some comfort Brenda would provide her daughter, Bridgewater thought, if she were anything like Edith. All a bunch of "I told you so's". This had been the therapist's thinking, too, because of the history of Sandy's parents' relationship with Brad, whom they scorned.

"She's not even getting any alimony!" Moishe said.

"Brad Reynolds is getting off scot free!" Edith cried, indignant at the idea. "Oh, I wish I could get my hands on that dirt! That filth! Bastard! I'd tear his eyes out!"

"Sid ought to be here," Moishe said.

"I could kill him! I could just——oh, that *dirt*! That *filth*! That *bastard*!" Edith said, her eyes pokers of fire stabbing at Rachael. She did not have to mention Docina Brown. Her message was unmistakable: Marry him and we disown you. Marry him, and the goy will doublecross you, leave you in the lurch, and we will have warned you. But we *won't* forgive you!

Tormented by prescience, Zippy bowed her head, refusing to look at her sister or mother. In private, to her husband, Zippy had claimed to foresee a time when Rachael and her parents would no longer speak to each other.

"Well, let's get back to the ten plagues," Moishe said, and Edith started to laugh hysterically.

"Yes! At least those won't be so traumatic!"

After the second cup of wine they laid aside their Haggadot and had dinner. To avoid any controversial topics, Bridgewater asked Moishe who he thought would win the American League pennant this year. The season opened on Monday.

"The Yankees. The Yankees and the Mets. It'll be a subway series."

"Not the Tigers?"

"The Tigers," Moishe said pityingly. "If they'd treated Gibson more fairly he wouldn't have gone to the Dodgers. They're okay, the Tigers, but they'll fade after the All Star Break. Evans is going to be forty-one in May. Tanana's getting long in the tooth. We've still got Witaker and Trammel, but two players don't make a team. Look at the Orioles in '84 when only Murray and Ripken were hitting."

"Who're they playing first? The Tigers."

"The Red Sox. In Fenway. The Tigers'll start Morris and the Red Sox'll go with Clemens, the two-time Cy Young Award-winner." Bridgewater marveled at the way Moishe knew all the names. "Geez, I wonder how they'll do this year without Gibson. He really filled the gap after Kaline retired."

"The Red Sox might win it," Bridgewater offered. "I've heard they've got the best pitching staff in baseball."

"Who said that? Somebody who don't know shit from shinola, if you'll pardon the expression. They've got Clemens and Hurst, and they got this reliever, Lee Smith, from the Cubs, but after that they fall apart. Oil Can Boyd's okay sometimes, when he doesn't go off his nut and start attacking his teammates, but they haven't got anybody after that. The Mets have the best pitching staff in the majors."

"What do you think of the Orioles?"

"They sure finished lousy last year. I don't see them doing much better this year, either. They've still got the same old team. I'm surprised they still keep McGregor around. I would have sent him to the knackers a couple years ago."

"They've had a mediocre spring, but you never can tell."

"Well, they better do something if Baltimore doesn't want to lose another team. They haven't come to any agreement with the owner about that new stadium yet, have they? Edward Bennett Williams. After the governor ramrodded the stadium idea through the legislature."

"They will before summer. Schaefer's still pushing it hard. He got it through the legislature and he got around a referendum that would have killed it, too. He'll get the signed agreement. You watch."

"Better hope so. Otherwise, the Orioles will leave town like the Colts and the Bullets did."

"You may be right."

"Say, is Johnny Unitas still around Baltimore? What's he do these days?"

"He's got a private detective agency, and he owns a Chinese restaurant in Towson."

"No fooling? A Chinese restaurant? Why not Greek?"

Bridgewater shrugged. "The Golden Arm it's called. It's in a shopping center on York Road." He turned to his food again.

The meal had begun with a boiled egg dipped in salt water, symbolizing the fertility theme of the Spring festival, and then they had matzoh, horseradish, charoseth, gefilte fish, and borscht. Turkey, dressing, potatoes, asparagus followed. Shulhan Arukh—the well-spread table. After dinner there was fruit, macaroons and tea.

"I wonder what gives Earl Grey this scent," Zippy said, sipping her tea. "It's like anise or licorice."

"The name of the scent, you mean? It's bergamot," Bridgewater said.

"Bergamot?"

"A small, sour, pear-shaped citrus fruit. The rind yields the scented oil."

"Sounds French. Bergamot."

"The word comes from the Turkish, *beg-armudi*, meaning 'prince's pear.'"

"How do you know all this, Pinchas?" Edith asked.

Bridgewater shrugged. "I looked it up once." In truth, he had once gone through a fascination with the names of teas. Earl Grey, Constant Comment, Lemon Lift, Cinnamon Stick, Red Zinger, Plantation Mint. Currently he was fascinated by the names of cat foods. Western Menu, Fisherman's Stew, Choice Cuts 'n Cheese, Ranch Supper. No doubt he would soon discover the names of baby products, once Susanna began eating solid foods. Already the names of disposable diapers were familiar to him. Pampers, Luv's, Huggies, Snuggles. But truly, when it came to names he was stumped about what to call his parents-in-law. Mom? Dad? No, sounded too cozy. Mr. and Mrs. Feldman? Nah, too formal. Edith and Moishe would have to do.

After the meal they said grace and had the third cup of wine. Sated and sleepy, they all picked up their haggadot. A cup had also been poured for Elijah. Edith asked Bridgewater to open the door for Elijah, which he did, and they recited the passages from the Psalms and from the Lamentations. Then Bridgewater closed the door and took his seat again. Twenty minutes into the post-prandial reading, the baby woke up in the living room and began to cry. Zippy excused herself to nurse the child, and the rest of the seder went fairly quickly. They had the fourth cup of wine, and at the conclusion of the seder, Moishe declared, "L'shanah habaah b'Yerushalayim!" Next year in Jerusalem, the traditional optimistic conclusion.

Afterward, Moishe, Edith, Rachael and Bridgewater sang a few traditional songs—"Adir Hu," "Had Gadya," and "Ehad Mi Yodea"—but since it was getting late and they had to go to the shul at nine the next morning, they did not continue the seder much longer. Besides, there would be another one the next night.

When he came downstairs the next morning, Bridgewater saw Edith sitting alone by a window in the living room; she looked old. Bathed in the dazzling white end-of-winter windowlight coming in from the east, she looked grayer and more wrinkled than he'd remembered. He felt compassion well up in his throat. The stubborn old shit, he thought fondly. He had slept quite soundly. He was used to being awakened much earlier by the insistent Ozzie, who demanded his Purina Cat Chow at the crack of dawn. He wondered if Ozzie had eaten all his food yet.

"Good morning!"

Startled by her son-in-law, Edith reached down for her knitting and concentrated on the action of the needles while she spoke. "Are Zippy and Ketzulah awake yet?"

"Zippy's changing her diaper now. Are Moishe and Rachael coming? We'd better go in two cars."

"Your father-in-law is out at the bathroom. I'll go call Rachael." The Feldmans' toilet facilities were not connected to the house, due to the mysteries of the septic tank and the water pressure.

"You look nice," Bridgewater said, as much to banish the thought of old age as to compliment his mother-in-law on her appearance. She wore a brown knit dress and a scarf tied loosely around the throat, and she had put on gold earrings and makeup.

"Thank you, dear," Edith said, moving off to call Rachael. These unexpected encounters with her son-in-law always made her feel uncomfortable, and she cut them short.

"Rachael!" she called. "Rachael! Are you still sleeping? Gevalt! You must get up, Rachael! Hurry! We have to be at the shul at nine!"

When they arrived at Temple Beth Chaim, Moishe and Bridgewater put on prayer shawls that they got from a cabinet outside the sanctuary. Bridgewater had brought his own yarmulke with him. Moishe used one of the synagogue's black nylon ones.

Inside the sanctuary there were already about a dozen people. The old people again. More came later after the morning prayers, drifting in in small groups, in time for the Torah reading. It was during the Torah reading that the baby-naming would take place. Several additional groups arrived before the morning service began. Counting the seven bar and bat mitzvah students there were about thirty people present. The young Jewish boys and girls struck an affectionate cord in Bridgewater. They were dressed in corduroys and khakis, wearing docksiders and tennis shoes. They assisted Rabbi Marx with removing and replacing the Torah scrolls from the Ark during the service and paraded around the congregation with him when the people touched their prayer books to the scrolls and then to their lips. During the prayers, Bridgewater noticed, some of the men bent and swayed, but the davaning was not as fervent as that of the young Chassids he'd seen in Baltimore. Beth Chaim was a Conservative congregation. He felt right at home, if that was the name for it.

During the prayers, an usher came around and gave Bridgewater a card that said CHAMISHI on it, the Fifth Aliyah. That was when the

Bridgewaters would take Susanna up for the baby-naming. There were seven aliyot during the Torah reading, when some member of the congregation would go up to the *bima* and recite the blessings for the Torah reading. The name of his aliyah made Bridgewater think of Japanese food.

When their turn came, they went up to the *bima*. Zippy also wore a shawl and a yarmulke. She carried Susanna, who blinked patiently in her arms. Edith refused to go up to the *bima* because she did not think women ought to do so; it was not the Orthodox custom. Moishe stayed behind to keep her and Rachael company.

At the direction of the gabbai, the rabbi's assistant, who was one of the older guys in the congregation, at the *bima*, Bridgewater touched the word that began the verse from *Exodus* with the tassels of his tallit, touched the tassels to his lips, and chanted the blessing, which started out as a call to prayer:

"Barchoo et adonia hamvorach."

"Baruch adonai hamvorach l'olam va'ed!" the congregation sang back the start of the blessing over the reading.

Confident, having rehearsed his lines for the past two weeks, Bridgewater continued in fluent Hebrew, *"Baruch adonai hamvorach l'olam va'ed. Baruch ata adonai elohenu melech ha'olam, a-sher ba'char ba-nu mi-kol ha-amim, v'na-tan la-nu et torahto. Baruch ata adonai no-tein hatorah."*

Then Rabbi Marx recited the Torah portion in Hebrew, and again Bridgewater did the bit with the tallit fringes and recited the Torah blessing to close the reading of the passage. He felt he deserved applause for his flawless performance, and afterward Moishe did say he recited splendidly, a little surprised and a little proud of his son-in-law and, Bridgewater suspected, a little relieved not to have been embarrassed.

After the Torah blessing, Rabbi Marx blessed the baby and said her Hebrew name, Shoshonah Golda. Later, he presented them with a certificate as a record that Susanna Geraldine Bridgewater (Geraldine was Bridgewater's mother's name), born on the 29th of Kislev in the year 5748, was given the Hebrew name Shoshonah Golda in the course of religious services at Temple Beth Chaim in the city of Potawatomi Rapids, Michigan, "AND HAS BECOME AN HONORED MEMBER OF THE FAITH OF ISRAEL." Rabbi Marx signed and dated the document, the 14th of Nisan, the first day of Passover. To "The

Midnight Ride of Paul Revere," Bridgewater improvised some verses in his head.

> Twas the twenty-ninth of Kislev in '48
> Hardly a person has felt so great
> As on that day the ecstatic father
> Of the beautiful newborn Susanna Bridgewater

He felt a moment of deep sorrow when the recurrent nagging question about Cecilia Nestorick's child came rushing back into his head, unwanted. *What if the child was mine? Would I be naming her now? Would she even be Jewish? Not genetically, for sure. Whatever that means. Besides, Jewishness is determined by matrilineal descent, and Cecilia wasn't Jewish. Then again, couldn't the baby convert, or be converted?* A whole series of questions flooded over him, but he was able to shove the door shut on them by concentrating on the service.

The sixth aliyah was read by a couple celebrating their fiftieth wedding anniversary, and then one of the bar mitzvah students read the haftorah. The concluding prayers were recited and the Kaddish for the dead. A prayer for the dew reminded Bridgewater that Passover was a fertility festival. Dew for the crops.

After the shabbos service concluded, they went down to the recreation room where Edith had set up the kiddush. She'd brought some Manishewitz concord grape wine and kosher cookies and macaroons. Bridgewater spoke with a young fellow named Mark Katz, a medical student at the University of Michigan who was visiting his grandparents for the holiday.

"I applied to Johns Hopkins," Mark said, when Bridgewater told him they were from Baltimore. "They accepted my application, and I got accepted at Michigan, too, which was where I wanted to go, but I went out to Maryland for an interview anyway.

"Man, the neighborhood looked—I don't know—threatening." He shrugged almost apologetically. He was a slim dark man with a boyish elfin beard growing in wisps on his whittled chin.

"Charles Village? Or do you mean by the hospital? East Baltimore?"

"Charles Village? Is that what it's called?"

"That's where the main campus is, the Homewood campus. The neighborhoods in Baltimore change pretty rapidly, though. One block may be a slum with abandoned buildings and boarded up windows, and the next block will be yuppies. How do you like Ann Arbor? My uncle lives near there. He got his doctorate in chemistry from Michigan."

"I like it fine."

When the kiddush was over, the Bridgewaters and Feldmans went outside, in front of the synagogue. Bridgewater had brought his Olympus 35-millimeter camera to take commemorative photographs. He took about half a dozen of Moishe and Edith and Rachael and Zippy, with one or the other of them holding the baby, the shul's symbolic menorah visible on the wall in the background. Bridgewater loved taking photographs of the Feldmans. They always looked so well together in photographs, so happy and supportive, like a cohesive unit, a four-ply family. Any stranger picking up a photograph could tell instantly that they were parents with their offspring. Then Bridgewater gave the camera to Moishe so that he could get into the pictures, too.

"Okay, so how do I make sure I've got it in focus and there's enough light?"

Bridgewater showed his father-in-law how to operate the camera.

"And what's this for?"

"That's the ASA film speed dial. It tells you the speed of the film."

"And this?"

"That's the aperture ring. The higher the f-stop, the narrower the aperture."

"And what's this called?"

"That's the shutter-speed ring."

"What's the name of this little lever here?"

"That's the exposure meter switch."

"This thing is called what?"

"Hurry up, please!" Zippy called. "Susanna's not going to be patient forever!"

"Just a second! It's called what?"

"That's the hot shoe. But you only need it for a flash attachment, which we aren't using."

Moishe laughed. "Hot shoe," he said, shaking his head. He was still wearing the black synthetic yarmulke, and in the sunlight the fabric shone with a halo of light. "Geez, there's a name for everything, isn't there?"

Person of the Week

Driving back down the Jones Falls Expressway to Baltimore from his job in Hunt Valley, Bridgewater reviewed the circumstances that had led to his present dilemma. He faced the unenviable task of dismissing Marlene McCoy, the day-care provider he'd been leaving his infant daughter Susanna with the past five weeks while he and Zippy went to work.

Every day, Monday through Friday, Zippy got up at 5:00 a.m. to nurse the baby. After putting the sated child back in her crib, she bathed, dressed, and went to work. Then at 6:15, having dressed and eaten breakfast himself, Bridgewater would get the baby up, change her diaper, wash her face, pack up the car and go to the McCoys' Remington home, where he left the child, though not without serious misgivings.

Marlene McCoy's home was a dreary hovel. The living room was dominated at one end by a monolithic steel-gray kerosene space heater and at the other by an enormous imitation-walnut color television set. After knocking for several minutes, Marlene's thirteen-year old daughter, Dolly, would open the door, yawning and rubbing the sleep out of her eyes. A blast of stale heat from the space heater washed over him, and already Bridgewater could feel the faint film of the fuel's fumes clinging to his face like a mist of cobwebs. A tattered sofa partially blocked the only window, and a shabby gray rayon curtain with a pattern of purple cup-shaped anemones concealed the remaining pane of glass. A bare, fly-specked overhead bulb lit the room, a vaporous dim yellow light. Dirt and water-streaked salmon wallpaper with a white, heraldic fleur-de-lis pattern covered the walls. It was hard to make out the wallpaper pattern in the dim, eerie, overhead light. When he stepped into the house, Bridgewater always broke into a sweat, and the baby began to whimper. No, this was not a good place to leave his daughter. He would have to make other arrangements, he always told himself, but then he'd procrastinate. After all, they weren't cruel to Susanna. They really did seem to care.

"Sorry to get you up so early," Bridgewater would say to Dolly, to be polite, even though he was annoyed to always have to wake her out of bed.

Gracious Dolly waved his apology aside with the hand that had been covering her yawn. Eyes slit like a cat's, she plucked the teardrops from the corner of her eyes. Then she stretched leisurely, showing a big patch of smooth white belly as her tee-shirt pulled away from her flesh with a great back-leaning yawn. She revealed a good six inches down below the bellybutton, to where the fine reddish-blond hairs started to curl and the edge of her frayed cotton bottoms began, hanging loose, held by the limpest of elastic bands. Was this innocence or provocation? Bridgewater could not decide. Dolly had a nymphet's flirtatious languor, a lazy beckoning in her pale green eyes—coy, bold, saucy, taunting, as if daring him to make a move, to take a chance with her.

Occasionally, on warm spring afternoons when he had come to pick up his daughter, Bridgewater had found Dolly and Marlene together on the front porch. He was always astounded by Dolly's sexual precocity. At thirteen she was no babe in the woods. Her older sister Raquel already had a baby at sixteen.

Dolly reminded Bridgewater of Cecilia Nestorick. Both were tall redheads with fair skin. While Cecilia had not been the amazon that, at six feet and still growing, Dolly was, she nevertheless had given the impression of great female height. Bridgewater wondered if it were the mental association he made between Dolly and Cecilia that tainted her with the stain of illicit behavior. Maybe Dolly was just an innocent kid, unaware of her sexuality. Yeah, right. An innocent thirteen-year-old kid who never went to school and smoked cigarettes in front of her mother?

Bridgewater felt a sneaky feeling of relief when he thought of Cecilia. He had gotten away Scot-free! But then he cautioned himself not to be over-confident. He frightened himself with the thought that one day a policeman would knock at the door and haul him away to the station, drag him into an ugly scandal. A Kafkaesque vision of being tossed into a cell and forgotten. But there was nothing that could link him to Cecilia that he could remember. No letters, no notes, no photographs. As far as the world was concerned, it was as if they had never known each other. Only impressions in gray matter. This thought, too, made Bridgewater feel guilty, especially when he realized there might be that other link, the dead blob of genetic material.

But the guilt was far outweighed by the relief. He felt grateful to God or Luck or Fate or Whatever for letting him get away with the mistake. He had learned his lesson. But what if? Could she reach beyond the grave, a la Von Humboldt Fleisher in the Bellow novel, to play one more of her little games, snare him in some insidious trap? Waves of nausea weakened his legs at the thought. Just what he needed, some Bellovian irony. But this was life, not literature! Von Humboldt Fleisher had said that, too.

"Mom, that man's lookin' at me," Dolly would say to Marlene, indicating somebody across the street who seemed to be minding his own business. "He's been passin' by here three, four times this week just lookin' at me!"

"Oh, Dolly," Marlene replied. "You're just so *dumb*! Just plain *dumb*!"

Another time it was, "That man over there's *funny*," waving her hand at the word "funny."

"Oh, Dolly," Marlene sighed, exasperated by the tendency of her daughter's thoughts. "I wish somebody would knock some *sense* into you."

"Well he *is*! You can tell by the way he walks. Just like a *girl*. That hanky he has comin' out of his back pocket *means* somethin', too. It's a sign to others just like him."

"You shut your mouth, Dolly, I mean it."

And then there was Marlene. She could have been anywhere between thirty-five and fifty-five but Bridgewater guessed from her name that she fell between forty and fifty. She had a younger sister named Paulette and an even younger one named Marilyn, and then there was the baby, Jayne. Named for the reigning movie queens of the day, they all looked like professional wrestling champions.

Dietrich was popular when? The forties? Marlene had three teenaged children. In addition to Dolly and Raquel, there was a hulking son, Ron, who skulked around the house like an ax murderer, dressed in a torn, too-small ZZ Top jersey with a fringe of light-brown adolescent mustache over his lip. He never greeted Bridgewater when he came to pick Susanna up in the evenings, sullenly ignored him when Bridgewater said hello.

Given her family, Marlene might have started dropping kids at the age of fifteen and still only be in her early thirties, haggard and worn though she looked. This was the same milieu out of which Bambi Warner had come, his brother Mark's fiancée, the aspiring actress.

Marlene had a tattoo on her meaty forearm. It looked like the kind a teenager spends hours digging into his skin with a ballpoint pen, plowing furrows in the flesh with the steel point. Strictly homemade. It appeared to be a man's name, though Bridgewater was never able to look too closely. But it might have been her husband's name, he figured, like a cattle brand establishing ownership. Why not put a ring through her nose?

Bridgewater had never met her husband, Larry, who was evidently disabled in some mysterious way that prevented him from having a job. The only evidence of his existence was the consumptive cough that came from a distant bedroom. Bridgewater assumed the poor bastard was bedridden. Possibly a Vietnam veteran blasted by shrapnel or Agent Orange. Once or twice, however, he heard Marlene telling Dolly that her father was "out."

"Where's he at? Zissimo's Bar again?"

"Don't get smart with me, Dolly! I'll slap that smile right off-a your face! Don't get smart with me, I'm telling youse!"

"I ain't bein' smart! I just wondered where he was at. He go to Roach's Cafe? He go someplace on the Avenue?"

"The Avenue" was 36th Street, the main commercial drag in the neighborhood, the heart of Hampden. Zissimo's and the Roach Cafe were both on the Avenue. Bridgewater had never been in either of them, though he occasionally made fantasy-plans to go to Zissimo's and to Ye-Eat Shoppe.

"You jis watch what you say if you don't want to get slapped," Marlene warned, and then she turned back to Bridgewater as if nothing had happened. A stage aside he was not supposed to have heard? But these brutal, savage exchanges were nothing out of the ordinary. It was like when Bridgewater and Mark were boys and they used to say, "I wish you were dead." A case of the bark being worse than the bite. They'd never do anything violent to Susanna, would they? Spank her, for instance?

Marlene usually did not come to the door when Bridgewater brought Susanna over in the morning. She explained that she'd broken her ankle a year before and getting up and down stairs was difficult, so she sent Dolly instead. But one morning he found her sitting in her nightgown next to the space heater stroking Missy, her calico cat. She said she didn't feel well but quickly assured him that she could care for the baby. She said she'd had a gall bladder operation the beginning of February and the doctor had told her not to eat greasy foods, but she loved french fries and deep-fried fish, and now her stomach was upset. But she could still take care of the baby, she repeated, and from this Bridgewater gathered that the pittance she earned from babysitting was critical to the household economy.

This troubled him now as he drove down the expressway. Should he sacrifice his daughter so that these people could eat and pay their bills? Was their welfare his responsibility?

Bridgewater had reached over to stroke the cat on Marlene's lap. He mentioned that he and Zippy owned a black cat they called Ozzie. Ozzie did not go outside.

"Missy goes out all the time, but we dit-n want no more kittens so we had her spaded."

"She have many litters?"

"Three, four. We drownded most of them in the toilet."

Bridgewater was horrified, but he did not show that it bothered him. He did not want to seem shocked or sentimental, afraid to seem too squishy in her eyes but also thinking it would be impolite to let her know how cruel and barbaric he thought her behavior was. Reluctantly, he handed Susanna over to Marlene, who made baby noises that Susanna did not seem to notice. Susanna looked at her father from within the suffocating circle of Marlene's heavy arms with a bewildered expression, and then the comprehension of betrayal and abandonment broke over her face, and she began to cry, to howl.

Bridgewater looked pointedly at his watch, smiled at Marlene and affectionately stroked his sobbing daughter. Then he slinked off to work, her cry in his ears, feeling like the world's worst parent. He did take a perverse pleasure from the fact that Susanna preferred him to Marlene, however.

Illness, surgery and death made up the fabric of events in the McCoys' life. On top of Larry's mysterious disability and Marlene's broken bones and missing organs, there were frequent deaths in the extended family. Since Bridgewater had known them, in fact, two had died. Paulette's seventeen-year old daughter Michelle had lost an infant in childbirth the first week of babysitting, and Jayne's husband Billy had committed suicide on Easter Sunday by taking 142 morphine pills. Marlene had been quite certain of the number when she told Bridgewater, who mumbled condolences and shook his head in sympathy. Apparently Jayne had been cheating on him—"foolin' around" was how Marlene put it—and he killed himself to punish her.

It was the fact that Marlene had no telephone that had brought the current dilemma into being. Marlene had promised the Bridgewaters that she'd have a telephone two weeks after she started babysitting. She did not have one yet, and it did not look like she'd be getting one soon. She did have a neighbor, Hilda Bartell, four doors down the street whom she said Zippy or Bridgewater could call if the need arose. The Bridgewaters were disappointed that the telephone had not been installed, and Marlene's evasiveness also disturbed them, but the problem did not come to a head until they came down with the flu the weekend they got back from Potawatomi Rapids, and then Susanna caught the bug, too. At least, she vomited up her mother's milk one evening and then again the next morning. That very day.

Bridgewater faced a deadline on a graphics assignment that morning. A proposal was going out to the state of West Virginia and had to be sent out by 9 a.m., or Maryputa could kiss the contract goodbye. Bridgewater's boss, Milt Spalding, the marketing director, was counting on him to put the finishing touches on the document they were sending out; a few flowcharts had yet to be done, and the cover needed to be typeset. But while Bridgewater sang to Susanna that morning, the baby sprawled out on the dressing table, waving her legs in the air, an arc of clear, translucent milk spewed out of her mouth as if from a Cupid in a fountain. Alarmed, Bridgewater changed her clothes and took her temperature, greasing up the rectal thermometer with vaseline and holding it loosely between her flaccid little baby buns for a minute. Normal. No fever. She smiled and cooed.

Should he go to work? Susanna seemed well. She certainly looked all right. He thought about work and the deadlines he faced, and he decided to take the baby to Marlene's. He knocked on the door for several minutes, and then Dolly finally answered the door. She was wearing a cheap, diaphanous cotton nightgown, and when she stretched, the nipples of her teenaged tits poked out the material. Bridgewater could even make out the brownish-pink color of the areolae. She closed her eyes, leaned back and yawned, and Bridgewater got an eyeful. One strap fell off her shoulder. She let it hang limp on her arm and reached for the baby.

"Sorry I got you up," Bridgewater said thickly. His tongue seemed to strangle him, filling up his throat. "Keep an eye on her, will you? She may be coming down with something."

Susanna began to cry. Tormented by the sound of her anguish, Bridgewater almost fled the house. He called Zippy from work and told her what had happened. Zippy said she'd call Marlene to check on the baby.

"You mean the lady down the street," Bridgewater corrected, his voice heavy with sarcasm.

"Did Marlene say when she was getting a telephone?"

"She hasn't said anything about it for a few weeks, as a matter of fact."

"Then that's it. We're getting another babysitter."

Zippy called back later to say she'd made an appointment with another day-care provider that somebody at work had recommended, a woman named Darnell Gilmore. It looked like they could start bringing Susanna to the new place right away. Meanwhile, she said she had called the neighbor lady, Mrs. Bartell, to get in touch with Marlene. Mrs. Bartell said she couldn't find Marlene but that the baby was sleeping.

"You mean she's not there with the baby?"

"That's what it sounded like."

"Was Dolly?"

"Mrs. Bartell was vague."

"I'll give her a call. We finished the proposal so the pressure's off for a while."

Bridgewater had never called Hilda Bartell's number before. The telephone rang four times before a rude voice answered.

"Hello? Who is it?"

"Peter Bridgewater. I'm calling to speak with Marlene McCoy. She's taking care of my daughter."

The sound of the telephone clattering on a table preceded the voice trailing off in the distance, as in a dream: "I toja that's who it was." Then, like a radio sound effect, the noise of a door opening and slamming shut. A few minutes later, Marlene's voice: "Yeah?"

"Hello, Marlene? Peter. Peter Bridgewater. How are you?"

"Okay." She waited for him to speak his business. Her truculent silence eloquently told him what she thought of his pussy manners.

"I'm just calling to see if the baby's all right."

"Yer wife called too."

"Yes, I talked with her this afternoon. She called me. And the baby's all right? Susanna's all right?"

"She's sleepin' back at the house."

"Oh. That's good." Bridgewater did not know what to say next. He wished Marlene were somebody he could *talk* to, confide in, joke with. "We were afraid she was getting sick. We wanted to call and check up on her."

"I don't mean to be smart or nothin'," Marlene said, "but don't youse and yer wife think I can take care of a baby?"

"Oh, it's not that," Bridgewater hastened to assure her. He felt like the ambassador to a foreign country whose customs seemed strange but whom he did not wish to offend. "It's just—we thought you were going to be getting a telephone."

"I gotta pay the bill on the last one I had before they'll put one in," Marlene confessed.

"Do you think you're going to do it? I mean—"

"I gotta pay the bill on the other one I had first," she repeated.

"Oh, I see. Okay. Well." He trailed off into silence. Now what? He put a tone of finality into his voice. "Well, I just wanted to see if Susanna was okay. Sorry to bother you. Bye."

The phone clattered on the other end. Marlene did not bother to say goodbye.

And now he had to fire her.

Bridgewater thought of his boss at work, Milt Spalding, and the business management seminars he was trying to push Bridgewater into attending. They could come in handy in a situation like this, he thought, taking the exit from the expressway that would lead him to Marlene's.

Milt was a bottom-liner; he thought of himself as Lee Iacocca. Every action he took he translated into dollars and made a snap, shoot-from-the-hip cost-benefit analysis to justify his behavior. He wanted to develop Bridgewater into a management type. Dressed in a suit and a tie, Bridgewater had the appearance of authority, but he lacked the talent to command. Sensing this shortcoming, Milt had suggested these training seminars. Maryputa would pick up the bill, he hinted darkly, as if in a backroom conspiracy. Milt thrived on the politics of departmental bargaining. "How to Handle Difficult People" was the title of one of the seminars Milt had in mind. "Hiring and Firing" was another. "Assertiveness Training for Managers" and "Assertiveness Training for Achievers" (what was the difference?) rounded out the options.

Milt was a short, tense, ferret-faced man who wore a toupee. The toupee was part of his strategy, and on more than one occasion he suggested that Bridgewater do the same to conceal his thinning crown.

"Bald guys just don't rate respect," he said. "They don't get the contracts; they don't get the raises; they don't get the promotions. They just get the shit. Everybody knows my wig's a fake, but fuck 'em. I'm not trying to fool anybody, just beat them."

As a hobby, Milt collected baseball cards. He had over 40,000; his prize was a 1963 Pete Rose. He'd had offers of up to $1,000 for it. Several times a year he went to conventions to make trades and bargain for new cards.

More than a head taller than Milt, Bridgewater felt like a boy around him, a gangly, awkward adolescent boy, not a 36-year old man still in the *selva oscura*, Dante's dark wood.

"If I'd gotten hold of you earlier, I could've made a pitcher out of you," Milt said, slapping Bridgewater on the shoulder. Though crafty and cunning, Milt could be warm and affectionate with those he trusted—to people who did not pose a threat. "With that spidery frame of yours you could have had a motion like Marichal's. I shit you not." Bridgewater wished his father-in-law could hear such talk!

Milt liked him, he could tell. He wanted to mold him, which made Bridgewater feel both wary and flattered. It wasn't that he just wasn't a threat to him, Milt actually *cared*. Yet Bridgewater felt an impulse to resist, even though he wanted to be guided (Milt as Virgil) and inspired (Milt as Beatrice).

When he thought back on the cavalier attitude he'd had about his job at the WPCC graphics lab, Bridgewater could hardly believe it was he who thought and behaved that way. He thought of the peremptory way he'd broken his business relationship with Franklin Wood, the poet, and he cringed inwardly. With the baby had come this strangling sense of responsibility.

Milt had a favorite slogan that he repeated endlessly. "Expand the pie! Enlarge the middle ground and identify the bottom line!" He was always in the middle of negotiations with printers and photography labs and advertising agencies, not to mention with his own management, all the way up to Gar Dickerson, the president of Maryputa. "Dickerson sees ours as an overhead operation," Milt told Bridgewater, Napoleon outlining the overall strategy to his troops. "But we're the ones who bring in the business, and we can't let him forget it."

Bridgewater tried to recall some of the things he'd seen in the brochures Milt had shown him, in case there was some tidbit of information he could use in dealing with Marlene. But all he could remember were the claims and promises. Learn the most effective way to fire somebody. Learn how to identify and handle the ten most common types of difficult people. How to say "no" and make it stick. How to manage with strength without appearing to manipulate. Learn how to stay calm under fire. Deal positively and effectively with conflict. How to overcome your fear of confrontation. How to handle employees' reactions when they're fired. Know your legal rights.

Sweet Jesus, it either sounded like a come-on for Transcendental Meditation or a television commercial for an anti-perspirant. They typically staged these seminars in a conference suite at a Holiday Inn off a numbered exit in the Beltway Wasteland someplace. Near towns called Linthicum and Odenton and Jessup—Tedium and Depressin' and Throw Up!

Bridgewater had talked about his dilemma to Milt after the conversations with Zippy and Marlene. Milt had told him he had to be tough. That was the bottom line. Cut your losses and don't look back. He drew an analogy with the recent problems of the Baltimore Orioles. The Orioles had lost their first nine games without a win. Already the manager had been fired and replaced. To many people it had seemed a little cold-blooded to fire Ripken, father of the star shortstop. Thirty years with the club, two sons on the team, he wasn't like an animal you put to sleep when he ceased to be useful. But Milt respected the organization for being tough when they had to be.

"You have to make these tough decisions sometimes. You can only jimmy the figures for so long before the facts start staring you in the face and you can't avoid the bottom line any longer. You gotta act decisively. If this Marlene McCrory woman starts to bitch and moan about it, you just say, 'You run your mouth, lady, and I'll run my business.' "

Bridgewater turned on the radio, looking for some distraction, but the news only sank him further in the muck of his dilemma. A news program was doing a story on the trade bill President Reagan was threatening to veto because of the provision it contained for businesses to give employees sixty days' notice before a lay-off. Depressed, Bridgewater turned the volume down. Know your rights, indeed.

But what about the McCoys' rights? Was it fair to stick it to them like this? Leave them high and dry without any warning? "Sorry, Marlene, but you and your family will have to do without food for the next few weeks until you get another job. Have a nice day!" He couldn't do a shitty thing like that, could he? After all, Susanna wasn't in any real danger was she? He drove past Zissimo's Bar and wondered if the lean hillbilly staggering around out front were Larry McCoy. Well,

Zippy had already found another sitter, so he had to can Marlene McCoy, no way around it.

Bridgewater tried to imagine the time after he had fired Marlene as a way of keeping the panic level down. This, too, would pass; it would only be an ugly episode in his life and pass like all the other pleasant and unpleasant episodes. This was Friday evening. He and Zippy would order a pizza and watch the evening news. ABC with Peter Jennings. ABC would have its usual "Person of the Week" feature since it was Friday. Who would it be? What had happened since last Friday? The Academy Awards had been presented. Cher won an Oscar for Best Actress in *Moonstruck*. Sonny Bono had been elected mayor of Palm Springs. Noriega still refused to leave Panama. Bridgewater took some interest in this ongoing international drama. Though it may not be in his authority to do so, President Reagan was trying to fire the Panamanian leader. Noriega had been indicted for dealing drugs and ordered out of office, but he refused to leave. The United States imposed economic sanctions, but still he refused to step down. What balls! This was so much more complicated than the piddling little anonymous dirty work Bridgewater faced; it made him feel downright relieved. Marlene McCoy was no Manuel Noriega. He told himself he needn't worry.

Or would the Person of the Week be affiliated with the IRS? Today was the deadline for filing income taxes, and after all the hoopla about the new tax law, there might be some human interest angle in profiling an anonymous government bureaucrat overwhelmed by paperwork, or the congressmen who had sponsored the legislation. Rostenkowski? Would he be Person of the Week?

A Person of the Week was somebody in the thick of existence. Somebody to whom an event had virtually chosen to happen but who, though ambushed by circumstances, behaved with dignity, honor, courtesy and courage. Noriega?

Bridgewater turned up the radio. Did the newsman say "designer" or "Zionist"? He listened closely, but the voice had moved on from the Gaza Strip to the New York primary, and Bridgewater pulled up to the curb across the street from the McCoys' thinking, "Zionist jeans, Zionist sunglasses, Zionist housewares. . . ."

They were all out front on the porch, Marlene, Dolly, Ron and Raquel, as on the veranda at an old-time western saloon. Showdown at the OK Corral. Dolly sat on a broken aluminum chair, coloring her toenails with a red crayon. Ron sat on the front steps with a Marlboro dribbling smoke from his lips. Massive, meaty Marlene sat on a wobbly wooden chair, holding Susanna on her knee in the embrace of her tattooed arm. Raquel lounged in the doorway, her hand on her hip.

Bridgewater waited for a snotgreen Chevy with an I BRAKE FOR BEER bumpersticker on its fender to drive past before crossing the street. It occurred to him that he could just take Susanna away without saying she would not be returning. Then on Monday he could just take her to the new babysitter, Darnell Gilmore Never see Marlene again. If Marlene called he could pretend she had the wrong number. Or he could just tell her then that he'd found somebody else. *If* she called, which wasn't likely, since she didn't have a phone. But no, that was too cowardly. Besides, she might have a legal right to another week's pay if he did that. *Know your legal rights! Learn the most effective way to fire an employee*! Assertiveness training for fathers. Learn how to say "maybe" and make it stick. Learn how to ignore somebody with patience and politeness.

Bridgewater caught himself losing his concentration. He tried to keep his wits fixed on the present and proceeded across the street after the car passed, fingering the wad of bills in his pocket that he would give to Marlene. Her week's wages. (It was annoying that she demanded cash; she did not have a bank account and could not cash a check.)

"Hi!" he called. "How's Susanna feeling?"

"Peter, I ain't gonna be able to take Suzie no more after today," Marlene said. She came right out with it. She was not one to pussyfoot around with pleasantries. Bridgewater felt stunned. Overwhelmed. *Deus ex machina*! He did not have to fire her! He could have smiled; the relief he felt was almost palpable—like velvet. A moral burden had been lifted from his shoulders. He brought the bills out from his pocket and thrust them at Marlene. Out of the corner of his eye he looked at the tattoo on her arm but still could not make out the word there.

"I'm sorry to hear that. You've done a really fine job. How come? Why can't you continue?"

"Got me a job in Droodle. Startin' Mundy."

"Druid Hill's kind of a long way from here, isn't it?"

"The twenny-two bus drops me right off at the door."

"What are you going to be doing?"

"I'll be workin' for this man my husbin knows," she said vaguely, her eyes wandering evasively to the floor, and Bridgewater knew she was making the job up. She was lying. She just wanted to quit. Did she suspect he intended to fire her and she just wanted to beat him to the punch? Save face? Or was she weak-willed, lacking in confidence? When trouble occurred as it inevitably does, was her instinct simply to bail out? Perhaps he should steer *her* into a seminar on something like "Stress Management for the Working Woman." Learn how to handle on-the-job pressures. Identify the physical and mental signs of stress! Handle the greatest source of stress: the drive for perfection! But did it matter why she was quitting? Giddy with relief, Bridgewater flirted with Dolly.

"How about you, Dolly? Think you'll get a job, too?"

Flustered by the unexpected attention, Dolly made noises of denial, turned pink and dropped her eyes to her toenails.

"Maybe in a burly-cue," Marlene mumbled.

They all laughed, even Ron. Across his knuckles, Bridgewater noticed, he had written LOVE and HATE in dark magic marker.

On that note of levity, Bridgewater gathered Susanna, collected her diaper bag, and took his leave.

"Thanks a lot for everything, Marlene, and good luck on your new job!"

He carried his feather-light burdens across the street to his Toyota. Buckling his daughter into the carseat, he looked at her closely for signs of abuse. Nothing but a smudge of cereal that had streaked across her fat, pouchy cheek and dried there. She smiled up at him with toothless baby glee.

"You don't look as if you've been damaged any, honey. You're a survivor!" He kissed her. "Let's go get your mother and check out the new babysitter, see what this Darnell Gilmore is all about. What do you say?" He kissed his daughter again and then got into the driver's seat. Bridgewater felt like a bona fide Person of the Week.

Escape

Rachael Feldman sat at her desk at the bank in Kalamazoo, staring at the photograph of her family that her brother-in-law Peter had sent her. He had taken it outside the synagogue in Potawatomi Rapids the day Susanna had had her baby-naming. Passover. Edith held the baby while Zippy, Rachael and Moishe all looked at the camera and smiled. How happy they all looked together! If only the camera could capture the inner turmoil, the gut-wrenching conflict, what a different picture it would show!

But even at that, she thought she saw something sinister, something evil, in the way her father's eyebrows arched, the hairs sprung loose in a Mephistophelean flair, like some kind of devil at a Halloween party, and the black nylon yarmulke he wore made her think of an executioner's mask. His brown eyes had a cunning ruthlessness in their warmth; that warmth, that *kindness*, was like something he had turned on just for the camera.

But no, she was just being unfair. Paranoid. Her father *was* happy. How could he help but be pleased with a granddaughter like Susanna? His smile was as genuine as Edith's wide-mouthed grin. So unselfconscious was *hers* that you could see the black gap where a molar was missing. Her tinted glasses, the kind that darkened in direct sunlight, hid the expression in her eyes as she gazed down at the bundle in her arms, but the scrunched-up leathery skin at the sides of her lenses told just as plainly the delight in her soul.

Zippy, too, looked well. She had not yet shed the weight she had gained during her pregnancy, and her breasts, especially, filled out the green-and-white striped blouse she wore beneath her turquoise cardigan. The extra weight was not unbecoming, even though Zippy had complained about it. Like her abundant, sun-spangled hair, it bespoke a maternal fecundity. Earth Mama. Only she, Rachael, with her toothy glued-on smile, the frog-like underswell of a double chin, and her slanty dark oriental eyes whose sheen of melancholy she could never quite disguise (or was that apparent only to her?) seemed unable to blot out her loneliness in the spirit of family gaiety. Or did it just seem that way to her because she knew the thoughts that had ground her to bits that weekend? The longing for Docina Brown coupled with the knowledge that her family would never accept him. The sort of shame she felt during the family religious observances, as if she had a dirty secret she could not share with the others. Or was it defiance she felt because the secret was subversive? So much confused emotion! Consciously, she knew it wasn't true, because she had no reason to *be* ashamed, but her parents' implicit judgement forced it on her. Always the favored daughter, she was now the black sheep.

And it was all so irrational! So unfair! After meeting Dody last fall, Moishe had denied any racial bigotry. But he had insisted that he did not like Dody *personally*. But how could that be? What was there not to like? There was absolutely nothing to dislike about Dody, and Moishe's claiming this only revealed the depth of his prejudice. Docina was a gentleman to the core, but all Moishe could see was the big black ram *shtupping* his lily-white ewe. Horrified by the vision, her prudish father mistook his primordial ethnocentric fear for personal enmity, the classic rivalry of the father and the lover.

Rachael remembered the first encounter between her father and her lover. The onliest time they ever met, she thought, using Dody's black slang to add poignance to her bitterness. On neutral ground, in a Kalamazoo restaurant, by pre-arrangement, Moishe had come to meet his daughter's boyfriend. A civilized setting. Yet Edith's refusal to even meet Dody already spelled disaster. On both sides, a refusal to ingratiate himself translated into a stiff politeness between the boyfriend and the father.

Rachael and Docina had arrived at Red Gordon's first, a whitewashed frame house with green trim whose appeal, from the homey building to the steak and seafood menu and white linen tablecloths—the family-style restaurant—seemed appropriately muted, low-key, convivial, promising polite, generous behavior. But had the non-kosher element offended her father? How could it? He only observed the dietary restrictions at home, the hypocrite. Moishe ordered lobster.

He had entered the dining room speaking to a waitress wearing the Red Gordon's trademark knee-length pleated dark skirt with the frilly white apron, his sharp dark eyes stabbing like headlights around the room until he spotted her and Dody sitting under the soft light of a brass wall fixture an instant before the waitress pointed them out. Typical. He could not be beholden to anybody.

The smile he put on when they recognized each other made Rachael feel fraudulent, as if, like a chameleon, she took on her father's false cheery manner. No, the smile in this photograph and that one in her memory were not the same. The smile that led Moishe to the table at Red Gordon's, that put-on-warmth, cut like a sharp, purse-lipped sabre. But the bitterness she felt now had only been a confused groping then.

"Here's Dad," Rachael said hopefully, by way of introduction, as her father approached the table. Naively, she had a vision of the two men discovering the noble qualities in each other and putting the matter to rest. The way it works in a Hollywood movie.

"Warts and all," Moishe's self-effacing humor fell flat, for all his showman's affability.

"Daddy, this is Docina Brown. Dody."

"Cap'm," Dody said, standing to shake Moishe's hand. Just the barest step-n-fetchit parody marked his tone, but enough to put Moishe on his guard. Already he felt Dody mocking him. Rachael dimly sensed this, hoping it was only her anxiousness and not her father's perception. But suddenly everything seemed confused and hopeless. Her pride in Dody diminished with his display of bad behavior, but then she blamed her father for this, mistaking her perceptions for her father's. Or at least Moishe goaded him to it. At last she had confused herself so thoroughly she was not sure what was real and what imagined. The entire scene yawned like a black hole, threatening to swallow her.

The evening had gone miserably, Rachael thought, sighing and putting the photograph into her purse. She could not now pick out any details; she'd been so confused. She began to go through her desk drawers, removing items and deciding whether to discard or save them. But her mind fought through the paralyzing fog, searching for memories it could call facts, to justify her feelings, seal her decision.

Afterward, when Moishe shook Docina's hand and made it plain that he wished to see his daughter alone, Dody graciously left them, pleading papers to grade. Of course, he knew that Rachael planned to come to him as soon as she could get away from her father.

"Your mother's very upset," Moishe said gravely, and though she knew his game, Rachael found it impossible to resist the guilt. "You know how she worries about the survival of the Jews."

The survival of the Jews! Must she sacrifice her life for her mother's absurd paranoia? This reminded her of a science-fiction novel. The survival of the Jews did not depend on Rachael Feldman! When she listened to her mother rant on about the survival of the Jews she did not feel anger so much as sorrow and a great fatigue. *Nothing* is permanent. All that is *is* nothing. Yet we refuse to believe it and have to experience loss after loss after loss of the people and the things we love, over and over again, until we finally lose ourselves, and then what good is the survival of an abstraction?

Yet she knew her father's principal motive was to make her buckle, and he was not above using her relationship with her mother to accomplish this. He didn't really care so much about Edith, let alone the survival of the Jews; he was only using Rachael's filial instincts to force her to do his will. Treating her like the naughty little girl.

"She refused to come," Rachael said.

"She's not feeling well." To make his position clear, Moishe added, "You're the reason she's so upset."

"Dad!" Rachael tried to maintain her composure. She could feel herself crumpling into the submissive, helpless, whining daughter role. It would be so easy! "Didn't you—*like* him? Didn't you *like* Dody?"

"It's not a question of 'liking' or 'disliking' him. Personally, I found him rather disagreeable. Boring and somewhat stupid. I don't see what you could possibly see in him, if you must know. I *didn't* find him attractive on a personal level. But the point isn't whether I like him or dislike him. He's just not good enough for you. If your relationship should become a formal one, you're only asking for trouble. Please accept this on the basis of my years of experience and my knowledge. My wisdom, if you will." He let out a single ripple of self-effacing laughter, though he made it plain he wasn't joking. The dead look in his brown eyes testified to his earnestness. "If you continue to see Dody, your mother and I want nothing more to do with you."

Why, in the grand scheme of life, drawn up before she was even born, the one her parents taught her, the Great Cosmic Struggle Between Us and Them—Jews versus Arabs, Jews versus Germans, Jews versus the Goyim—Jews versus *Everybody*—why did she feel that her main opponents, her real enemies, were *her parents*? *They* were the only ones who found fault with her, not the Arabs, the Germans, the goyim. Why, instead of wanting to be a part of life, did she increasingly want to flee from it?

Fighting back tears of impotence and rage, Rachael had stalked blindly back to her car and driven away without so much as saying goodbye to her father. How long ago that seemed now! The meeting at Red Gordon's had taken place last fall, before the first snow, in the midst of the turning leaves and frosty nights. Her parents' pressure had only added to the ambivalence she felt, to her indecision. One influence among many. But instead of trying to win her parents' approval, Rachael kept her love life secret from them. Then, shortly after Pesach, she discovered she was pregnant!

Rachael never took risks with birth control; she could not understand how this had happened. Afraid of pills and IUDs, she used a diaphragm and contraceptive jelly. Nothing is foolproof, she realized—the ace shoplifter tackled outside the department store with the blouse stuffed into her bag; caught in the act.

Dody was pleased when he heard the news. He wanted to marry Rachael and have a family, get on with their lives. Smug as the department store detective who captures the thief, he almost led her away in handcuffs to the Justice of the Peace.

But Rachael balked. She wanted to think this over, she said. Pregnancy wasn't a good reason to marry. Though loving and supportive, Dody tacitly handed down his own ultimatum; at least, he raised the question of their future together. He wanted a family. Maybe she should get an abortion now, since the pregnancy had not been planned, but when would they put an end to the continual postponement? How long would they remain hostages to the wishes of her parents?

Rachael sought advice from her sister in Baltimore. Zippy had no doubts; Rachael's only alternative was an abortion. She was not ready to have a baby, not with the unresolved situation with Dody and their parents making that ambivalence even more complicated. "You know what they'll say, Rachael. You know exactly how they'll act."

But Peter Bridgewater urged her to keep the baby. Well, perhaps "urged" wasn't the word, but he did seem to think she should keep the child, if only as an act of defiance, an assertion of her will, as if to jumpstart her own personal history as a human being.

"It's a lot of work having a baby, and you don't always get a lot of sleep. It's especially tough for you, being a single parent. Unless you plan to marry Dody. And why not do that, too? In for a penny, in for a pound. I mean, he *is* the father, after all; he's got to care about the child. From what I've seen, he's a responsible sort of guy, isn't he?

"And then of course your parents will care about the baby, too, no matter what they may say before. An innocent baby, after all. Your mistakes aren't the baby's fault. If you want to *call* them 'mistakes,' I mean, and I guess Moishe and Edith will. But then, who knows, maybe your parents will come to accept Dody. Unless they just ignore him. They used to do that to me, remember. Still do, in a way. But then we had Susanna and things changed.

"Well, bottom line is, you won't find out unless you keep the baby. So, go for it, as they used to say a few years ago."

The contradictory advice compounded Rachael's indecision. Should she keep the child or get an abortion? Should she marry Dody or not? Rachael was inclined to follow Zippy's advice. Her sister knew what she was dealing with. Her parents. Her brother-in-law didn't know.

Peter Bridgewater evoked a string of memories then. While inarticulate memories—inchoate images—swirled through her head about the bank, seducing her to melancholy, the image of her brother-in-law filled her mind. The pads of paper she dug out of desk drawers, with virtually meaningless abbreviations and notations, reminded her vaguely of the people she worked with, antagonists as well as allies, colleagues and clients, one nebulous composite of the work that had filled her time for more than six years. Images she stored up against the onslaught of nothingness, when yearning would unexpectedly grip her. That would inevitably happen, she knew. But Rachael's conscious memory retrieved incidents form her association with Peter.

Normally a quiet, reflective, introverted type, he could become animated and loquacious at the most unexpected times. Even giggly. Then he fought so hard to maintain a straight face—a bored, world-weary dignity; he became, when swept up in the childish hilarity, a schoolboy caught breaking the rules. Rachael remembered visiting her sister and brother-in-law in Baltimore once and driving down Howard Street to get to the glitzy new mall, Harborplace. Unenthusiastic about the excursion, Peter sat quietly in the backseat, staring out the window while Zippy drove. But when they passed a small adult film theater called the Little X, he suddenly became amused, and his mouth split open in a wide, madman's grin.

The marquee advertised Alexis Firestone live onstage, and Peter, trying to suppress his gleeful madman's laughter, told them about "a friend of his" (couldn't have been Peter himself, could it?) who had gone to one of these live onstage appearances, this one by a porn queen named Bunny Bleu. He related his friend's description of the dancer prancing across the stage in a striptease act and especially dwelt on the furtive, sweaty guys with boxes of popcorn in their laps; they applauded enthusiastically like religious devotees hoping to be singled out for their special fervor; their transfixed adoring eyes never blinked; behind steamy glasses that reflected the glint of stagelight their eyes stared, riveted to the buxom blond with the intensity of the Ancient Mariner's. After the stage performance, Peter said his "friend" said, for five or ten dollars you could get your picture taken with the porn queen, and for an additional fee you could get your picture taken licking one of the pasties and affixing it to the nipple of one of the starlet's enormous breasts.

Rachael remembered the county fair in Potawatomi Rapids, the big summer event held each August to compare corn and hogs for prizes. The favorite attraction for the local yokel teenage boys was the striptease show where skanky hillbilly girls kicked off their clothes to raunchy jukebox music. Outside the striptease tent the oily barker promised that inside Kelly Rae would wind up wearing nothing but nine beads—"Nine beads of sweat on her brow."

When she was a junior in high school, some of the local boys sneaked into the show, under the tent flaps, and afterward boasted loudly about it at the local teenage hangout, a Miller's Ice Cream store run by Ka-thump and his wife. Ka-thump was the cruel nickname with which the Potawatomi Rapids boys taunted Jim Harris, a somber, grumpy old man with the loose, wagging jowls of a beagle and dead serious gray eyes; he was forever calling the police about them for lounging around the parked cars outside and, they suspected, sending anonymous postcards to their parents saying they drank beer and smoked cigarettes. The nickname, Ka-thump, referred to the fact that he had once had a serious heart attack, and they taunted him with his mortality, a sort of death wish. (In fact, Harris had died from heart disease only a few years ago.)

"Man! You could see her great big black bush!"

"That pussy was *sopping* wet, man! *Sopping* wet!"

"And she had the biggest God damn tits, man!"

"Bigger than Rachael Feldman's?"

"Nobody's got bigger tits than Rachael Feldman!" she heard a voice say, and she recognized Dougie Holdren talking to his friends. A blond boy with buckteeth and hair falling in his eyes, a spray of pimples on his chin. "Rachael Feldman's built like a brick shit-house!"

"There she is! Over there! She heard you, Dougie!"

"You just cut a fart," Dougie accused his pal, Bobby Berkheimer, trying to shift the spotlight of embarrassment to the other boy.

"Skunk smells his own ass first!" Bobby chortled, unperturbed.

What little beasts those high school boys were! Rachael shuddered.

No, Peter's interest in the Little X was not as prurient, so immediate and unreflecting, as theirs. He seemed to be entertained by the grotesque aspect of the spectacle, moved by the intrinsic baseness of human nature. He'd even mentioned a painting he planned but which he never actually got around to doing. *Swine in Circe's Garden*, he said the title would be, depicting these same sweating men staring in their seats as a girl on the stage twirled a bra in the air over her head. He said he wanted to suggest the same sort of bedlam you might see at a prizefight.

Several years later, having given up trying to complete high school, Dougie Holdren had gotten drunk with a group of his friends—two girls and one other boy—and had driven the wrong way down an off-ramp onto the interstate. They'd collided with a car driven by an elderly couple from Hillsdale, who'd been killed instantly. Dougie was flung thirty feet from the car spinefirst into a metal light post and was now paralyzed for life. Before that, during his endless junior high school career, he had spent some time in a boys' reformatory in Terre Haute, Indiana, for stealing cars.

The blinking red light on Rachael's computer kept watch as she continued to clean out her drawers and inspect the shelves. Her fingers probed the keyboard to display electronic mail messages one final time. Once, years ago, when she was still in graduate school in Urbana, before she met Docina, she had made a pilgrimage to Terre Haute. Though her father had steered her into economics, Rachael's true love had been art. Her favorite painting was one by Mary Fairchild MacMonnies called *Five O'clock Tea*, a detail of which decorated the cover of a paperback copy of a Henry James novel (*The Europeans*), which she had torn from the book and mounted over her computer console. She looked at it now, at the fine young lady in the garden with her hand on her hip, touching the bright orange sash at her waist, staring imperiously down at her seated companion, a blond young woman in a blue gown whose chin rested on her left hand and who gestured toward the standing woman with the palm of her right hand open. A gesture of appeal. Rachael identified with the disdainful dark-haired lady in orange.

On her way back to Urbana from a visit to Potawatomi Rapids, Rachael had gone by way of Terre Haute to visit the Sheldon Swope Art Gallery, where the original painting was on display. Usually she went back to school by way of Chicago, but this time she had sacrificed the excitement of the Loop and her friends on the Near North

Side to behold the artwork. She smiled at the memory. She had felt like a religious devotee at Guadeloupe walking on her knees across the cobblestones to the shrine of the Virgin—or the sweaty, furtive guys at the Little X applauding Bunny Bleu—but at the same time, she reflected, she had never felt so free, so *unencumbered*, as she had that time travelling through Terre Haute.

"You'll be getting an IBM XT PC," a loud, confident voice suddenly said in an adjacent office. "You'll still interface with the mainframe with the Forte board we'll install, though. It forces a download when you select the menu option."

The voice was smug, self-satisfied, and Rachael thought how this exaggerated amazement at the capabilities of computer programs passed for conversation at the bank. In fact, Rachael customarily talked that way herself. She had marveled that way about computers to her sister, Zippy, during the Passover holiday, while her brother-in-law clammed up and lost interest. Now her pregnancy seemed to put all this shoptalk into perspective, and she saw it for the shallow surface-skimming exchange it really was. Only noise. Noise to fill up the silence. Noise to avoid making a decision, a commitment. In her current state of mind, it was as if she were watching herself die, reviewing the truly significant events of her life and separating them from the chaff, the noise, the stuff that not even an omniscient mind would bother to remember.

And now that she had gone ahead with the abortion, what did she have left?

Nothing. Not even Docina Brown. They had not formally broken off, but Rachael sensed that he was pulling away, wedging formality, distance, between them. She had called him only the day before, Sunday, before she went up to Potawatomi Rapids for Mother's Day, but he had not answered his phone. Then she called his mother's place. Dody's sister, Vonzella, answered the call. She said Dody had gone down to Chicago to see the NBA playoff game between the Bulls and the Cleveland Cavaliers. She gratuitously added that he had gone with Sequanda Watts. Von's voice sounded cold, even cruel, when she said it. Sequanda Watts was the daughter of a neighbor of the Browns' that Dody's mother had been trying to match him with for years, since they were in grade school together. Rachael felt as though she'd been kicked in the stomach. She drove up to Potawatomi Rapids fighting back the tears all the way.

Menacing thunderstorms swooped around the state all that day. Out on the lake the water was the sickening violet gray of churned sewage. The lake tossed and turned, surged in turbulent, white-frothed, spittle-sudsy waves that thundered endlessly against the shore. The ominous gray sky hovered over the fresh-leafed trees, and a strong, cool wind licked at the virginal branches; the saplings swayed, and the pines stuck out their thumbs, hitchhikers going south, leaning in the direction they intended to take. Down by the shoreline, she saw, the lake boiled around the huge smooth boulders, sleek with wetness. Down there, she knew, the roar of the waves would have a hollow sound, not unlike the sound of a cork coming out of a bottle: *th-nawk . . . th-nawk . . . th-nawk . . .* slapping the sand and the stone, whipped into a fine, misty, spackling spray by the wind. Off in the distance, on the tip of Potawatomi Point, she made out the ghostly pepper shaker outline of the lighthouse, and she imagined she heard the mournful tolling of a ship's horn somewhere unseen out on the lake. *Did* she hear it? She concentrated on the sound and almost ran over a gray squirrel loping across the road. She turned down the mailbox road feeling as if the world conspired against her.

In her distraction, Rachael drove too close to an ancient oak tree in the Feldmans' drive and the goose-pimpling screech of wood against metal finally broke her down to the inevitable tears just as the wind and water blustered and foamed in a prelude to a storm. Almost with relief she pictured the long fingernail marks the bark had left across the red Datsun's side: a perfect excuse to cry. She leaned over the steering wheel and wept with great, convulsive, body-shuddering sobs. The crying had a cathartic effect, and she stayed that way for several minutes while the rain freckled the windshield and a stray branch from a locust tree swatted the rear fender over and over again with a dull, rhythmic *scritch-scritch*. She held onto the steering wheel like a survivor draped across a life preserver, until the door abruptly came open, and Edith's voice, vaguely alarmed, slightly annoyed, announced, "Rachael! You're crying! Gevalt! Are you all right?"

Rachael reached over to the passenger's seat and grabbed the crinkly yellow paper that held the bouquet of flowers she had brought, dabbed her eyes with the sleeve of her leather jacket and, sucking back snot, said, "Happy Mother's Day, Mom!"

She laughed at her own joke and dabbed at her eyes again. She still had her sense of humor, at least. "I just scraped the hell out of my car on that old oak tree in your drive. The paint job is probably ruined. I'm afraid to look."

"Oh, what a pity," Edith said. "Maybe your father can suggest something." She took the flowers—pink and yellow tulips—and brought them to her face. "Lovely!" she said, inhaling their fragrance. They went toward the house, Edith talking over her shoulder to Rachael.

"Zippy called to wish me a happy Mother's Day. She's a mother now, too, of course. She said Ketzulah's cutting her first tooth! She and Pinchas think it could come tomorrow! Think of it! Shoshonah's first tooth!"

"I ought to call Zippy and wish her a happy Mother's Day," Rachael said, mostly to herself.

"Wait till you get home. The lines are all tied up. You'll never get through."

"Ah, Rachael! How are you, love?" Moishe said when they entered the kitchen. This was the kitchen the Feldmans used all year long, except during Passover.

"Rachael said she scraped her car against the oak tree when she came in."

"Oh, no! You didn't!" Moishe said sympathetically. The way they could feel genuine pity over a scraped car and not even care about her broken heart dismayed Rachael. "Did it scrape the paint off?"

"I didn't have the heart to look."

"Maybe there wasn't any damage," Moishe said hopefully.

"Oh, it doesn't matter anyway," Rachael said, her despondency almost palpable, sloping her shoulders and slumping her back like a physical force.

"Doesn't matter! Oy vey! You should have seen her out in the car crying, Moishe! And now she says it doesn't matter!"

Her mother's nagging, querulous voice went on like that all afternoon, Rachael recalled, tossing out a batch of notepaper with the heading:

MEMO FROM RACHAEL FELDMAN, ASST. MGR.

All through lunch and the thunderstorm and the smalltalk and the family gossip, the same contrapuntal stylized rising incredulity in her voice. Like a parrot or some exotic bird with blue and orange wings. The high-pitched voice was as shrill and relentless as a teakettle. She went on and on about how stupid Zippy was to leave her child with goyim. Before long Shoshonah would be celebrating Christmas; she would want gifts from Santa Claus. She would want a tree in her living room. She would scorn the menorah, be ashamed of her heritage, unfamiliar with her Jewish tradition. Edith refused to believe Zippy's reports about the difficulty of finding babysitters; she just wasn't looking hard enough and certainly not in the right places. Why couldn't Zippy leave little Ketzulah with a good Jewish family?

And Sandy! What meshugas that girl had brought on herself by marrying a shagitz! That pisher Brad Reynolds! That big nothing! The latest on Sandy was that she had impulsively left her job one afternoon in Beverly Hills and got on a flight to New York. She had seen her estranged husband Brad walking hand-in-hand with his blond idiot girlfriend on Wilshire Boulevard and had felt seared by the sight. She had to get away! But when Sandy arrived in New York she had a nervous breakdown in La Guardia airport.

"All because of that swine, Brad Reynolds! May he rot in Hell!"

On an impulse, Rachael told her parents she had broken up with Dody, both yearning for the approbation she would receive and hating herself for seeking their solace, knowing that finally she would receive no solace from them ever again; she held her parents guilty for taking even *that* away from her.

"My Mother's Day present!" Edith shrieked in the high-pitched voice. "Oh, it's the greatest gift a mother could ever ask for!"

"You've done the right thing," Moishe said sagely. "I'm sure it will hurt at first, but you'll see in time that you've made the right decision."

These congratulations only inspired hatred and self-loathing in Rachael. Primly pursing her lips and looking at both parents with gleaming eyes, she said, "What would you have said if I'd told you I was pregnant?"

"*Zol vaksen tzibeles fun pupik,* Edith exclaimed, half-joking. May onions sprout from your navel.

Moishe attempted to appear casual, though the thought disturbed him, and his eyes betrayed him by tick-tocking a little faster for a moment. He ignored Rachael's hypothetical challenge and looked out the window. "Well, it's stopped raining. I think I'll go over to Detweiler's."

"He's closed," Edith said. "Mother's Day."

"Detweiler closes for Mother's Day?"

"You need something for your *muhgen*? Have some dried fruit."

"What do you think? I'm constipated? I just want to go get a newspaper." Moishe fidgeted around in his chair. Then he bent toward his daughter.

"You aren't, are you?" He sat on the edge of his seat, leaning forward, the effect of hemorrhoids or anxiety.

"I'm not what? Constipated?"

"Pregnant."

"No, I'm not."

"No, I'm not," she repeated now in her office in the bank in Kalamazoo. "No, I'm not pregnant."

In a sudden rage she picked up her coffee mug and hurled it against the wall. A fragile, white clay cup with blue letters that said: "Today Is the Tomorrow You Worried About Yesterday".

Purged but alarmed, cautious now, Rachael grabbed the newspaper from her desk to scrape up the broken pieces. She hoped nobody had heard, or paid attention. In the next room she heard the voices going on, oblivious of her outburst:

"How much memory has she got?"

"Six hundred and forty k."

"Wow! My Apple IIc only has a tenth of that!"

Rachael swept up the broken pieces. "Pistons Dust Bullets, Bulls Beat Cavs, Hawks Knock Out Bucks" the smaller boldface headline said over the main headline. Rachael thought of Docina and Sequanda sitting together on the bleachers at the Chicago arena, their thighs pressed together. Did they have bleachers at professional basketball courts? Or did they have individual seats?

The main headline blared the news that Nancy Reagan consulted astrologers, according to the new kiss-and-tell book by Donald Regan. This was news? This sort of book was so ubiquitous and boring, it was like all those baseball books Moishe had with the latest star's analysis of the relationship between George Steinbrenner and Billy Martin. Who cares? It was all just noise! Just meaningless noise, like the computer jargon of her colleagues. Sound and fury, signifying nothing.

Besides, you really can tell the future. Or some people can, anyway. Zippy could. Zippy had predicted this—this rupture with her parents. Zippy, too, had fled, Rachael thought. Just a year ago. Over the same traumatic dilemma of pregnancy and abortion, too—though for different reasons.

Rachael threw the paper-wrapped cup into the wastebasket before surveying the office one last time. Anything else? In another week somebody else would have this office, and her presence would be blotted out entirely. As if she had never existed. These few bits of memorabilia stood between her and nothingness. How flimsy a life is! How insubstantial! All props and mirrors. At base a big zero. Emptiness.

She was a stranger in a strange land about to go off on her own private diaspora. Rachael remembered reading the obituary for Robert Heinlein, dead at 80 on Mother's Day. Was that a sign? Something out of astrology? She packed the torn book cover into her bag, and now she looked at the pastel office walls. The wall poster. A birthday gift from her staff.

LACK OF
PLANNING
(on your part)
DOES NOT
JUSTIFY
AN EMERGENCY
(on my part)

She felt an impulse to take it with her but decided against it. Were her own plans fully formed? Hardly. But this *was* an emergency! She had to save her own life!

In My End, My Beginning

The beginning of June. Bridgewater lay in a chaise longue by the side of the Wyman Park Pool Club pool thumbing through *Time Magazine*. President Reagan had just returned from the summit in Moscow; Gorbachev's stylish wife smiled on the cover. The magazine groaned under the weight of stories and reports on arms control negotiations, perestroika, refuseniks, Star Wars, human rights, and the famous feud between the wives of the American and Soviet leaders. Everybody said the summit was a success.

Good press for the president, who had recently taken it on the chin. Only a month ago Reagan's former chief of staff had written that Nancy Reagan consulted astrologers, and the month before that his former press secretary had published a book with the same sort of unflattering claims about the president. This sensational stuff reminded Bridgewater of the grocery store tabloids. Those had gone downhill since the time they used to print stories about Adolph Hitler being seen alive in South America, he thought. Now they just ran ridiculous stories about pilots photographing heaven and husbands confessing to wives that they were really aliens. Only I SAW ELVIS—ALIVE! came anywhere close to the blend of horror and history they used to achieve, and it was only a pale comparison at that. Bridgewater never read them in the checkout lanes, anyway, going for *People* and *Time* instead. Only yesterday he had purchased this copy at the Giant when he had gone to the store for some diapers.

Bess Myerson nabbed for shoplifting (nail polish, batteries and shoes jammed into her purse at a Pennsylvania department store); Billy Carter hospitalized for treatment of pancreatic cancer; Harry Reasoner married to an insurance executive in Iowa. Michael Dukakis would nail down the Democratic nomination in the upcoming California primary.

Locally, Bridgewater mused, looking up from the magazine to the scudding fleecy clouds overhead, Hampden was celebrating its 100th anniversary as a part of Baltimore, He imagined a story appearing in the "Behavior" or "Living" section of the news magazine—a sociologist could go wild in Hampden. The most inbred neighborhood in the whole USA. Poverty, racial prejudice, child prostitution. Hordes of dirty children everywhere, like something out of a Dickens novel. The Artful Dodger on the prowl. Recently, Hampdenizens had been hounding a black Muslin family on Keswick Road who had had the audacity to move into the neighborhood. Gangs of whites harassed their children and threw rocks at their windows. (Bad enough that they were black and kinky hair covered their skulls, but what really infuriated the neighbors was the robes and fezzes and that they called each other "Abdullah" and "Mukhtar.") Consequently, a 24-hour police guard had been assigned to watch over their home. Bridgewater shuddered, both because of the strong cool wind and theatrically at the thought of Marlene McCoy and Darnell Gilmore, the Hampdenizens in whose care he had left his daughter Susanna for a total of ten weeks.

Darnell had turned out to be as bad as Marlene. Even worse. A pretty young woman, despite her brown, twisted teeth, with clear, tawny skin and wild, intense, angry gray eyes, Darnell had treated Bridgewater and Zippy almost like recalcitrant employees. A regular martinet, if she wasn't demanding some sort of equipment in the rude, impatient tone of an employer who hates to remind his workers of the obvious—a stroller, a playpen, a walker, a swing (didn't babysitters usually have these things?) – she was calling their abilities as parents into question. Having raised two children herself —Richie, a quiet four-year-old and Patti, an athletic six-year-old – she set herself up as the expert and regarded her style as the only way to raise a child. Even in warm weather she insisted that the baby have a T-shirt on beneath her onesie; she regarded a T-shirt as a sort of bulletproof vest against germs. "Richie and Patti always wore them, and they never got sick, not once."

Bridgewater would often collect a sweating, whining child at the end of the day, a condition for which Darnell took no responsibility, irrationally blaming Zippy for the way she cared for Susanna at home. "If she'd just give that baby formula, she wouldn't be whinin' and cryin' all the time. I put Richie on the bottle when he was three months old and Patti when she was one month, and they never got sick after that, not once."

Darnell didn't care what the pediatricians said about nutrition. Those doctors changed their minds every year anyway, she sneered. They oughta listen to what people say who actually *raise* kids! Shoot, she knew more about raising kids than any book did. She'd given Richie and Patti mashed potatoes since they were two weeks old, and there wasn't nothin' wrong with them. They'd never gotten sick, not once. Darnell demanded that Zippy stop breastfeeding the baby; she said it would make her job easier as well as being better for Susanna, because if Zippy didn't stop, the baby would not take a bottle from Darnell since she was used to the titty at home.

"You tell Zippy to put her breast back in her bra where it belongs!" The furious, frightening look in her eyes leaped out at him like a tiger, and again, as with Marlene, he wondered if his daughter was safe, if he were being a negligent parent. If those eyes of Darnell's were water, he thought, you would be able to see minnows swimming above the ridged sand at the bottom. "She can't be workin' at a job and nursin' that baby, too. It's just not fair. If she wants to quit her job and stay at home and breastfeed Suzie, that's fine. But as long as I'm the one that takes care of the baby durin' the day, no way. Pete, she just cries all the time, and there ain't nothin' I can do about it neither, because she ain't learned how to hold a bottle. I love her just like one of my own, but I don't have the time to be holdin' her all the time. I got housework to do, and Richie and Patti ain't been feelin' good, and I gotta take care of them, too." Like Bambi Warner, Darnell had the savage streak of a mean junkyard dog.

Bridgewater said vaguely that he'd talk to Zippy about it. But weren't they paying her to take care of the child no matter what it took? A baby demands a lot of attention. Darnell wasn't there just to pick up some extra change, was she? But then again, he thought, they weren't paying her all that much, it was true. Moreover, she seemed diligent. She claimed she wanted to pass the high school equivalency exam, and she talked about her plans to go though the process to become a licensed daycare provider. Bridgewater supposed that Darnell, now in her late twenties, had dropped out of school at a young age to marry and have babies but was now determined to develop her talents. She seemed resourceful.

Darnell's husband, Hank, a fat guy who worked for the state, operating computers, also seemed like a responsible person, in contrast to Larry McCoy. The Gilmores were buying their own home, too, not just being negligent about paying the rent, as had been the case with the McCoys. Hank Gilmore's only indulgence consisted of staying up late watching the Orioles lose on television. He had to be at work at 4:00 AM, but he loyally stayed up watching the games, sometimes past midnight. When the team's losing streak reached 12, Hank put on a jersey that said:

BALTIMORE ORIOLES, 1983 WORLD CHAMPIONS

Hank vowed not to take it off until the Orioles won a game, which they did some two weeks later.

Also in their favor, the Gilmores had a telephone. An enormous improvement over the McCoys, especially in light of the circumstances of *that* business arrangement. Not that Darnell appreciated people calling and checking up on her, she made it plain, but if the Bridgewaters needed to get in touch with her, they could.

Zippy called once soon after they'd begun leaving Susanna with Darnell. Darnell was laconic and she barked into the receiver.

"Those Hampden and Remington people are pretty rude, you know?" she commented at dinner that evening.

"How do you mean?" But he knew what she meant.

"They sort of growl at you. They're very rude, but I wonder if maybe they don't realize they're being rude; that's just the way they talk to other people."

"Probably," Bridgewater assented.

"I don't *think* Darnell was angry with me for calling – I mean, why should she be? – but she sure sounded annoyed. Busy, maybe."

"Well, you should feel free to call her if you want to."

"Well, I'm pretty busy at work . . ." Zippy never called again.

Because she seemed like such an improvement over Marlene McCoy, the Bridgewaters tried to meet Darnell halfway. They tried weaning Susanna by giving her more cereal, mixing it with breast milk, but the baby wanted the contact with her mother, and Zippy nursed Susanna in the morning and in the evening. Then, after another two weeks, Darnell demanded that Zippy quit cold turkey and that they feed Susanna formula from a bottle.

"I got people callin' me all the time wantin' me to look after their child," she boasted. "So you tell Zippy she better stop cold turkey this weekend or I ain't gonna look after Suzie no more, Pete. I don't have to put up with it if I don't want to, you tell Zippy that. You tell Zippy I won't take no more breast milk from her, neither. You tell her Suzie's gotta drink formula or I ain't takin' care of her no more."

It was a seller's market, all right, but at that point, to use Milt Spalding's words, the Bridgewaters told Darlene she could run her mouth but they'd run their business, lady. She'd handed them her ultimatum on a Friday, and the Bridgewaters spent a frantic weekend calling and interviewing sitters to whom they had been referred by friends, neighbors, and colleagues at work.

The sitter they chose was Bernita Simms, a licensed nurse in Charles Village, who, with her sister, Vondalair, took care of several small children at Bernita's house on Calvert Street. Right away Bridgewater and Zippy had liked her, not just for being so patient with small children and for having a sense of humor, but because her house looked well cared for, unlike Marlene's or Darnell's. Not just her housekeeping but her taste recommended her as well. Bernita collected antiques. A crystal chandelier hung from the ceiling in the living room, and Bernita transacted her business from a mahogany secretary in the foyer. An oak dining table dominated the dining room, against whose wall a mahogany china cabinet stood with polished glass doors.

Bernita's husband, Waverly, a city bus driver who helped out with the children when he was home, had set up the basement for the children. A thick carpet covered the floor, and playpens and swings and bassinets were everywhere. The room would be cool during the hot Baltimore summers. Bernita had a couple of parakeets named "Kids" and "R Us" that fascinated all the babies. She had a swingset and a sandbox in the backyard. While not as oppressive as the McCoy home, Darnell Gilmore's living room had been decorated with a six-foot poster of Cal Ripken drinking a glass of milk and depressing black-and-white Olan Mills portraits of the family. Richie's and Patti's toys littered the floor like a minefield. The neighborhood where Bernita lived was marginal, but the household indicated finer sensibilities and more practical experience.

"The onliest time Susanna cry is when she wake up from her nap," V said to Bridgewater at the end of the first week. They called Vondalair "V." "That other babysitter don't know what she talkin' 'bout." Indeed, Susanna seemed to like her new surroundings. She smiled and waved her warms when Bridgewater came to get her after work, sitting amid a group of other babies in walkers and swings. Bridgewater thought of the other little babies as Susanna's colleagues. He found Bernita and V easy to talk to, and he often spent half an hour or more with them when he came to get Susanna, listening to Bernita's stories about growing up in Virginia, how her parents raised their children with old-fashioned values, or V's account of how much money she had saved that week with the coupons she clipped from the newspaper, or how their brother Isaiah had videotaped his graduation from the police academy. V was a slender, freckle-faced woman who chain-smoked Salem cigarettes. Two years older than V, Bernita weighed at least seventy pounds more than her sister; her skin, more yellow than brown, was lighter than V.'s.

Such were the cares of a parent, Bridgewater reflected grimly. Day care. Babysitters. Bodily needs. Food and shelter. Apart from whatever satisfaction he took from his work as Maryputa graphics coordinator, he had long ago ceased thinking of himself as an artist. He felt trapped if he dwelled on the thought too much, though, and he tried not to. A slave to necessity. A prisoner of the mundane. Stuck in Baltimore. Forever. Not like his brother Mark, who was making plans to move out to California.

Mark had married Bambi Warner in a private ceremony in Key West, Florida. He and Bambi eloped without telling anybody their plans. Frank, of course, was delighted that his son had married. He had retired from city government at the end of May and was planning to move to Arizona in the winter. As a wedding gift, he gave Mark and Bambi his most prized possession, the electric train set. While Mark was effusive in expressing his gratitude to Frank for his thoughtfulness and generosity, in private to his brother he let the old man have it.

"That asshole! What the fuck does he think I'm going to do with a fucking electric train set?" Mark stormed around the sunken den of their father's house. Frank had gone out to buy some champagne to celebrate. "An electric train set! A fucking electric train set! Of all the lamebrained gifts in the world! That old dumb fuck!"

"Well, you've always praised the damn thing," Bridgewater pointed out. "Ooo-ed and ahhh-ed over it. What did you expect? To him it's a great sacrifice."

"I was just being polite!"

"You sounded as though you really meant it. 'I'd give anything for a set like that, Dad,'" Peter quoted back to his brother.

"Oh, Christ!" Mark groaned. He held his head in both his hands and closed his eyes, as if this were all a nightmare. "Maybe I can sell it. Maybe I can find some other old fool who likes to play with toys. You see those loony bastards all the time at F.A.O. Schwartz or hanging around playgrounds."

"You mean you'd actually sell it?"

"Damn straight I'd sell it! If only I can!"

Mark and Bambi planned to move to Hollywood to promote her acting career. Also, it was a good place to be in the real estate market, Mark said. His friends in Miami had friends in L.A. who could set him up in business.

Mark also had an idea in the back of his mind to discover some useful, revolutionary invention and promote it, market it, make a killing. He was in his Mister Wizard mode, in which he tinkered with pseudo-scientific gadgets – pedometers, prisms, boomerangs, stopwatches, kaleidoscopes. Captivated by them much as his father was captivated by electric trains, he spent hours twisting dials and pressing buttons and measuring effects. He had an idea he might find some equally arcane oddity that would answer some deep psychological need of the population, and then he'd exploit the hell out of it. In grade school, Bridgewater remembered, Mark had had similar ideas about creating something with the chemistry set he'd received for Christmas.

But this invention project was not a high priority. Something on the back burner to mull over and nurture if it came along. The main thing now was to promote his wife's career.

"She only wanted you for your name," Bridgewater joked, winking at Bambi. "Bambi Bridgewater is a much more memorable screen name than Bambi Warner."

"I'ze gonna say," Bambi blurted.

"Yeah," Mark agreed. "Like Gail Force or Bunny Bleu or Alexis Firestone. Annette Haven. Dolores del Rio. Linda Lovelace. Maybe we should work on a name, Bam. Maybe something like Bambi Starr? Bambi Comet?"

"Do you know any of those people? Gail Force or Linda Lovelace?"

"We've met Bunny Bleu. She starred in *Dial F for Fantasy*. We met her at the opening. We've also met Nina Hartley, briefly – no pun intended."

"I'ze gonna say."

"Nina was in *Breakin' All the Rules*. We also met Angel Kelly, who starred in *Fatal Passion*. Who else, Bam?"

"Barbara Dare."

"That's right. She was in *Roman Holiday*. Also Nicki Knights. I sort of met her, anyway."

"I'ze gonna say." Bambi's voice was faintly resentful.

"I paid a few bucks to have my picture taken with her," Mark explained. "She was in *Out of Control*. So was Angel Kelly, for that matter."

Did Mark actually go to porn movies regularly? Like the furtive guys with the popcorn boxes? He felt a wistful sense of regret remembering the painting he had planned to do but never did. *Swine in Circe's Garden*. Or was it *Turning Men Into Swine*?

Well, the alternatives stunk, too, Bridgewater reflected, considering the current offerings in Baltimore theaters. The first wave of summer junk comedies and sensational horror films. Chevy Chase in *Funny Farm*, Sly Stallone in *Rambo III*, something called *Maniac Cop, Crocodile Dundee II, Big, Willow, The Milagro Beanfield War*. The Charles Theater was temporarily closed for renovations, but *Au Revoir, Les Enfants*, the Louis Malle film, would be showing there in a few weeks. He and Zippy would not be able to go to the movies again without getting a babysitter, though, so they'd probably just stop going. They'd taken Susanna to *Good Morning, Vietnam* a few months ago; Zippy had nursed her in the dark theater when she wasn't asleep. But now, almost six months old, she was too rambunctious and noisy to bring to the movies. Sigh.

"California may be just the right place for you, Mark." The end of the continent where all the crazies and retirees ended up. Bridgewater had read somewhere that a group of conservative Christians out there was getting up a petition to send to the White House urging President Reagan to "just say no to astrology." A play on the First Lady's anti-drug slogan. They claimed that President and Mrs. Reagan's failure to reject astrology legitimized the occult and "set the nation on a collision course with God."

"Well, the way you're going, it may be the place for you, too," Mark said. They heard Frank's car pull into the driveway. "The whole family'll be gone from Baltimore without a trace. We'll be out in See-Ay, and dumbfuck will be vegetating in Ay-Zee."

The way he was going. Mark referred to the fact that Bridgewater had been complaining about his job. He wanted to quit. He had grown quite sick of his boss, Milt Spalding. In fact, he had nightmares about the guy; he felt overwhelmed by Milt's manipulative personality, as though he had to be constantly on his guard. He liked the idea of belonging to an organization, but he did not want to be absorbed into it and dominated by it. That was what Milt seemed to have in mind.

He bugged Bridgewater to take those silly management seminars with the fervor of a priest urging a hoodlum to go straight.

The latest ones he'd been pushing advertised "Basic Supervision" ("Learn from an Expert about Boosting Productivity, How to Handle Problem Employees, Developing Communications Skills. . . ."), "Powerful Presentation Skills," "Powerful Business Writing Skills," "Criticism and Discipline Skills for Managers," "How to Manage Multiple Priorities" ("How to Handle Conflicting Calendars, Planning and Organizing Skills and Techniques that Work, How to Get Right Things Done – Done Right on Time!"), "Skills for Managing the Office," "Team-Building Skills for Managers." Skills, skills, skills! Bridgewater thought he would scream if he heard that word one more time! Develop enough "skills" and they promised you would attain "power." How laughable! Power to do what? Intimidate employees? Fuck secretaries? If only you took enough of those seminars, you would develop those precious skills. Fuck skills! He wanted nothing to do with skills! Life was not a machine that you learned to run by pulling the right levers and twisting the proper dials!

"Remember your BATNA," Milt had been saying lately. "The Best Alternative To a Negotiated Agreement."

"Shouldn't that be called a BATANA, or maybe just a BANA – don't capitalize the 'to' or the 'a'?" Bridgewater had joked, but Milt didn't see the humor.

"Always keep the Best Alternative To a Negotiated Agreement in mind, Pete, I'm tellin' ya. It's one skill you can't do without when you're dealing with the fucks around here, like Dickerson – determining the BATNA." Milt marched around the room like Groucho Marx, the ultimate schemer. "You gotta be aggressive, Petey boy, remember that! Like when you drive a car. Never look at the car that's ahead of you to decide what you're going to do. Look at the car that's *ahead of* the car that's ahead of you. That's the bottom line." On his part, Milt had started to lose patience with Bridgewater, to become disenchanted with him. He did not like Bridgewater's laissez-faire attitude, his lack of get-up-and-go.

It was maddening. Yet Bridgewater knew he could not quit and pursue a romantic dream, like painting. Nor could he go out to California. He had a child now, and all he could do was keep his eyes open for some other opportunity, stick it out until something came along. In the meantime, he just had to endure.

The strong wind tugged at the copy of *Time* in Bridgewater's hands, threatening to whip the pages shut. He closed the magazine and placed it under his towel and sketchpad so that Raisa Gorbachev's head was visible beneath the word, TIME. The corny illustration of her against a blue background made her look like Carol Burnette with a hammer and sickle beside her.

The breeze whipped the water in the pool into little wavelets. The sun reflected off the ripples, creating a zillion little yellow-flashing mirrors, like the multiple facets on a *traje de luces*. Each spangle seemed individual on the surface, but they all merged into one yellow light. Under the aqua blue of the water, the stripe down the center of the bottom wavered, like something under a microscope. Bridgewater watched the stripe wriggle beneath the surface; forming recognizable objects; the stripe became first one thing and them another; shapes emerged and dissolved. At one moment the outline of a head formed – Roman nose, heavy-lidded eyes, full lips, protruding chin and forehead – and in the next instant the head became a fish with flickering fins and cold mobile lips, only to become a fire-spewing spike-backed dragon and then a singing, wing-flapping bird, a galloping horse with flowing mane, a hilly, undulant landscape, a mass of scudding clouds. Earth, air, fire, water. Like an expanding and contracting amoeba the jellyish blob contained everything. The amoeba changed shapes, protean, but everything was the amoeba; the substance remained constant. All the individual shapes partook of the single substance. Like some sort of mystical Eastern religion, Bridgewater mused. Hinduism. The shapes were maya, illusion, but part of samsara. *Tat tvam asi*. That art thou. Somebody said that to somebody else in *The Bhagavad Gita*. Krishna to Arjuna? Everything is Brahman. Brahman is everything. I am Zippy. I am Susanna. I am Moishe. I am Bambi. I am Marlene McCoy. I am the walrus. Goo goo ga joob.

Watching the stripe wriggle and the wavelets shimmer, Bridgewater thought of the old saw, the more things change, the more they stay the same. Last year the sports press had been full of the number of homeruns being hit in the major leagues; this year they talked about the number of balks umpires were calling on pitchers. Last year it was the cicadas; this year it was the gypsy moths and tent caterpillars. Last year it was Reaganomics, Greenspan taking the Federal Reserve over from Volcker; this year in was perestroika and economic reform in the Soviet Union. Last year Zippy had fled, disappeared. This year it was Rachael. New names, same events.

Same events, true, but every time they seemed new and individual and with an original urgency and vitality. You really could almost sum up all of life in that pithy little bumpersticker phrase he'd seen on the backs of cars recently, white sans serif letters on a red background:

SHIT HAPPENS

How can you anticipate reality? You set up expectations, and your plans get trashed. So you plunge ahead, open-eyed and open-minded, as into a grand adventure.

Bridgewater glanced around the pool. The lifeguard, a new boy this year with the same muscular torso and brushcut sun-bleached blond hair, flirted with a gorgeous, curvy blond college girl, a vision from a beach movie in a one-piece, scoop-backed swim suit. Like the lifeguard, she, too, displayed a deep, late summer tan. The boy, Bridgewater noticed, wore a tee shirt that said:

YUCK
FOO

Bridgewater felt no resentment or jealousy as he watched the boy and girl flirting at poolside. She was twisting her long blond wet hair over her shoulder, and the boy was self-consciously stepping on one foot and then the other, scratching his ear and nervously brushing back his hair. With both hands the girl squeezed the long rope of hair, pressing her breasts together between her shoulders to form a prominent cleavage in the low-cut bathing suit. The wrung water spilled over her collarbone, clung momentarily to her nylon bathing suit, and then slid sensuously down her glistening legs to darkstain the last white patches of cement around her. The boy could not help but ogle.

Last year Bridgewater had found the clumsy mating rituals of the young maddening. He'd been upset about Zippy's absence, of course. Jealousy springs from self-pity. Or had it only been those annoying bugs, after all? Bridgewater recalled the shrill, steady tremolo of the cicadas; the single high-pitched note had made the atmosphere seem almost liquid. This year's bugs weren't nearly as exciting. The gypsy moth nests looked like cobwebs or abandoned hornet-nests in the branches. The strips people tied around their tree trunks were not nearly as dramatic as the tents people had draped over their small trees a year ago. Life seemed much saner now. Duller.

Zippy had taken Susanna to the synagogue that morning. Pleading a headache, Bridgewater had come to the pool instead. Actually, he wanted to begin a painting of his daughter, do some preliminary sketches from photographs. Not since his drawings of Cecilia Nestorick had he picked up pencil and paper with the thought of creating something personal. As if purged or something, he no longer felt critics looking over his shoulder or the awesome weight of his reputation in the eyes of posterity; he just wanted to paint a picture of his daughter.

Bridgewater looked around the pool area. Because it was a windy, chilly day, not many people had come to the pool, and nobody swam or played in the water. Most of the chaise longues were unoccupied, and the cabanas where people changed their clothing all stood empty with their slatted wooden doors flapping slightly in the wind on rusty hinges. The creaking noise reminded Bridgewater of Susanna's low-grade moans of displeasure. *Ehhhh . . . ehhhh . . . ehhhh . . .*

A few people lay in the sun, trying to get a tan, and here and there somebody read a paperback book, pressing the pages flat against the wind. The lifeguard and the girl lounged together now in the shade of the lifeguard station, drinking Pepsis and listening to the Eagles on a portable tapeplayer. A group of middleaged women played cards and gossiped at a glass-topped umbrella-table by the huge wooden fence at the back.

A potbellied woman in her early 60s shuffled around the edge of the pool in flip-flop sandals like an ancient family dog clickfooting around the house under a sad, sagging spine. The woman's leathery brown skin looked like it might crack; it had been baked and wrinkled by years of overexposure to the sun. Where had he seen her before? Had she come here last year? The lady looked vaguely around the pool like an old, watery-eyed collie and then took a chair out of the sun beneath an umbrella. Who was she? Or did she just remind him of somebody? Somebody he'd met in Potawatomi Rapids, perhaps? A beach lounger who had spent her life in a bathing suit on the sand? Some friend of Edith's and Moishe's? He gave up speculating and thought of his parents-in-law.

They'd had several telephone conversations with Edith and Moishe lately. Edith had heard from Brenda that Sandy, who was living in a halfway house in New Haven, still trying to get over Brad Reynolds, had received a postcard from Rachael, who was staying with Uncle Sid in Tel Aviv. Rachael had burned with indignation at the thought that her parents were using her as a sort of cat's-paw – a dupe, a fool, their snot-nosed daughter who still did not know what was "good" for her. A real blow to her self-esteem. She wanted nothing more to do with her parents. But Moishe did not seem to mind.

"As long as she's not involved with Dody, that's all I care about," he said. "She'll get over it, and then she'll see that we were right all along." History would justify him. He really did think he had Rachael's best interests in mind, that he knew what was best for her – better than she herself did. Bridgewater hoped that he would not fall into the same arrogance with Susanna when she was older, but he probably would. Rachael should have gone ahead and had her baby, he thought, instead of getting an abortion. Put another generation between her and her powerlessness; maybe she'd have a better understanding of Moishe if she did. He wondered if she would come back to the United States. Zippy had, after all.

Bridgewater smiled, remembering that Edith was currently pissed off at him and Zippy. Temple Beth Chaim in Potawatomi Rapids had had a "Bounty of the Babies" ceremony on the first day of Shavuot two weeks ago, the Sunday before the Memorial Day weekend. Edith had nagged them to bring Susanna out to Michigan for it. On the first day of Shavuot, Jews gather to read the Ten Commandments and to thank God for giving them the Torah. A Midrash has it that after God chose the Israelites to receive the Torah, He demanded some security in return to guarantee that the Jews would cherish and study the Torah for all eternity. Collateral. A shrewd trader, God. The legend goes on that God refused the priests, the prophets and the elders of the community when Moses offered them but finally settled on the children. The Bounty of the Babies ceremony, which commemorated this, took place during the Torah reading, before the third aliyah. All the babies born of members of the congregation during the last year were carried up to the *bema*, a tallit held over them, and the congregation sang a Hebrew song of mazel tov and thanked God for the babies.

"But we aren't members of your congregation, Mom!"

"Ketzulah is my granddaughter! She was named at the shul! Gevalt! Bring her out here! Are you afraid to spend a little money on an airplane ticket?"

"We already have plans for that weekend."

"Pinchas!" Edith cried. Bridgewater was listening in on the other line while his mother-in-law badgered her daughter. "Could you please try to persuade your anti-Semitic wife, Zipporah, to bring Shoshonah out to Potawatomi Rapids?"

"Anti-Semitic! Because I can't come out to Potawatomi Rapids? If you wanted us so bad you'd offer to pay for our tickets, anyway, if it means so much to you."

"Anti-Semitic because you refuse to make a contribution to CAMERA to stop the lies and the distortion of the facts the press makes about Israel!" Edith cried in shrill irrelevance, ignoring her daughter's remarks. Bridgewater always marveled at the woman's *non-sequitors*. CAMERA—the Committee for Accuracy in Middle East Reporting in America—was another of Edith's current obsessions about which she hectored her daughter. She kept sending magazine advertisements for the organization with little clip-out coupons, urging them to donate.

"Come now, children. Afterward we can schmooze with the other parents and grandparents," Edith said, resuming her wheedling about the Shavuot service.

"And listen to all the babies kvetch."

"They will not kvetch. At least, Ketzulah won't kvetch. Not Shoshonah. Come on, it'll be a real simcha. Pinchas, be kind to your *shviger* and bring your wife and daughter out to me."

"Well," Bridgewater began, not sure what to say, but Zippy interrupted him.

"Why should he be kind to his mother-in-law? She hasn't always been kind to him."

"But now we have *shalom ha-bayit*, Zipporah. Come on out to Potawatomi Rapids."

But Bridgewater and Zippy demurred and postponed the final decision until it was too late to go out there. Edith was still angry about it when Zippy called on Memorial Day, but she'd get over it, Bridgewater knew, until something else came along to anger her. Why worry? They really did have *shalom ha-bayit* now, and there was no real crisis. *Shalom ha-bayit*. Household peace.

Bridgewater remembered his conversation with Zippy that morning, as he lay in bed, feigning a headache he knew she didn't believe for a moment that he had. But she went along with the sham, anyway.

"Do you ever imagine Susanna dying? For some stupid thing you did or failed to do?" he asked, watching her get dressed. She still carried the extra pounds from her pregnancy, but Bridgewater enjoyed looking at her naked, anyway.

"All the time. I imagine never being able to see her ever again and spending the rest of my life yearning to see her, to undo whatever it was I did and knowing I can't."

"Crippling, isn't it?"

"Paralyzing. You hear about people who lose their children in some tragic accident, and for months afterward they do things like set a place at the table for them or call out to them, and then they remember. God, it must be horrible."

"Or thinking they see their children on the street and waving to them and calling their names, and then they realize that's not their children they see. Can't be. Will never be. You know how sometimes you think you recognize people, until they come closer and it's not who you thought it was at all?"

Zippy nodded. "When I worked at the Burger Chef after school in Potawatomi Rapids I kept fantasizing a celebrity coming in for a Big Chef or a Super Chef or a cheeseburger and fries. Pretty soon everybody looked like a celebrity. Rock stars, actors, politicians." *Mick Jagger!*

"Sometimes I want to pinch Susanna when she's asleep to make sure she's still alive. With a subdued longing Bridgewater watched as Zippy leaned forward and reached behind her to fasten her bra.

"She's so alert when she's awake! Everybody comments on it. It's part of her charm."

"I guess that's the big fear parents always have about their children, that big sense of responsibility. Whereas a child tends to think its parents are immortal, that they'll never die."

"Do you really think so?"

"I suppose I shouldn't generalize, but those are pretty common emotions, I think. I remember I had a hard time accepting my mother's death. Couldn't really believe it."

"I remember my worst nightmares were being abandoned by my parents. That's like them dying." She watched herself in the mirror buttoning her blouse.

"Listen. Do you hear her?"

"No, that's just Ozzie. He wants to be fed again. The baby's asleep in her room. I just fed her. Hear that? That's Ozzie meowing." Bridgewater nodded and settled himself in bed more comfortably. Odd how he listened for his daughter's cry, even in his sleep. It was like convincing yourself you could hear the telephone ringing when you were running water or when the washing machine was running.

"So you were afraid your parents would leave you? Abandonment. Flight. Diaspora. A universal theme in your family, no?"

"A tribal instinct, you mean? Genetic response? Don't read too much into what I just said."

"Well, all I mean is, there's Sid, you, now Rachael. Even your cousin Sandy fled to get away from the pain of her estrangement. All of you took off. Sure, there's a difference between Babylonian captivity and exile, the Zionist movement – all that – and spending a summer in Barbados looking for Mick Jagger."

"Mick Jagger!" She turned and stared at him, puzzled.

"Don't deny that you used to write all those erotic fan letters to him."

"That was for a novel I was writing, Peter! Did you think I was serious?"

"You *mailed* them, for Christ's sake!"

"I sent a few, sure. I wanted a reply. I thought the story would be more authentic that way."

"Do you expect me to believe that?"

"No, but it's true."

"But what about the therapist? What about all that . . . you remember, all that. . . ." He gestured vaguely with his arm, sweeping the insubstantial air before him.

"I can't be depressed and write a novel at the same time? It was therapy itself to be writing it."

"You never told me."

"You never asked."

"Well, then, where's the manuscript? You must have written something."

Zippy laughed and peered into the closet for the pair of shoes she wanted. "The manuscript is in the same never-never land as all your canvases," she said, retrieving a pair of polished red pumps.

So what was he supposed to believe? Shaking his head, Bridgewater reached down for his sketchpad, having suddenly reminded himself of his project, and as he did so, the wind nearly blew his *Time* away. He lunged for it as it lifted into the air, and he caught it blown open to the "Medicine" section. Beneath an article about a new FDA-approved contraceptive—the age-old cervical cap—was a small item about antiandrogens, the drugs used to treat sex offenders. A paragraph in the article announced the resignation of Betty Nestorick from a fund-raising position she held with the American Mental Health Fund, the organization founded by John Hinckley's parents. Since the death of her son and daughter she had lost interest in the committee's work, she said. The article went on to relate the bizarre murder-suicide of her incestuous children, Roger and Cecilia Nestorick. There was also a small black-and-white photograph of her talking with John Hinckley Sr., outside St. Elizabeth's, the mental hospital in Washington where Hinckley's son was being treated. Where had Bridgewater seen that face before? All at once, he knew.

Bridgewater counted five beats to be sure of his composure, and then he casually glanced over at the worn-out old woman sitting under the umbrella at the table fifteen yards to his left. She caught his glance, and they both smiled briefly. Bridgewater did not pause but continued his casual survey. Could that really be Betty Nestorick? Impossible! The coincidence was too fantastic! He had never met her; he had only seen her photograph in the newspaper. Could it really be she? No! It couldn't! Bridgewater wondered if Cecilia had ever mentioned him to her – or to Roger – and he supposed she had. It was a good bet. He tried to keep from looking at the building where Cecilia had lived, but it was impossible not to. He fantasized a sign across the entrance:

LASCIATE OGNE SPERANZE, VOI CH'INTRATE

Abandon all hope, indeed. Hardly a day passed when Bridgewater did not feel some searing regret that he'd ever gotten mixed up with Cecilia Nestorick and wondered if she'd been carrying his child, a question whose answer he would never know. While his fears that he would be criminally or legally implicated had diminished over the past six months, he still found himself wondering about it and wishing he could erase it all somehow.

He would catch himself pleading his case in a desperate interior voice, pointing to the mitigating circumstances of Zippy's departure, his ignorance about Cecilia's involvement with her brother—*for so long she had led him to believe Roger was only a distant cousin!* They had been lovers only for two months—"only" two – *less than two!* Sometimes he would dream about it, the way he had dreamt about smoking cigarettes after he'd quit. In the dreams about Cecilia, a policeman would knock at his door to lead him away. He'd hang onto the door frame while the officer pried his hands loose. Then he'd wake up, relieved it was only a dream, just like when he'd had the cigarette dreams.

Bridgewater never told Zippy the extent of his involvement with Cecilia, and she never asked. Presumably she had forgotten all about it. They had other things to think about. All she knew about were some art-class drawings. Nothing to it outside the guilt in his own mind. The Raskolnikov of a wild oat!

Bridgewater lay aside his *Time Magazine* and picked up his sketchpad. He opened the pad and removed a packet of photographs of Susanna. Though her head was covered with a film of hair at birth, her fine dark hair had only recently begun to grow. Bridgewater was not certain, but it looked like it had a reddish tint. Susanna had his eyes, his mouth, Zippy's nose, Zippy's hair. A beautiful child. Lightly with his pencil he shaded in some hair on a tentative curvature of skull on the pad of paper, then looked again at the photographs. He made a bold curve for the soft, pouchy baby cheek, and then he looked at the photographs again.

One of the group pictures he had taken in front of the shul in Potawatomi Rapids after the baby-naming ceremony caught his eye. How happy the Feldmans all looked together! Especially Rachael, he thought, with that amused twinkle in her big brown eyes, as if she promised to let you in on a secret or share a joke with you. What enormous breasts she had, too, he thought, looking at her chest. Moishe under his shiny black yarmulke and Edith behind her obsidian eyeglasses, beaming. How *triumphant* the whole group looked! He could almost hear Moishe calling him "Gazookis." Smiling, he turned back to the sketchpad to look at what he'd done.

Bridgewater worked carefully at shading in the wings of Susanna's nose. They unfolded sharply in the Feldman manner, a trait recognizable in the father and his daughters. Moishe's genes. The wings sloped down to the thin upper lip and the bulbous lower lip that could have been plucked off of him or Mark or Frank and stuck onto Susanna. Bridgewater genes. He shaded the lower lip to give it a full, wet, ripe look, and he hatched in dimples at the corners of her mouth.

An aluminum chair scraped the cement with a grating screech, and Bridgewater looked up into the sun-ruined face of the woman who might be Betty Nestorick. She stood up from her chair and seemed to turn in his direction. Was she coming toward him? Wasn't she looking at him meaningfully, like the family dog asking to be petted? No! Couldn't be! He just imagined it. But still, she was coming toward him, as if she wanted to speak to him. Could it be? Speak with *him*? Why? Maybe she wanted the *Time*, to read the story about herself. And wasn't that exactly how Cecilia had come into his life? Pestering him for his *Time* so she could read the review of the Saul Bellow novel? It was all starting to feel too weird, a kind of déjà vu in a room full of distortion mirrors.

Bridgewater tried to maintain his composure. He tossed the *Time* onto an adjacent chaise longue, as if tossing a piece of bloody meat to a guard dog, a gesture to show he was done with it. A breeze blew it onto the cement and against the legs of a pool chair. She could have it if she wanted it. He stood, stretched, yawned, as though he were bored, as if he were a man without a care in the world, and he went over to stand by the edge of the pool. He looked down into the shimmering spangle of wind-driven water. He glanced around casually. Damn! The woman was coming closer! He no longer dared to look directly at her. But *she* was looking at *him* . . . he'd swear to it! Could it really be Cecilia's mom? Bridgewater turned back to the pool. He stared for a moment at the water, and then he dove straight into the wavering amoeba.

Coda: Born Again

Born Again

"I was only dead about a minute before they got my heart going again. That's been more than twenty years ago, 1977."

Bridgewater counted several beats before looking casually around at the speaker in a seat on the bus a few rows behind him, across the aisle on the right side. It was still before dawn. They were all being transported from wardrobe to location, everybody on the bus an "extra" in a synagogue scene, all outfitted in dark suits, white yarmulkes and prayer shawls draped around their shoulders.

"I was trying to kill myself," the man continued to his seatmate. He looked like he was in his late fifties or early sixties, pudgy, gray-faced, but with an alert eye. "I drank like a fish, smoked a couple packs a day, ate fried foods, didn't hardly exercise—the whole nine yards."

Bridgewater remembered the conversation he'd had with Zippy early that morning. The alarm had rung, and Bridgewater was about to leave the warm nest of the bed when they heard the distinct sound of their ancient cat, Ozzie, urinating on the floor at the foot of the bed. At seventeen, Ozzie was blind and incontinent. He did not seem to be in any pain, though he was frail and distracted. Bridgewater jumped from the bed and scooped Ozzie up. Ozzie had already finished, but he took Ozzie down to his litter box nevertheless before coming back up to mop up the piss. After he'd washed his hands he lay down for a moment longer.

"Our whole house is going to smell like pee," Zippy said. It sounded like an accusation. "It's annoying when he does it in the kitchen, but at least there I can mop it up."

"Well, what can we do about it?"

"If Ozzie were a person, we'd have to put him in a nursing home, where somebody could take care of him."

"God, sometimes I wish he'd just die, you know?"

"Well, when you get to the point of wishing an animal would simply die – you know, either we go on like this and let our whole house turn into Ozzie's litterbox, or – or we have to make a decision."

"You mean kill him."

Zippy started to speak, but she couldn't get the words to sort out the complexities. She tried again but once more the words failed to come. They lay silently for a while and then Bridgewater got up to go to the filming. Downstairs, Ozzie lay on the couch, curled in a fetal ball. He looked gaunt. Surely he'd used up most of his nine lives.

The scene they were filming was Rosh Hashanah in an old Orthodox shul, ornate wooden pews carved with Stars of David, a balcony for the women, a stained glass domed ceiling with a Tree of Life. The director told them all to remove their watches and eyeglasses and to put away their cell phones. This was supposed to be 1954. No anachronisms allowed.

The movie starred Hillary Nixon, whom Bridgewater had known as Bambi Warner, now a legitimate actress. She'd divorced Mark about the time Mark and Peter's father, Frank, had died. A massive heart attack at an exercise club in Phoenix. Just like his wife a quarter of a century earlier. Both of these events had sent Mark on a Christian revival. He'd found Jesus. Death and divorce had driven him to it. Born again.

In fact, Mark had accused Peter of "not having invited Jesus" to Frank's funeral, and he had adopted some nasty anti-Semitic rhetoric with his new-found Christianity. The brothers had not spoken in five years, though Bridgewater had heard from Uncle Ben that Mark had joined some sort of cult in Colorado.

It had been seventeen years since Bridgewater had converted to Judaism. Now his older daughter, Susanna, was about to become a bat mitzvah.

It didn't feel all that different from what he'd known before. Sure, the holidays weren't the same—Rosh Hashanah and Passover instead of Christmas and Easter—but in America, the differences didn't seem that important. "Converting to Judaism must be like emigrating to Canada." He could still hear Cecilia Nestorick's voice over the years.

The star of the movie came down the aisle while the cantor sang a prayer at the end of the traditional Rosh Hashanah service. He stopped next to Bridgewater and gestured up to the balcony where Hillary stood, unseen. They shot the scene a dozen times from different angles, moving huge expensive equipment around for each shooting. Bridgewater wondered if he would appear in the film when it was released in a year. Maybe his left shoulder would be visible, or maybe he would recognize his left hand, with the gold band on the ring finger, where he had clutched the back of the seat in front of him.

"I'm going to be in a movie this weekend," Bridgewater had told Myra Malachevsky, a Russian woman at work. "I'm playing a Jew." Bridgewater was the Director of Communications for a non-profit heath-care advocacy group, a job he'd taken after being laid off at Maryputa during the recession at the beginning of the decade.

He was subtly teasing Myra, who never really bought his conversion as anything but a gimmick. To her, Jew was something stamped on an identity card. It meant hardship, ostracism. It meant you were marked. You were born a Jew. You didn't "decide" to be a Jew or not be a Jew.

"Peter is going to be Jewish this weekend," Myra said in an ironic tone to her boyfriend, Tom. They were all walking to the parking lot together after work.

"We can show him how to be Jewish, if he needs some help." Tom wore a beard and long hair. A man in his late forties, he had probably been a hippie.

"What do you know about Jews?" Myra said. Her voice dripped scorn. She'd escaped Russia during the Brezhnev years, going first to Israel and then to Baltimore.

"I know plenty of Jews."

"But you don't know what it means. You can't know what it means."

Bridgewater parted company with them at the lot. They walked to Tom's car, still quarrelling about the meaning of Jewishness.

But I am a Jew! For the past seventeen years I've been living in a Jewish household, observing all the Jewish holidays, Friday night candles, Saturday morning synagogue services; both of my daughters go to a Jewish day school! What more does it take to be a Jew?

Filming had begun at seven in the morning and was over by two. Although they'd filled out W-2 forms, they weren't being paid. What they would have earned was being donated to the synagogue. They were given a cafeteria-style lunch in the basement of the synagogue, however. Bridgewater had learned about the movie through his children's school. A notice had been distributed to the students to give to their parents. ("EXTRA! EXTRA!") Others had learned about the event through other Jewish organizations and by word of mouth. Not everybody was Jewish. Bridgewater had overheard one man telling another that this was the first time he'd ever been in a synagogue. They were all just bodies wearing yarmulkes, dark suits and prayer shawls, enough to fill all the pews in the shul for a Rosh Hashanah scene in a movie.

Bridgewater filled his tray with salad, some sort of pasta dish ladled out by a film crew member, and tuna casserole—a kosher dairy luncheon catered for the occasion and he carried it over to an empty seat at one of the long folding dining tables. A minute later, the gray-faced man he'd seen on the bus that morning took the seat opposite him. They nodded a greeting. Bridgewater wondered fleetingly if the man were "really" Jewish and then fell briefly into the abyss of wondering what a "real" Jew was.

"Interesting experience, huh?" Bridgewater said.

"Yeah, but I don't think I'd like to do it again. Once is enough."

"How long do you think that scene will be? Ten minutes?"

"Five, tops. It'll probably be cut with the outdoor stuff they shot yesterday."

"A lot of work for five minutes of film."

"Where do you think those huge production costs come from?"

"I wonder if we'll recognize ourselves in the movie."

"Immortalized on the silver screen, eh?"

"Gives new meaning to the phrase, 'born again.'" Bridgewater looked at the man to see if that phrase had any other special significance for him, but his expression didn't change.

"I didn't even see what's-her-face, Hillary Nixon," he said. "Did you?"

"Nope." Bridgewater thought about telling him she used to be his sister-in-law, but he decided against it. Why bother?

When he got home, Bridgewater was greeted by his daughter, Susanna. She was sobbing.

"What's the matter, honey?"

"Ozzie's dead!" she shrieked. "Zoë and I found him in the basement!" Susanna could barely get the words out. "I was calling for him, and he didn't come, and I started to worry, and I looked all over the place, and then I saw him in the corner of the basement, and I called him again, and he didn't move. He didn't even move!" She burst out sobbing again at the memory.

Bridgewater hugged his twelve-year old daughter close to him. He felt ineffectual, but he hugged her tightly anyway.

"I picked him up and he just—he was just like an empty bean bag. Just completely lifeless. His head just hung there!" She started to cry again, sobbing harder and harder.

"Poor Ozzie. He was just so old, honey. It's probably better for him this way. It really is. He was just so tired, you know? He was such a good pet."

Bridgewater's last words of comfort triggered another bout of sobbing, and he held Susanna close until she calmed down.

"Can I help you bury him?"

"Sure you can. We'll do that today. This afternoon." Azazel sent away with his cargo of sins at last. Symbolic of the fresh start the Jewish New Year signifies. Born again. They'd get him into the ground quickly and simply, Bridgewater reflected. Jewish-style.